PRAISE FOR
GIRL TALK

"Baggott's brand of witty psychological observation is dark
and corrosive . . . [she] has a knack for finding the oxy-
ronic in any situation."

—The New York Times Book Review

"And it is *GIRL TALK*—a breathless novel that manages
to be both funny and bleak, poignant and bitchy—that
will make Baggott famous."

—Poets & Writers Magazine

"Baggott's debut novel is a touching coming-of-age
story . . . [a] multilayered, psychological tale. . . .
Appealingly quirky characters will charm readers."

—Publishers Weekly

"A first novel by a woman with a strong new voice and a
splendidly eccentric and comic tale to tell. . . . It is a
vibrant, fascinating story, full of humor and pathos. The
sort of novel which one finds difficult to put down—I
enjoyed it hugely."

—Publishing News

"Julianna Baggott's first novel is a dazzling fountain of
surprise. . . . With *GIRL TALK* she bursts into the liter-
ary scene like someone carrying a Roman candle into a
murmurous tea party."

*—Fred Chappell, author of Look Back All the Green Valley and Brighten the
Corner Where You Are*

"A wise look at mother-daughter legacies."

—Library Journal

"Filled with the kind of eccentric characters found in Vonnegut or Pynchon."

—*Shout Magazine*

"An endearing coming-of-age story and a love song for mothers and daughters alike."

—*Asbury Park Press*

"Baggott's deft movement of her material is often lyri and poignant."

—*Kirkus Reviews*

"*GIRL TALK* is fast-paced and funny, a catty, witty look at the mistakes all too easily made in the name of love."

—*The Sunday Oregonian*

"*GIRL TALK* is a wonderful story. I was hooked with the very first sentence and yet was never actually sure where the story would lead. What I was always certain of was that I was in capable hands. The subtle twists and turns are remarkable and the characters, especially the mother, are vivid and memorable. This is the work of a very talented writer. It was a pleasure to read."

—Jill McCorkle, author of *Carolina Moon* and *Crash Diet*

"A warm, touching book about relationships between mothers and daughters, the past and the preset."

—*Hello*

"Cruising along with the rhythms of a comedy, *GIRL TALK* is at heart a dead-serious analysis of the often-disastrous choices women can be forced to make."

—*Baltimore Sun*

"Baggott's descriptions of Lissy's experiences are colorful and provide the careful details that allow female readers to closely relate to the awkward motherly moments bound to make any fifteen-year-old wish for an escape."

—*USA Today*

"I couldn't put this book down. *GIRL TALK*'s hilarious, relentless truths are well-served by its author's tough lyricism. Baggott trains a stern and tender eye onto our cultural markers, using them to signpost her lively trek toward the revelations of love—lost, rediscovered, and most satisfying of all, unconditional."

—Carol Dawson, author of *The Mother-in-Law Diaries*

"Just in time for the eighties revival, *GIRL TALK* is a sweet-and-sour re-creation of American teenagehood during that fast and furious decade. Lissy Jablonski is the daughter of a one-legged gynecologist and a mother who tries, as best she can, to communicate just what it means to be a woman, and a clever one at that. Smart, lyrical, and funny chick lit."

—*Eve magazine* (U.K.)

"This is the story of Lissy, who's pregnant by her married ex and facing her father's imminemt death. The arrival of an old flame sends Lissy back to the ill-fated summer her dad ran off with the red-haired bank clerk. *GIRL TALK* is a divinely written and moving read about love, life, and mothers. Do yourself a favor, read it!"

—*B magazine* (U.K.)

GIRL TALK

Julianna Baggott

WASHINGTON SQUARE PRESS
PUBLISHED BY POCKET BOOKS

New York   London   Toronto   Sydney

A Washington Square Press Publication of
POCKET BOOKS, a division of Simon & Schuster, Inc.
1230 Avenue of the Americas, New York, NY 10020

Copyright © 2001 by Julianna Baggott

Originally published in hardcover in 2001 by Pocket Books

ISBN: 0-7434-0083-6

First Washington Square Press trade paperback printing January 2002

10   9   8   7   6   5

WASHINGTON SQUARE PRESS and colophon are registered trademarks of Simon & Schuster, Inc.

For information regarding special discounts for bulk purchases, please contact Simon & Schuster Special Sales at 1-800-456-6798 or business@simonandschuster.com

Cover design by David Scott, front cover photo by Luigi Ciuffetelli

Printed in the U.S.A.

TO MY MOTHER AND FATHER,
Glenda and Bill Baggott

AND TO MY HUSBAND,
David G. W. Scott

Acknowledgments

I thank Nat Sobel, whose encouragement prompted me to lie about having already started to write this novel and without whom there would be no novel. I thank all of my readers—Elise Zealand, Rachel Pastan, David Teague, Quinn Dalton, Kathy Flann, Eric Fine; all of the readers at Sobel Weber, especially Judith Weber; and, of course, my editor, Greer Kessel Hendricks. I thank my research help, the fabulous Isabelle Murray, Kay Scott, Dr. David Fink, Father John Grasing, Gina and Don Ostmann and the Mardi Gras diners, Mary Sawicki, Joe Zealand, Donna Wolfe, Clare Anne Darragh, and Kristin Rehberg. I thank Andy Spear at *New Delta Review* for publishing "Girl Talk," the short story, and my teachers, especially Fred Chappell, Lee Zacharias, and Michael Parker, as well as the Virginia Center for the Creative Arts, Ragdale Foundation, and Delaware Division of the Arts for all their support. Jim Clark and Barbara King have been invaluable.

I also thank Kathleen M. Middleton for writing *Images of America—Bayonne* (Arcadia Publishing, 1995) and Alan Shapiro for writing *The Last Happy Occasion* (University of Chicago Press, 1996) and for consenting to his appearance in the Woodstock scene. *Popular Beliefs and Superstitions: A Compendium of American Folklore* (Puckett, Hand, Casetta) was also a great help.

GIRL TALK

1

One month before my father died in the fall of 1999, Church Fiske appeared at my door. I hadn't seen him since the summer my father disappeared with a redheaded bank teller from Walpole when I was fifteen, the summer my mother decided to teach me the art of omission, how to tell the perfect lie, or more accurately, how you can choose the truth—with a little hard work and concentration—from the assortment of truths life has to offer. But for me to truly appreciate her art, my mother knew she would first have to give me the bare, naked truth so that I could see how she'd altered it. Like a gangster who has to tell his child he doesn't play violin, that the case is used for concealing a semiautomatic, my mother, Dotty Jablonski, spent the summer of my father's disappearance opening violin cases, showing me her guns.

Of course, Church brought a lot of that summer back to me. We had clumsily lost our virginity together in a back-

yard pool in Bayonne, New Jersey. But I'd been decon-
structing and reconstructing that summer ever since it happened and everything that I'd learned about my mother—
her weepy, fish-stained father and drunken, arsonist mother;
her first love, Anthony Pantuliano, from the Bayonne Rendering Plant; the convent school where she almost drowned
for the love of a polio-stricken nun; and why she married
my father, her passive accomplice. And recently it dawned
on me, nearly fifteen years later, that I am more like my
mother than even my mother, that I have spent my life
trying to live out her sordid life, taking on the various leading roles.

When Church showed up, I was living alone in downtown Manhattan in a tiny two-bedroom apartment with a
bathroom so small you'd think you were in an airplane. My
life was a disaster. I'd just kicked out a newspaper-found
roommate—a Korean stripper, self-named Kitty Hawk.
Half the furniture was missing—her beanbags and futon.
There were big blank spots on the walls where she'd hung
old movie-star posters—Bette Davis and James Dean; she
was a kind of fucked-up romantic. I was screwed out of half
the rent for two months. I was fast approaching thirty and
had just found out that I was pregnant, my bathroom shelf
filled with pregnancy test sticks, pink and blue lines shining from behind their plastic-covered windows, all pointing out the obvious. I'd sworn off men, having just gone
through a breakup with a married one, Peter Kinney—who
still didn't know he was the father.

It turns out that Juniper Fiske, Church's mother, had
called to talk my mother into going to their twenty-fifth
reunion at Simmons College in Boston where they'd been
roommates their freshman and sophomore years studying
nursing before they both got married. Although they both

finished up the four-year program eventually, on their own schedules as the wives of Harvard men, they considered themselves, at least as far as reunions went, members of the class in which—had certain life events not taken place—they would have graduated together. Juniper had finally kicked the Valium habit and was into tai chi, self-help, and vitamins. My mother declined the invitation for the reunion on the grounds she thought reunions were creepy (Juniper Fiske being a perfect example)—classmates having turned into themselves in such disturbing folds and twists, one element of their personality taking over until a tattletale becomes a cop; a nerd, a techie millionaire; and a cheerleader, an aerobics instructor.

My mother was comfortably back to the calm routine of life with my father as Dr. and Mrs. Jablonski in Keene, New Hampshire. My father came back, you see, at the end of his summer with the redheaded bank teller, and the three of us never spoke of that summer again, or of redheads, bank tellers, or anything to do with nearby Walpole. Once, when I was nineteen and bent on revealing my family's dysfunction at the urging of an inept nose-tugging therapist, my mother stated flatly, "You never really had a fifteenth summer. It was the summer that never happened." But I have to admit that although my mother never talked about that summer, it was always there between us.

Instead of going to the reunion, she prepared a statement that she mailed to Juniper for her to read to anyone who inquired about her at the roundtables for their year. Juniper called my mother upon receiving the letter. The conversation, according to my mother, went something like this:

"I don't feel comfortable with this," Juniper said.

"With what?" my mother asked.

"You say that you weigh one hundred fifteen pounds and you've never had a gray hair."

"And?"

"Well . . ."—Juniper hesitated—"it isn't true."

"How do you know how much I weigh? We haven't seen each other in ages."

"I can tell in your voice. It's padded. It's a fat voice. Hear my voice? *My* voice is the voice of someone who weighs one hundred fifteen pounds."

"And I have a gray-haired voice, too? I sound like an old fat witch?"

Juniper went on. "You need to be honest with yourself. I wouldn't be telling all of this to you if I didn't think that our relationship deserved honesty."

"Oh, for the love of God!"

Juniper swerved away from the letter and the reunion and to a safer topic: the kids. It turned out that Church was finally heading to New York and wasn't Lissy still there and wouldn't she help Church out? "He's a bit of a lost soul these days," Juniper said.

"Sure thing," my mother said. "You know, Juniper—I'd do anything for you. For better or for worse, you're like a sister."

And so it was arranged that Church would come to stay with me, for a while. Although I needed the rent money he'd be dishing out, it was a crazy time for Church to visit. My eyes were ringed with smeary eyeliner. I'd just gone to a yoga class, trying to center myself, but the room was lined with mirrors, and I tangled myself into pretzel contortions that forced me to stare at my bloated face and my widening ass at the same time. I left in tears. In addition to being pregnant and alone, I was feeling old, thirty looming. It had hit me that when my mother was my age, she had a nine-year-old kid, but I was incapable of any sort of normal lasting relationship. I'd started suffering from a recurring nightmare of winning Most Well-Preserved at a reunion of my own, only to find out in true Carrie-horror-prom-night fashion that it's a joke and I look ancient. I stumble around in the dream only able to chat with classmates about my walnut-sized bunions, my recalcitrant bowels, my imaginary husband's prostate, and how the palsied camera angles of these new cop shows make me dizzy. "Who's the cameraman, Katharine Hepburn?" I hear myself saying in this Billy Crystal–impersonating-his-grandfather voice.

When Church knocked, I was in deep: I was wearing a dress from 1987 that had once been sloppily big but now I couldn't zip. I was sorting out the shit Kitty Hawk had left behind—spiked thigh-high boots and leather tap pants. I wanted to be drunk at noon, had searched the cabinets for liquor, but found only a bottle of peach schnapps. I carried it to the sofa but couldn't drink it. I was, after all, a pregnant woman.

I saw Church's face, distorted by the peephole—that tiny rich-person's nose grown broad, eyes tightly packed into a pointed forehead—and I could barely open the door, I was so weak. I scrambled through the ritual of locks and bolts, flung the heavy door open dramatically, and collapsed onto Church's tweed jacket.

"Jesus," he said. "And I thought I was fucked up."

Church was now twenty-eight. He'd been in and out of an assortment of fairly well-to-do colleges. Nothing Ivy League, but the almost-Ivy—remote, small colleges designed particularly for the well-educated, if-not-extremely-naturally-gifted rich. Bowdoin comes to mind, Colby, Colgate. He'd been a ceramics major because he wanted to get dirty, a philosophy major because he wanted to be allowed to think dirty, a forestry major because he wanted to be one with the dirt, and a psychology major because he wanted to help people deal with their dirt. But nothing suited him. To understand Church Fiske, you have to understand that he'd never liked being rich, although he came from deep pockets of family money; he was infatuated with the middle class. I hadn't seen him in nearly fifteen years, but we'd talked on the phone every few months, always picking up exactly as we'd left off, flirtatious, smart-ass teenagers. He'd say, "It's all bullshit. It's not real. Ceramics is about function in art, mutually exclusive. And philosophy about look-how-clever-I-am, and forestry run by bitter environmentalists pissed off because they're not rich, and counseling, well, it's the biggest crock of all—how to fix fragile little wrecks like my mother." And now he had no job, no direction. He'd started the habit of looking for the perfect career way back, wanting to drive the big rigs when he was fourteen. More recently, he'd look at the want ads and circle things like *lounge singer, tarot card reader, movie extras—no pay.* He kept saying that he wanted to be in the city to meet real people, to have an authentic experience, snorting, "Whatever that means!"

But there he was, Church in his tweed jacket, his hair rumpled and windblown, his cheeks ruddy, holding his suitcase, and I was relieved to see him.

"Thank God you're here, Church. Everything's turned to shit. The place is a wreck." I scooped up an armful of Kitty's clothes, more of her G-strings and spangled bras and Catholic schoolgirl miniskirts to clear a space on the sofa.

"What's this?" Church said, picking up something so skimpy and lacy that I wasn't really sure if I could identify it.

"Kitty," I said. "My ex-roommate's stuff. I promised to take it down to the Fruit, Cock, Tail Strip Club for her." I sighed. "Jesus, I'm in love with a real dickhead."

"I know. Love is the worst thing of all. It's how life kicks you in the balls." He put his arm around me. "But this guy's not worth it. I can tell. He's a son of a bitch." He didn't know anything about Peter, of course. He was just on autopilot. I certainly wasn't going to tell him I was pregnant. I couldn't believe it myself. "That's why I'm so glad I like women, Lissy. Men are such assholes."

And then Church stood up. "Let me help you. What can I do?" He paused. "Here," he said, picking up Kitty's underthings and overthings, "let me cart these down to the club for you."

I started laughing and then he smiled his Church grin, knowing I'd nailed him. But the truth was, I was in no mood to see Kitty Hawk, and the club was just over on 14th Street, not far. It would give me a chance to throw the extra crap out of his soon-to-be bedroom. I said, "Okay, Church, you asshole, do me a favor and go to a strip club."

He packed the clothes up in a brown paper bag and headed out of the apartment like a proud six-year-old helping his mother with the garbage for the first time. And that's how he met Kitty Hawk and fell in love with her, which eventually led to their short, unstable marriage. Things were at their worst when Church showed up, and I'd thought he'd make it all better. Five hours after he had left for the Fruit, Cock, Tail Strip Club, he showed up again at my door. "And look who I bumped into . . ." he said, doing a drumroll on the doorjamb and then hitting an air cymbal. "The amazing . . . Kitty Hawk." He was drunk. She stumbled into the room in spiked heels and a short coat with a fur-lined hood, jabbing him with her elbow, giggling, "She no like me, Churchie-boy. I tell you."

He whispered to me in that loud, drunken whisper, "I think I'm in love!" He pressed one hand to his heart and batted his eyes. "I want to be a hopelessly romantic pervert when I grow up."

I said, "Welcome to adulthood." I felt a surge of nausea— morning sickness, a misleading term, since it seemed to have a mind of its own, coming and going whenever it pleased. I scrambled out of the room to dry-heave over the toilet.

The summer my father had an affair with the redheaded bank teller, 1985, my parents had been married for nearly sixteen years. We lived in a nice Colonial house on Pako Avenue in Keene, New Hampshire. They'd met at Guy and Juniper Fiske's wedding on Cape Cod. My mother doesn't dance and my father had lost a leg early in the Vietnam War, and so they met at the punch bowl. They knew right from their very first encounter that they were going to get married. My mother strolled out of the reception on my father's arm, and just before Juniper drove off with Guy in his father's antique roadster, she thanked Juniper, as if my father were a large, overly lavish party favor. My parents were married two weeks later by a justice of the peace. She'd grown up the daughter of a fish-shop owner in Bayonne, a quick ride from New York City. She'd told me that my grandfather died of a heart attack shortly before their wedding and my grandmother died shortly thereafter from what, in retrospect, seemed to be a suspiciously generic and vague illness. She said she'd already begun to feel like an old maid. It was 1969. My father was twenty-four and she was twenty, ten years younger than I am now.

I'm sure there were some snags in the marriage, but at fifteen I wasn't aware of them. I can recall only that my mother didn't like the way my father whistled while washing his hands in the bathroom and that he complained her perfume was asphyxiating. Aside from these minor annoyances, they seemed happy. I remember seeing them kiss under mistletoe. They linked arms when out walking in town. But I didn't know anything, really, about my mother then.

It was all a surprise to me, beginning that one night when I stumbled from bed, a gawky fifteen-year-old girl (back when gawky was just on the verge of being sexy, but not quite yet) and found my mother in the kitchen, wearing a black bathing suit, standing in the glow of the refrigerator light. She was bent over, leaning in, her head slightly lifted to cool her neck. I can still see her lit up in the refrigerator in that pose, like an immodest starlet on an otherwise dark stage. She was thirty-five and buxom and had full red lips and slightly buck teeth. She'd been weighing her food for a month or so on a little Weight Watchers scale, eager to take off some of her extra padding, but I was jealous of the padding, the soft breasts and full rump. I was all limbs and had already spent many hours that summer eating peanut butter straight from the jar with a spoon, trying not to move, so I could put on some weight, willing it to just the right places, with no luck.

I was used to my mother, on her sleepless nights, rousing me from bed—purposefully dropped toilet seats, ignored kettle whistles—for "girl talk," as she put it. It was a term that by the time I got to college with my new-found feminism, I would find insulting, demeaning. I'd see it as a generational distinction between us. I remember constantly reminding her that the women who worked for my father were adults, that calling them girls made them sound like their mothers dressed them every morning in little lacy dresses, shiny Mary Jane shoes, their hair in Bopeep curls. But at fifteen, I loved the idea that my mother and I were equals. And now, looking back, I've come to love the words she chose offhandedly, because I think that in many ways, especially this one summer, we were both still innocent, each on the verge of becoming someone else or, maybe more accurately, growing more into ourselves.

Of course, my father, as a gynecologist, might have been the better choice for teaching me the anatomical goings on of my body. My dad had been raised in Boston by an uptight circle of women: his mother, whom I called Tati, and an unmarried aunt, whom I called Bobo, along with his three primly unattractive sisters. The Vietnam War had been his first experience living with men, aside from a scout camp where he'd lit firecrackers behind the scout leader's back and was sent home in shame, his eyebrows singed. I imagine he decided to be a gynecologist as a retreat, in a way, back to the gentler organs of the female body and the more protected world of his childhood. Despite his expertise in female anatomy, however, my mother never relinquished what she thought of as an educational duty. She was passing on a lifetime of womanly experience and found my father wholly unfit.

"My God, Lissy," she liked to say, "he's a dentist with no teeth, a psychologist without hang-ups. Would you trust a blind eye doctor?" I loved it when she talked to me this way, lowering her head, with her eyebrows lifted, her eyes half closed, the same way she talked to the ladies at the Keene Country Club. I loved it because I was a lonely kid, I guess, restless and bored. I loved my mother's confidential tone, even though at this point she hadn't really begun her confession spree. And I listened to her. I soaked her knowledge up like a dutiful sponge, tagging and filing all her little tips that I now find myself referring to as if they were scientifically proven, forgetting their offhanded, often illogical origins. For better or for worse, my dentist has teeth, my eye doctor has eyes, the only psychologist I ever had was insane, and my gynecologist has a vagina.

But I have to say that up until this one summer night in 1985, my mother's girl talk had been vague and generic. She'd told me not to sit on boys' laps because it gave them stomachaches; she'd mumble "blue balls," a term that, left undescribed, made me envision fragile Christmas decorations. When I got my period for the first time, she laid out all of the necessary hygiene items on my bed, a box of pads and tampons, even a pair of my underwear with a pad already in place. (Evidently, she'd been prepared.) She gave me a hand mirror to help me figure out where a tampon should go, and then she held me for a moment by the shoulders, looking deeply into my eyes. She tilted her head and smiled, then turned, picking up a basket of laundry, and left the room. She preferred to discuss the polishing aspects of lipstick. Occasionally she'd allude to sex and womanly issues, but she told distant blurry stories as if she didn't have sex and she wasn't a woman, really, but she had a good friend who did and was. I could tell that she wanted to give it to me straight, but she was a converted New Englander, tight-lipped and rigid, and, as in any arena, the converts are always the most firm in their beliefs.

That night when she heard me shuffle into the kitchen, she straightened up. "Do you think this suit is flattering?" She swiveled and pivoted, asking in a tone that suggested midday, ignoring any hint that she might have awakened me, no "Did I wake you?" or "Oh, you're up, too?" It was the beginning of summer vacation and, without the threat of early morning wake-up, the breakfast scramble and busstop hustle, there was no reason, really, not to be awake.

I told her that it was okay, but she didn't seem convinced and she shut the refrigerator. I reached for a plastic-coated kitchen chair in the dark and sat down, pulling my bony knees up into my T-shirt, where they stuck out in place of breasts, a knobby shelf for my elbows. I was ready for her to start our regular lessons. But this time, she lit a cigarette—an occasional weakness about to become more than occasional. The kitchen was dark, a little light thrown in from the hall. The struck match lit her face for a second. She sat down at the table and said, very calmly, almost sweetly, "Your father, the bastard, is sleeping with a red-headed bank teller in Walpole. What do you propose we do about it?"

I wasn't altogether shocked by my mother's language. After all, no one can absolutely shake her roots. I certainly haven't. I had imagined her upbringing in Bayonne, her father's fish shop on Avenue C, where he'd made enough money to send her to a convent school for her last two years of high school and then on to Simmons, a pristine women's college in New England that tidied up anything over-looked by the nuns. But sometimes when she was angry or chewing gum, she became the fish-shop owner's daughter from Bayonne. This was one of those moments. She sat down and pushed back a cuticle with her thumbnail, waiting for my answer.

Once I had finally processed what my mother had said, my first reaction was disbelief. My father seemed too clumsy to be a doctor, much less to have an affair. Sex alone seemed thoroughly complicated to me, but to have it with someone with unfamiliar parts seemed nearly impossible. He seemed to lack both the necessary coordination and bravery. My mother once moved a coffee table three inches farther from the sofa and my father repeatedly nicked his wooden shin, and the real one was bruised for weeks. He was completely unhandy—and handiness seemed necessary, for some reason, in pulling off something like an affair.

"He doesn't even have a toolbox." It was all I could think to say. "He keeps his screwdrivers in a cut-open milk container. Are you sure he's having an affair? How do you know?"

"He's your father. He gets frazzled pumping gas. You can imagine him in the midst of an affair." She sat down and crossed her legs. "He's all but written it in lipstick across his forehead."

Strangely, I didn't think my father was immoral. I didn't think of sin or anything of that nature. My mother was fairly religious, not above taking the Lord's name in vain, but a constant at weekly Mass and confession. The nuns at the convent school had made an indelible impression. She didn't speak of them often, but when she did, she was reverent. My father, on the other hand, was moderately religious, less likely to swear, but also less likely to attend church, and as far as I know, he never went to confession. We'd always attended a cinder-block church decorated in the fallout from the '60s, orange shag carpet, abstract ren-

ditions of the stations of the cross—spiders on purple
felt—and a chubby Jesus that a parishioner-artist had vol-
unteered to do for the cross, his loincloth so skimpy that
whenever I looked up, I felt dirty, as if I were trying to
catch a glimpse up his skirt and fearful, too, of what might
pop out. In the church's basement, I attended the manda-
tory CCD classes where I was taught the Hail Mary before
I could read. There was a posterboard with pictures of hail-
stones and the Virgin Mary and because someone didn't
know how to draw grace, there was a picture of grapes. And
we recited: "Hail, Mary, full of grapes." I went through a
devout stage at thirteen, when I was confirmed. I chose
Joan of Arc for my confirmation name. In the eyes of the
church, my name is Melissa (Lissy) Katherine Joan of Arc
Jablonski. The three other girls in the class chose Theresa,
as in the Little Flower of Jesus, but she was much too sub-
servient for my taste, finding God while scrubbing floors.
But somewhere between my grandiose confirmation at
thirteen and the summer of my father's affair when I was
fifteen, my religious fervor began settling into murky dis-
interest, which has since turned into a detached appreciation for my failed attempt at spirituality. I thought that my
father's affair was scandalous, incredible, but I wasn't really thinking of it as unethical. However, because of my religious upbringing, I felt comfortable thinking that his
affair was so unbelievable that it was nearly miraculous.

Often when I'm remembering my fifteenth summer and,
especially, this one particular night, it's as if my mother
and I are underwater. The kitchen takes on that thick,
underwater feel, that slow, unsyncopated sinking. My
mother and I are not strong swimmers. She learned eventually at the convent school to frog-kick with her neck

stretched away from the surface like a collie's. And on summer vacations at Lake Winnipesaukee, she taught me the same awkward stroke. I can still see my father, a non-swimmer, on the dock, basking in a foldable aluminum lawn chair, his stump dangling, his fake leg propped idly against the arm of the chair, his good leg resting on its heel. My mother stands breast-deep, her shoulders pink from sun, pinched by the thick straps of her suit, her painted toe-nails dusted in lake silt. She waits for me, with her arms outstretched, to tip off the sandy shore and paddle into deeper water; my legs churn frantically beneath me, my hands pawing. I had always feared slipping under and settling on the bottom of the silty lake, and this is what I feel in the kitchen, underwater, next to the luminescent refrigerator and under the slow-motion ceiling fan. And although we were sitting there calmly, it's as if my mother and I are holding our noses, the air tight in our lungs, our clipped heartbeats racing in our ears, the panic of the water pressing in.

I remember I asked her straight out, "Do you love him?" I asked it because it seemed like an adult question, and I very much wanted to be adult or, at least, to have my mother respect me like one. And I needed to know. It seemed the most important thing.

My mother stopped and stared at me. On the one hand, she was the fish-shop owner's daughter, the girl who grew up in Bayonne, hard, no-nonsense, the identity she wanted desperately to shed but never really could, and on the other hand, she was the person she dreamed of becoming, that she was promised she could become, the person that I'd believed her to be, for the most part, when I was fifteen: the type of woman who taped down her nipples with Band-

Aids under strapless evening gowns, who taught me how to pee without making a tinkling sound, who still believes that a woman should reveal as little as possible about herself. And yet this was when she started to crack; this was the moment, if I were pressed to choose one, that she decided to go ahead and reveal everything, and there was no turning back.

Her cigarette shook between her fingers, her eyes shimmered, and she whispered—almost mouthed, "He breaks my heart."

2

It was nearly midnight by the time we pulled on to Route 12, heading north, and the summer air pouring in the car windows was cool. Walpole was only a half hour away, and we zipped along in the blue station wagon, each streetlight pulsing over the car.

"In the old days," my mother said, pushing the cigarette lighter, "you waited till they were drunk, tangled up in bed sheets, and you beat the hell out of them with a cast-iron frying pan, or, depending on your class, a polo mallet." She sighed. "Of course, my mother never had this problem. My father was a sap. My mother was a drunk with a mean, superstitious heart. She beat on him all right, but she didn't need a frying pan."

My mother almost never spoke of her parents, so I was surprised to hear them described this way—or any way at all. I'd never given them much thought. There was a black-and-white picture of them in the living room, a man with a push-broom mustache, a somber woman with light brown hair and a small, tight mouth. They were smudgy and small and collected a good bit of dust. I had imagined if they'd been alive, they'd have looked like typical grand-parents, talk about phonographs, and wear cardigans; that maybe he'd have taught me to bait a hook and she'd have taught me to cross-stitch. But because I had little interest in fishing and needlework, I'd decided I hadn't been cheat-ed out of much by their early deaths.

"They seemed nice, in their picture."

"Do you believe everything you see?"

I didn't respond. It wasn't really a question.

At the time, I didn't wonder why my mother had brought me along. She'd presented it as family business, the way she consulted me on the color of new carpeting when it was really her decision entirely. I also didn't ask where she'd gotten the address of the redheaded bank teller. In retrospect, I wish I had, because I was young enough to get away with that kind of question. Now it's a gaping hole in the story. I assume that it was a piece of information that wound its way from secretary to neighbor, from teller to customer, from this source to that, until there were so many ways for it to travel to my mother that it was just a matter of time.

That night, however, I was concentrating on the image of my father in bed with a redheaded bank teller. I was try-ing to piece it together with things I'd read in Judy Blume books and seen in bits and pieces in the movies, *Summer of '42* in particular. But as soon as I saw the faceless woman loosen his tie, I was stopped by the saggy skin at his throat. As soon as he took off his trousers, I was stopped by the sock garter on his real leg and the pinkish shine of the fake one. For a long time growing up, I thought my father had actually *lost* his leg in Vietnam, that he'd misplaced it, hopped off, and left it behind, and I remember being aware of my body as a child, in a way other kids probably weren't, on shopping trips around town, taking quick inventories of my limbs. But I wasn't really afraid of losing a part of myself. I knew that I could just get another arm or leg, just pick up a spare on one of my mother's errands. Eventually, I realized that my father's leg hadn't been left behind like a sock forgotten under a motel bed, that it probably had been blown off while he was hauling bodies away on stretchers, but he never spoke of it. I began to envision the leg that used to hang below his calloused stump, his youthful leg with its fine blond hair. I tried to imagine him rounding bases, taking stairs two and three at a time. By my fifteenth summer, I'd become afraid of the fake leg, how it suddenly appeared, sticking out from behind a sofa or leaning casually against a wall, like a predator, part of a lover that might take me one day, and also like loss. In any case, no matter how much I tried to envision my father in bed with the redheaded bank teller, my father was still my father—the man who took pride in a straight hedge and an evenly sodded lawn, a gangly gynecologist with a lopsided grin and hobbled gait, a wobbly tune whistler.

"Why would he have an affair?" I asked.

She lit up, took a drag. Smoke curled up from her nose. "The man has women undress for him all day long. He's bound to slip."

I cringed. I'd been to his office only as a visitor, not a patient. I'd seen the legless, headless, bloodless model of a woman's body cut open and with moveable parts, the tissue paper—covered tables, the silver stirrups. I'd opened the thin drawers filled with shiny instruments and had spun around on his little seat on wheels. I knew that women came in and he examined their privates, but I decided to focus on the large standing lamp with its wide bulb, which helped me pretend that his job had more to do with warming baby chicks than staring at vaginas.

"Really? You think she's a patient?"

She nodded. "He's a very handsome man, you know," she said. "I just wish I'd been prepared."

"How?"

"Oh, God," she said. "I've had my opportunities. Frank Mertog has been after me for ages."

"Oh," I said. "His daughter, Linda, wears a lot of eye shadow. She globbed it on all last year during social studies."

She looked over at me then and she seemed surprised, as if she'd just realized how young I really was. Maybe she thought that she'd made a mistake, that I should be at home reading Nancy Drew mysteries in my canopy bed. She started to cough, stubbed out the cigarette, and then said, "Don't smoke cigarettes. If I ever catch you smoking, well, that'll be the end of it, Miss Lissy."

My mother had the redhead's address scribbled on a piece of paper that was spread open on her thigh. We were snaking through side streets, my mother squinting up through the windshield. "I can't see a thing," she said, changing the subject. "Can you make out any road signs? Do you see Hamilton Avenue?"

I started to get nervous. I had to pee. "Can we stop at a McDonald's or something?"

"Not in this part of town," she said. Walpole was rinky-dink at best, with a town common, a few ball fields, houses, barns, and churches, and most of all the stink of chicken farms. New Hampshire is a strange state. I've taken an informal poll of people from across the country and asked them what they think of when they think of New Hampshire. They say, "Skiing. Turtlenecks. Nice sweaters. Summer homes on lakes. The primaries. Money. Syrup." Of course, if they're from Boston or thereabouts, they know it's a shabby state of run-down farms, codgers on porches, and county fairs with eight-legged calves soaking in jars of formaldehyde. I was embarrassed when I first went off to college in Baltimore and someone asked where I was from, but then after each glowing response, I realized that nobody seemed to know the truth—that we have the highest alcoholism rate in the nation, for example; that people kill themselves in droves each devastatingly long winter—and I wasn't going to make anyone the wiser. And no one has ever really caught on. Nashua, for God's sake, was recently voted the best place to live in the nation. Walpole is your typically trashy New Hampshire town.

I pointed to the sign. "Hamilton Avenue!" And then I slouched down in the seat. "What are you going to say?"

"Oh, don't you worry. I know exactly what I'm going to say."

We stopped in front of a town house with empty macramé plant holders swaying in the breeze, two rusty folding chairs sitting on a tiny square of front yard, a cat curled by the front door. My father's Toyota Corolla was parked in the driveway.

"My God," my mother whispered. "Jesus."

And suddenly I saw my father clearly in my mind in bed with a redheaded bank teller, his white hands gripping the pillow beneath her head, his pale body, the taut cords of his neck, her bright hair splayed on the pillow. It was an image that I couldn't fully understand, but there it was, clearer in my mind than if I'd walked into the room with them.

"Get out of the car," my mother said. She fiddled with the keys on the ring dangling from the ignition.

"What? What are you going to do?"

She took two keys from the ring and said, "Get in your father's car, start it up, and put it in reverse. Pull out of the driveway."

"I can't drive!" My father had taken me out on a few Saturday afternoons to the church parking lot for driving lessons.

"I'm not asking you to drive. Just pull out of the driveway."

"And what are you going to do?"

"I'm just going to switch cars with your father, that's all."

My father's car smelled like him, like his aftershave and coffee. The radio came on as soon as I started the engine. It was an old pop song, "Sugar, Sugar" by the Archies, and I knew then that he was a stranger to me, that he was not the man I had known as my father. I wanted to be older, to be a part of that other world just out of reach. And so even from this early point in my father's betrayal, my overwhelming emotion was not anger at being betrayed but envy. Yes, he was a traitor, but by my teenage definition of the tedious life in Keene, New Hampshire, it was a mutinous situation. *I* wanted to be the one to disappear down a highway with the radio blaring, "Oh, sugar, sugar," to be careless and in love.

I put the car in reverse and backed out of the driveway, bumping it off the curb, then yanked it into drive and tugged at the wheel. I watched my mother, white-

knuckled. She scooted her car in, glancing around excit-
edly, a cigarette poised between her lips, and she was a
stranger to me, too.

My mother jumped into the passenger's seat and started
laughing. "Drive," she said. "Just drive."

I stepped on the gas, and the car jerked down the street.

I don't know how my father got involved with the redheaded bank teller. I admit that there's only a tiny sliver
of this story that I can tell with any precision. I assume that
she was a patient, that my mother's information was right.
It had, in fact, led us to the right house. But I can't imagine his affair had anything to do with the fact that women
undressed for him every day. I can see my father having to
tell the redhead some sad news, because this was often his
job, in his office behind the heavy wooden door. Maybe she
began to cry and he comforted her, and there was a con-
nection between them, a mixture of heartache and sympa-
thy and safety. I can only guess.

About four blocks from Hamilton Avenue on our way
home, I blew through a stop sign, and my mother took
over at the wheel. The Archies had stopped singing "Sugar,
Sugar," and my mother switched off a weekend weather
update. It was still dark. We flew by a cop ticketing a convertible. My mother smoked cigarettes, one after another.
Neither of us spoke.

When she pulled into our driveway, I asked, "Now
what?"

She said nothing and walked into the house. I followed
her to the kitchen. She started to brew a pot of coffee, the
thin white filter shaking in her hand.

"What's the rest of the plan? What's next?"

"Now we sit and wait," she said.

"For what?"

"Now he knows that I know. Now I wait."

We both sat down at the kitchen table, the coffeepot gurgled, and my mother stared at me almost desperately, her eyes wide. She glanced around the kitchen, as if she were a lost guide admitting a failing sense of direction. I reached across the table and took her hand, as if I knew just what to do next.

We waited quietly in the kitchen for a couple of hours, and then we went to bed. I lay awake, waiting to hear my father unlock the front door, for the closet to rumble open, his coat to rustle and loose hangers to chime, for the sound of his feet on the stairs, the coins in his pocket jingling. I finally dozed off but kept startling awake all night, wondering if I'd heard the click of the light switch, my father peeing in the bathroom, his whistle as he washed his hands. I convinced myself that it was possible for him not to notice my mother's car at all, that he could simply drive home almost blind or that the car itself could find its own way to the our house on Pako Avenue like a horse at the end of the workday.

But this is the moment I come up for air, the clearest of my memories: I am staring at the one moonlit wall of my dark room. I stare at that bright square until my eyes sting and tear. I feel the water again, my mother and I, our arms pushing, our legs scissoring beneath us. Each motion takes on a new heaviness—waterlogged, almost leaden. We tread together breathlessly. My father didn't come home, not that night or the next or the one after that. He disappeared for an entire summer.

3

The redheaded bank teller was a tragic figure even before my mother began collecting all the necessary facts. I suppose she was tragic because I couldn't imagine someone having an affair with my father just for a romp. He was a serious man, not a drinker or a smoker. He believed in God—although not fervently, as far as I could tell—and I thought that, if my father was having an affair, it was for some almost holy reason, as part of a Catholic outreach program of sorts, not out of passion. He was not a passionate man. He left Fourth of July fireworks displays early to beat the traffic home. And so I figured that the redheaded bank teller was needy and that he was responding to that need.

The first factual thing that I knew about her was from the tattered little note we found slipped under our door the morning after my mother's switcheroo—a dismal failure, in retrospect, an unprecedented miscalculation. The note was written on the back of a receipt for Lucky Stripe chew-

ing gum and eyeliner from The Apothecary, a drugstore on
Main Street. It said:

> *Dear Mrs. Jablonski,*
>   *We are leaving town, and so's not to upset you and Lissy,*
> *I am leaving this note. Bobby left instructions at his office*
> *for Bonnie and Kay on what to do with his patients and*
> *checks and that sort of thing. I guess there's really not much*
> *else to say.*
>
>   *Sincerely,*
>   *Vivian Spivy*

The "Mrs. Jablonski" was all wrong, of course. My mother took it as a slap in the face. "She's saying, 'I'm young and
you're old, Mrs. Jablonski. Old,' " my mother said. But I
thought the note sounded shy and embarrassed and humble,
like the "sincerely." It was, I think, her way of saying, *I'm not
trying to take your place.* And, now, looking back as an adult,
the "Bobby" reference showed a certain naïveté. My mother
rolled her eyes when she said it out loud. Calling him
"Bobby" was a poor choice in what I had already decided was
a string of poor choices Vivian had made, within perhaps a
lifetime dedicated to poor choices. She had no idea that my
mother never called my father Bobby, that it was a pet name
that Vivian had invented, a persona that perhaps he had gotten so attached to that he couldn't let go of it, that maybe
the entire affair had more to do with my father's being
Bobby than it had to do with his love for Vivian Spivy.

I'm not sure why my father didn't write. It was unlike
him, perhaps one of the clearest signs that he'd changed or
was trying to change. My mother read the letter that my
father had left for Bonnie, his nurse, and Kay, his recep-

tionist. She said it was businesslike, explaining that the
leave was indefinite and unexpected and that they'd be
compensated. I imagine his not writing to my mother and
me—at least a list of instructions on issues of upkeep,
house and car and bills—was an act of will. For whatever
reasons, he decided not to write, and he doggedly stuck to
his decision.

My mother was a detective, wired for gossip, and I didn't
question her sources. There were obviously entire networks,
CIA and FBI types of women's information organizations
in Keene. Every day of that first week, my mother came
home from the store, the post office, the fabric shop with
new information about the redhead: Her parents were dog
track bettors with a brood of children ranging from adults
to infants; her brothers laid concrete. She'd been taking a
class in accounting at Keene State College and had been
living with a woman who had fifteen cats. She'd taken tennis lessons that spring through the Department of Parks
and Recreation but wasn't athletically inclined. She was a
patient of my father's. She'd had her tubes tied by another
doctor in Boston. She was twenty-four.

My feelings for Vivian Spivy were complex. I'd just
started to get all sweaty around boys, and so the visions I
had of the naked body of Vivian Spivy were confusing. My
feelings for her weren't really sexual, although they were
rooted in sex, sex with my father, but they were feelings of
love. It was, actually, a motherly or fatherly (it's hard to
say) kind of love. I wanted to take care of her, to raise her
up from dog track bettors and concrete layers. I wanted to
give her tennis lessons the way I'd been taught privately on
Tuesdays by the aged Mrs. Tutwhiler, who'd once been on
the women's Olympic team. I wanted to brush the cat fur

from her clothes and the tangles from her red hair, help her get into a good college, full time. I wanted to untie her tubes and make her a mother, clean and whole and beautiful, like my mother. And I felt guilty about this, because I knew that I shouldn't love Vivian Spivy, that this love was betraying my mother, just as my father had. I loved Vivian and I hated her, too, for taking my father, for hurting my mother. I hated myself for loving her. I knew that my love for Vivian Spivy wasn't natural, wasn't a normal reaction, but there was nothing I could do about it. In retrospect, I believe I was in love with her because that love allowed me to understand my father.

The only therapist I've ever had—it was during college at the end of a string of sour romances—said that this love of Vivian allowed me to fantasize being Vivian Spivy, which allowed me to have sex with my father, for whatever that's worth. I don't go around saying that when I was a teenager I wanted to have sex with my father. I certainly did not. The mere idea would have made me gag— gagging being popular in the '80s. But what I'm saying is that my father's affair and the subsequent events concurring with my sexually impressionable age were not something I overcame easily. These were the kinds of things that force you to rethink every decision from there on out. It was a pivotal moment, a psychoanalyst's field day.

I'd like to add that the whole Electra complex business is also a result of my generation, my time and place in history. Freud was shoved down my throat. Of course, my generation has been brainwashed to look for cocks and tits masquerading as everyday household items. My sophomore year of high school, a Catholic high school even, I was analyzing vodka ads in a sociology class for genitalia among melting ice cubes. By college, I was trained to actually read *sex* in the swirled cigarette smoke of a menthol. I knew that, if you fold the Land O'Lakes butter wrapper the right way, the Indian's knees become nippleless breasts, that Joe Camel's face was really just a flaccid penis lying on its balls, and that halfway through a certain Mickey Mouse ice pop, you'd find yourself sucking a purple dick. It was a conspiracy theory that made advertisers look like perverted geniuses, which is one of the reasons I like advertising, my chosen career. People of my generation and social and educational background are fluent in cocktail Freudian theory, maybe even are able to speak a little pidgin Jung, enough to throw out the word *archetypal.* We're a generation of crackpot analysts, self-analyzing. Imagine the horrifying array of self-haircuts there'd be if we all thought we were professional hair stylists because we owned a pair of scissors. Now replace haircuts with psyches. It's not a pretty picture. My point is that because my father had an affair, I was forced to think of him sexually, which led to a crackpot diagnosis. It may very well mean nothing. My therapist, by the way, was a troll-like woman who, whenever we approached the subject of sex, had the habit of tugging at her nose, which I—being well trained—thought of as her own little penis. So who's the stable one?

I was fairly sure that everyone knew what was going on. Mrs. Defraglia came over for unannounced visits and invited the family to a little barbecue for the sole purpose, as far as I could tell, of hearing my mother come up with an excuse to decline. As luck would have it, our bank was the bank that Vivian Spivy worked for. When we went in to check the account and found $1,041 missing—exactly one third of the total—I was convinced that the tellers were whispering, *Yes, he took it so he could escape with Vivian,* each one of them secretly rooting for Vivian, sizing us up, deciding what we had done to run him off.

My father's receptionist and nurse called from the office, bewildered by the instructions my father had left them. They wanted to know if it was some kind of joke, not that my father was the joking kind, but neither was he the kind to disappear suddenly. My mother told them that his mother was sick and that he was in Boston, because she'd been asking to see her son.

"She's an old crow," my mother said, convincingly irritated. "He could be there for days, weeks. We'll call it a holiday."

My Grandmother Tati and Aunt Bobo were a sticking point, however. Tati especially was an intimidating woman. And it was their impending Sunday-night call that my mother most feared. My mother knew that she couldn't fool them, and that without their boy's voice, they'd suspect the worst of my mother.

"They'll think I've got him locked up in the basement or something," my mother said. "They'll think I've killed him. They've never liked me."

On Friday afternoon, I was practicing the clarinet, flipping through a book of popular sheet music, "You Light Up My Life" clipped to my metal music stand. I was a terrible clarinet player, always letting out some dying-duck call, some cats-at-sex squeal. My mother sat on the living-room sofa in front of the bay window to listen. She said it soothed her, but I can't imagine she was telling the truth. It was hot and she'd drawn the curtains all but an inch or two. Occasionally she'd peer out and shake her head at the sight of Mrs. Defraglia digging in her flower garden in short shorts. Sometimes she'd mutter, "The son of a bitch is in my car with that woman. My car!" As if she'd forgotten that it was her little scheme that had provided him with her car. I had trouble imagining my father in the family car. It seemed so embarrassing to run off with a woman in a station wagon, so middle class and suburban. I felt sorry for them, cruising along interstates in a big boat built for car pooling, not love affairs. I imagined her huddled up against him, trying to make a little nest within the wide body's bench seat.

"We won't be here when Tati and Bobo call," she said finally out of the blue. "He should have to explain himself to his own mother."

I squeezed out a final wheezy note. "Where will we be?" I asked. I didn't much care for being fifteen, for the long claustrophobic summer days, and it was only the beginning of summer, the whole lazy vacation stretched out in front of me like a fat lady in a bikini. I was knobby and awkward and had only one friend, Louisa Eppitt, another clarinetist who lived across town in a shabby little house with linoleum peeling up from the floorboards and slit screens, the living room cluttered with broken toasters, radios, clocks, and lamps, what she referred to as her father's "projects." Her mother was dead and her father sat in a La-Z-Boy with a cable box duct-taped to its nappy arm. My father's affair had offered me some much-needed excitement. I didn't doubt he'd come back eventually. There were moments of reality to the situation, but I had trouble understanding the seriousness. My mother was agitated, eating little, chain smoking. But more than anything, I was curious as to what was going to happen next. And I thought a trip would be good, that when my father

pulled into the driveway and plopped down in his own easy
chair to catch the next Red Sox game (I fully expected him
from one minute to the next), it might do him good if we
weren't there.

My mother didn't answer the question. She rose up
abruptly from the couch, staring with fixed intensity out
the window. I could hear the growl of a rusted-out muffler,
and I quickly kneeled on the sofa next to her to peer out the
window just as a yellow Nova heaved itself into our driveway. An old woman in a brown coat, on a day much too hot
for a coat, stepped out of the car, which was still sputtering
and coughing. She looked up at the house with a pinched
face and slowly walked to the front door.

"Shit!" my mother said. I glanced across the street and
saw Mrs. Defraglia, one hand on her hip, saluting with her
trowel to keep the sun out of her eyes as she squinted at the
woman on our stoop.

The woman was wrinkled and slightly hunched. She had
sandy gray hair and wore orange lipstick, which led me to
believe she'd once been redheaded, and there was a sharp-
ness to her in the tight chew-chew of her gum and the
tense knot of muscles flexing in her overworked jaw. She
was thin. Beneath the coat she wore blue jeans and a thin
pink sleeveless T-shirt. A big wad of Play-Doh stuck out
from under the sole of one tennis shoe, as if she'd just
stepped in neon dog poop. It crumbled a bit as she vigorously rubbed her shoes on the mat. We stood behind the
screen door, saying nothing.

Finally, she looked up. "Ruth Spivy," she said. "Vivi's ma."

My mother hustled her in the door and away from the
intense gaze of Mrs. Defraglia.

Ruth Spivy went on to say, "Dudley can't sleep—not
since they're gone—and Tig won't wean, you know how

that goes. And he's too big, too, you know, near five year old. There's a lot of tears, you can say, 'tween Tig and Dudley." She had a way of speaking that made her seem very important, as if everyone should know exactly the daily goings-on of Ruth Spivy, know everyone by first name, because we'd just read about them in the newspaper or watched the soap-opera drama of their life on television, and the accent was hers alone entirely, one I'd never heard before, nor since. "Bilxo come in first place last week. We made up some lost time with that, yes did. Dud said he's going to give the winnings all to Vivi if only she'll come home, even if she takes up with that witch again with all the kitties. As long as she's home and given up on all this foolishness with the good doctor. Although he cured her, yes did. And she stopped all the crying jags and sleepless-ness. Thank the good doctor." She was a little breathless but went on. "Vivi called up last night, you know, yes did. Only told us she wasn't telling us where she's gone. Dud loves her. Maybe he loves her too much." Her eyes filled up with tears for a second, but then she wiped her nose fierce-ly with the back of her hand and looked at my mother.

I was wide eyed, but my mother just stood in the hall-way and listened. Ruth Spivy had removed her coat. But my mother didn't offer to hang it up. It was there like some ugly peace offering, but perhaps not peaceful at all— maybe more like the Trojan horse. And it was all the more suspicious because it was so out of season. Ruth had kind of pushed it toward my mother at one point in her speech, but my mother had refused to take it, and now it hung awkwardly in Mrs. Spivy's arms. Without it on, she looked even smaller. Her shoulders were bony and so slouched they couldn't keep up either of her bra straps, which slung down around her elbows like flopped rabbit ears. Mrs.

Spivy had momentarily run out of steam, although she seemed prepared to explain more, if necessary.

My mother didn't let her go on. "Are you asking me to rein in my husband like he's a neighborhood dog who's knocking over trash cans and spreading garbage around people's lawns with his big wet nose?"

Ruth Spivy was a bit confused. She cocked her head momentarily, like a spaniel. She had a knowledge of dogs, it seemed, but maybe not the same knowledge of pets and neighborhood politics as my mother. "Not sure what you mean there. But I'm asking you to do something, as the good doctor's wife. The girl's gotten too old for me." She paused. It was quiet, and then she urged, "Go and collect what's yours, missus."

"Let them go, Mrs. Spivy. That's my advice to you. Don't be ignorant."

Ruth Spivy looked around the house with raised eyebrows. "All ways you can explain ignorant," she said.

My mother opened the front door and ushered the little woman out onto the stoop, where Ruth Spivy angrily tugged on her shabby brown coat. As I watched her shuffle to her car, I felt suddenly woozy, the woman's body seeming to tilt, the car to lean, the grass and trees smearing into a wet, greenish blur. My mother shut the door behind her and pressed against it. I listened to Mrs. Spivy's car labor out of the driveway and down the street. I stood next to the hall closet door and then slid down it, kicking my feet out in front of me, straight legged. I was shocked most, I suppose, by the idea that my mother was so willing to let them go, that she was powerless. I pinched my eyes. My nose started to run. It was the first time I'd cried since lying in my bed that first night waiting for my father to come home.

I must have looked at my mother in a way that caught

her off guard. She straightened up and pulled her loose curls on top of her head into a messy ponytail tied with a rubber band from her wrist. She looked at herself in the hall mirror, tugged at the shirttails of her pink oxford, and said, "Don't cry. He's my husband, but he's not your real father."

It's funny, but at the moment that my mother told me that my father was not my real father, I must have been thinking about Ruth Spivy's son Tig, almost five years old, whom she was trying to wean, and Dudley, her husband, loving Vivian too much. I was wondering what it all meant, why Mrs. Spivy was holding on to everything so tightly. I'd even imagined her home as one like Louisa Eppitt's, a junk-filled, run-down house brimming with knickknacks and carnival trinkets, the yard littered with chicken wire and cement slabs and refrigerators, that she was unable to let go of even the simplest and most useless and ugly things. And then the news came that there was another man, my real father, and my first thought was a physical one: How did my mother let him go? I envisioned my mother and a stranger slipping away from each other, something dreamlike. I envisioned them naked, spinning off and away from each other in space, my mother swelling with me inside her. I wondered if she was joking.

"What?" I said. "What did you say?" I didn't know yet that my mother was a professional liar, my origin being one of her best lies—not a lie really, as my mother would let me know, but a lack of truth. But she had developed such a full and complete life around deceptions that I didn't recognize the truth of her tone, the cock of her head, the hands so squarely on the hips. Although this was one of the most truthful things she'd ever said to me, I wasn't sure I believed her. I wasn't sure if I knew exactly who was talking to me.

4

My mother never liked Juniper Fiske. Put together by chance as roommates their freshman year, they each stuck it out like a good daughter in an arranged marriage. Juniper's maiden name was Shriver; she was somehow related to the politicians and socialites and tennis pros. She was wealthy, and I'm sure this impressed my mother. I got the idea that they were so wealthy that Juniper took my mother on as a charity case in the grand tradition of volunteerism among the women in her family. She'd dressed my mother in her outdated angora sweaters in the previous year's colors. She taught my mother how to daub perfume, ride horses, play tennis, and flirt: the fine points of tittering and gazing.

But I don't think it was easy work. I have a picture of the two of them together at a homecoming football game at Harvard, visiting Juniper's friends. Juniper was not an attractive girl. Her nose was too high on her face and her eyes were too close together, but in the photo she's impeccably dressed, a boutonniere on the lapel of her tailored wool suit, her hair an inch above her shoulders and pulled back in that rich-girl style made popular by the likes of Gloria Vanderbilt. My mother, on the other hand, was a natural beauty with shiny black hair that always looked wet and eyes so large and dark they could make you dizzy, as if you were standing next to a deep hole. Her long hair was pulled back into a loose chignon with soft pincurls in front of her ears, the type nowadays seen only on Hassidic Jews. She had a huge smile, inappropriately large, with dark lips and oversize teeth that rose slightly from her face. My mother seemed to be yelling something to the person snapping the picture. She and Juniper were holding hands, but it was more like Juniper was holding her down, the only thing keeping my mother from leaping out of the picture.

My mother hadn't kept in touch with Juniper personally but had heard through the grapevine that she and Guy had divorced and that Juniper and her daughter Piper and son Church were still living on Cape Cod—the Cod, my mother called it, which even *I* knew was wrong. I had the impression that my mother thought it a good idea to see an accomplished divorced family, that Juniper would educate her in the ways of single-motherhood, as she had in college in the ways of the upper crust. My mother called it a vacation, but I had the idea that she viewed it more as a crash course.

She called her alma mater for Juniper's current number and then called Juniper. She said that Juniper was elated to hear from her. In fact, they'd hastily arranged a trip. We packed our bags that afternoon. My mother carried her little Weight Watchers scale in a brown bag and I brought my clarinet. I called Louisa Eppitt to cancel our practice session for later that week, but she wasn't there, and I was forced to leave a message with her lazy father, a message that I was pretty sure she wouldn't receive. My mother told the cleaning lady, Mrs. Shepherd, a trustworthy old woman with a frog's down-turned mouth and a bosom like the cowcatcher on a freight train, about the spare key on the hook in the garage. She instructed her that Dr. Jablonski would be coming home sometime soon but to work around him.

We waved to Mrs. Defraglia, who was now sipping a little golden drink with lots of ice—a drink that could pass for iced tea, but as my mother said on the way out of the drive, "She's not kidding anyone, drunk midday."

Mrs. Defraglia pretended quickly to be looking at the sky. "Looks like rain," she shouted across the street.

We smiled and nodded, but the sky was bright blue, not a cloud in sight.

My real father, Anthony Pantuliano, was a small man, only five foot four, with an oversize head and a penis of mythically large proportions. I learned this while my mother and I were driving the three hours from Keene to Juniper Fiske's house on Cape Cod in my father's Toyota Corolla. The light blue sedan was clean, recently vacuumed, with half a roll of Certs in the sparkling ash tray, and the whole car smelled sweet from his aftershave. Of course, I was thinking by then that the aftershave was for Vivian, the Certs for Vivian, that he'd vacuumed the car out for Vivian. He was spruced up for dating. I imagined him nervous and excited, driving to her place in Walpole like a sixteen-year-old who'd borrowed his dad's car. It was all very disconcerting.

My mother had started the discussion about my biological father as if she were the head of a PTA question-and-answer meeting. "I'll talk a bit and then open it up for questions. Please feel free to ask me anything."

But she was rusty and her speech was clumsy and ill prepared. He'd been a presence in her mind for so long—a person with no words, only thoughts, attached to him—that it was hard for her talk about him. She jumped around so much and was so sketchy that I wished she'd conducted it even more like a PTA meeting, complete with the hum of an overhead projector glowing with a tidy timeline of events.

She began, "I was a Verbitski, Polish; he was Italian, Pantuliano. My family was against it." But all of this sounded like Romeo and Juliet, the Capulets and the Montagues. It had begun to dawn on me that maybe she was trying to make me feel better, that for some twisted reason, a made-up father was better than one who had run off with a redheaded bank teller from dingy little Walpole. On top of that, she was used to her station wagon. My father's Corolla had more zip, and my mother drove all automatics two-footed, one foot on the gas and one on the brakes, and sometimes, I swear, both at once. She wasn't the best driver even under the best circumstances, but now she seemed to be overcompensating, alternating brakes and gas just to go forward in a straight line. I felt nauseated, jerking and speeding down the highway, the warm air flipping my hair into my eyes.

"Look, I don't need this little story you've made up," I said. "I can handle the truth."

"What truth?" she asked.

"That my father's a two-timer, that he's left us," I said.

My mother pulled the car over onto the shoulder and put the car in neutral. "Listen to me: Your father and I met and got married in twelve days. I supposedly conceived you on our honeymoon and you were born seven months later. You were two months premature and weighed seven pounds eleven ounces with a full head of hair? It doesn't take a genius to smell something wrong with that stew."

We sat there for a while not saying a word. The car was suddenly airless.

"So does my real father know about me?" I asked.

She shrugged. "I have no idea where he is."

"Okay," I said. "Tell me something you do know."

"Anthony Pantuliano wanted to experience everything. He was an idealist with a big head and a giant penis."

I think my mother, perhaps subconsciously, was telling me all about Anthony Pantuliano to get back at my father. They'd made a silent pact, of sorts. He broke the pact by leaving her and so she was free to tell me anything she damn well pleased. She was angry, and she began to tell me the story of her first love out of that anger. She was getting even. But I think that my mother believed she was telling me everything for my own good. Her own mother was a silent, ogrelike woman who told her nothing until it was too late and she was shipping off her teenage daughter to be raised by nuns. My mother realized, at the start of that summer, that she had to raise me the opposite of the way she'd been raised. My father's affair woke her up, I think, made her open her eyes and take a look around at what she'd thought a good, solid life. That's when she found me already fifteen with little breasts and a sweet if not pretty face, on the verge of becoming a woman, prepared to figure it all out with or without her. But she had no role model for giving it straight. In retrospect, I think she'd agree that she went overboard. But she was doing the best she could. She was dogged about being truthful. She was winging it.

An eighteen-wheeler rumbled by, making our car shiver, sucking the wind from the windows. "His fully erect penis was the size of a loaf of French bread," my mother said. "He had only one eye. He was a visionary."

I'd never heard my mother say the word *penis* before. Our previous girl talks had been failures of communication, flopped attempts at bonding. She seemed to take on a sudden matter-of-factness, a strange calm, as if she'd finally and absolutely resigned herself to telling all of the sordid details. Perhaps she called on the detached professionalism she'd practiced studying nursing at Simmons. In any case, the news was startling to me. I'd only glimpsed penises— the anatomical health book and coarse, comical, desk-carved varieties. I'd once walked in on my father after a bath before he'd wrapped up in a towel. I'd always thought of the penis as an odd dangling, bobbling pink thing or a sturdy salute. But to think of it suddenly in such graphic terms, so large, it was breathtaking, deeply disturbing. I knew that it was something meant to go inside of a woman, and, at fifteen, this was a scary enough thought with the previous notions I'd had of penis sizes. I'd just become comfortable using slender/regular tampons. I thought, *My God, it could have punctured her lung.* The part about his having only one eye went virtually unheard.

After the initial shock of my biological father's distorted proportions, my thoughts turned to the man I'd always known as my father, Bob Jablonski. I wanted to defend him, as if my mother had been the one who'd had the affair.

I began to wonder exactly what Bob Jablonski knew about my paternity, if anything, and, if he did, what he thought of it. From my birth, he'd played dad rather convincingly. "Does Dad know he's not my dad?" I asked.

"Sure," she said. "Of course. He's not a blockhead, and it *is* his field of expertise."

"How did you break it to him?"

"Well, I didn't announce it like the Virgin Mary did to Joseph. It was a little different situation, being that no angel passed the word onto me, and he'd had no inspired dream like Joseph to prepare him."

"So? What did you say?"

"Oh, I hate this feminist crap," she said. "This idea that my husband is my best friend and I've got to confess, spill my bleeding heart out all over him. It's really a load, if you ask me. Listen, Lissy, this is my point: Don't tell the truth. I'm not telling you to lie, although lies can be very important. Just don't go around telling the truth every minute, spouting out a play-by-play of what you're thinking and feeling."

Strangely enough, if you look at Mary in the Bible, this is kind of her motto. She is constantly keeping things in her heart, pondering them. Check the Gospel according to Luke, the stuff with the shepherds and finding Jesus in the temple. I imagine Mary making her way through the Bible, keeping all of her sorrow locked up in her heart until it swells from the size of a pocketbook to a suitcase to a steamer trunk, the angels sent in for the regalia of her ascension, hauling her into heaven, their cheeks red from effort, her heart *Guinness Book of World Records* heavy, so much heavier than, say, that woman with the 303-pound tumor wheeled out of the operating room on its own stretcher. My mother wasn't a virgin, her conception wasn't immaculate, but her anticonfessional habit was Mary's all the way.

"So you didn't tell him?"

"No," she said. "It was just something we both knew. That's all."

I thought of my father sitting through my clarinet recitals, my softball games, the endless hours of tortured dance performances where I scuffed and teetered across the stage in a herd of pink-tutued girls. When I was nine and desperate for a sister, my parents told me they'd tried, but it wasn't meant to be. I wondered how it must have been for my father, a possibly sterile man. (My mother had proven *her* fertility.) Maybe, I thought, he had to believe I was his more and more as time went on, because I became his only shot at fatherhood, and maybe he didn't want to accept that someone else, a stranger, had upstaged him this intimately. If I play out the Mary metaphor, my father makes a wonderful Joseph, solid and dependable (aside, of course, from the Vivian escapade). Upstaged by the Holy Spirit, Joseph knew Jesus wasn't his own son, and yet he raised him all the same. Don't get me wrong. I don't think I'm some Christ figure. The metaphor should not extend to me as some unintentional, fumbling Jesus or to Anthony Pantuliano as God. I certainly wouldn't want to play Jesus, and even Anthony, with all of his mystery and power couldn't have pulled off God Almighty. But my father was an excellent Joseph. He knew that I wasn't his and yet he must have forgotten it at the same time. I can still see him in the audience beaming, his apple cheeks shining just beneath his wet eyes. It made his love all the more miraculous, and his leaving, too, more understandable. He could have walked out on my mother and me the day I was born, the seven-pound-eleven-ounce premature child who obviously wasn't his. My head wasn't glowing like Jesus' head; there was no star; there were no wise men. But he stuck it out as best he could for fifteen years. And then there was a temptation. I was on his side, though. I thought temptations were bound to occur and I figured that a temptation—named Vivian Spivy—had hit at just the moment he was feeling the most weary of his role as Joseph. This is what I wanted to believe. It was a slip. He'd be back.

Ever since my mother had told me about Anthony Pantuliano, I would sometimes see a puny, dark-haired kid with an oversize head and I'd catch myself looking for the bulge in his jeans, his sealed eye. I'd catch myself saying *Anthony Pantuliano,* my heart skipping, my stomach doing a little flip as if I were the one who'd fallen in love with him.

You can look at this idiosyncrasy many ways. My therapist decided that I had not just one Electra complex but two, one for each father. (Modern families with divorces and remarriages are a bitch, by the way, for the whole Oedipus-Electra thing.) But you know how I feel about Freudian theory, its pervasive nature cuckolding an entire culture into believing we're perverted, a force so paralyzing we can't chew ice without analyzing our sexual anxiety. So I've decided that any Electra complex could be the figment of a Freud-obsessed culture, adding more simply that I was young, hormonally imbalanced, and impressionable and the stories of Anthony were as romantic as any movie I'd seen. I fell for a character, not a person, a sixteen-year-old romantic lead, certainly not my father.

But since it was my father, genetically, and my mother, I couldn't help but take the leap that their story was a part of me. My mother started out telling me about her life with the best of intentions, but her plan, in some ways, back-fired. I was bound to hear the stories not to learn lessons but to follow her.

The first time I realized that I was living my mother's life was after I left home for college—Loyola in Baltimore. I took up with a guy named Joey Pedesto. He, too, was short and big-headed like Anthony Pantuliano; his cock, however, was more proportionate with the rest of his body, and he had both of his eyes. He was a bartender and two-bit pot dealer who'd done a stint in the navy and was taking classes at Towson State so he could eventually go on to law school. We first got together on my birthday. I'd just turned twenty-one, and although I'd been going to the bars for a long time—Gators in particular, on a corner on York Road just outside of Baltimore—it was nice to final-ly be legal. And I was letting Joey in on the little secret that I was not—as my fake ID claimed—Nancy Espiritu, a five-foot, 100-pound smiley American Filipino woman, but, in fact, taller and a little more buxom, with a dark, cool sense of humor.

"I'm not Filipino at all," I told Joey conspiratorially, quite drunk. "All I know about the Philippines is that General and Mrs. MacArthur never had a second honey-moon there."

He was taking a break from tending bar. It was late,

probably midweek. My friends and I were regulars, duti-
fully putting in hours as if it were a library. We wore
tapered jeans, sometimes pinning the cuffs, and I had a
black leather bolero jacket with a hundred zippers. My
partner in crime, a wild and intensely bright young woman
named Liza Merchum, was chatting up some Hopkins guys
wearing argyle sweaters who'd mistakenly wandered in.

"If you're not Filipino, then what are you?"

At home, I didn't tell the truth, that I'm half Italian,
half Polish. My father, Bob Jablonski the gynecologist from
Keene, came back after the summer that never happened,
and I was again his daughter, two Polish halves—Verbitski
and Jablonski—making a whole. I was eight hours away,
though, and on my own I could tell the truth without any
betrayal. I didn't. My mother would have omitted, danced,
retained some mystery. It was what she believed in. But I
went for the lie.

"My mother toured with a flamenco troop. She was a
Spanish dancer. She met my father, a Brit, in Samoa where
he was a struggling painter. They had sex on a veranda and
I was born nine months later."

Joey had placed a cigarette between his lips, and,
although I didn't smoke, I took it from his mouth and put
it in mine. He lit it. I thought it was all terribly sexy. After
last call, he drove me back to his place. (Liza had already
taken off with the Hopkins boys, sitting up on the backseat of a convertible Saab, wearing one of the boys' argyle
sweaters wrapped like a turban on her head.) I remember
Joey's roommate had a cargo bag filled with little bags of
pot. We passed a joint back and forth on his bed, taking
long, tight-lipped, sipping drags. Our eyes puffed up. We
got naked. A month later, I was living there, and, every

once in a while, I'd look at Joey Pedesto and I'd think, *Anthony Pantuliano.* I'd watch him come, his eyes squeezed shut, his hot breath on my face, and I'd mouth it: *Anthony Pantuliano.*

One day I drove up to the apartment building with a bag of groceries in the passenger's seat and saw cop cars in the parking lot. I didn't stop. I kept on going. I couldn't reach him on the phone, no answer. A couple days later, I came back for my belongings, and the place was empty except for an older Mexican man painting the walls white over the white. He spoke no English. And I spoke no Spanish; I wasn't the daughter of a flamenco dancer after all. I wondered what it must have been like for my mother to lose Anthony Pantuliano, to think that she would never see him again. For the first time, but not the last, I realized that I was trying to live my mother's life. I knew it was wrong, a bad idea, but one I would continue to repeat.

By the summer of 1999, I was well rehearsed in the roles of my mother's life. I had started an affair with Peter Kinney—who would become the father of my child—not playing the part of my mother but, worst of all, playing the part of Vivian Spivy. I had, in fact, dyed my hair red. It had been a Halloween prank to make me look more like the lead singer for the B-52s, but I had used permanent dye, and in retrospect, it's all too obvious. I guess I'd recently come to the conclusion that Vivian was the most sympathetic character, although now I'd argue they were all sympathetic, not one of them truly in control. I had played my mother's part a number of times, the Joey Pedesto affair being only one of many examples, and here I was as Vivian.

I had no doubt that if I married, I'd end up playing the part
of my father and have an affair. At the arrival of Peter
Kinney into my life, my ugly college therapist with the
nose-tugging twitch would have raised her tiny fists in the
air, vindicated, my Electra complex having led me to a
married man, a fatherly type, a Bob, at last. But in my
defense, I thought I was truly in love—for the first and
possibly only time in my life—with Peter, and things had
taken a bad turn. There was no divorce in sight, as was the
case for Vivian; he was going back to his wife.

Once upon a time, I'd loved men, their broad hands,
their narrow hips, their muscled thighs, tough jaws, and
soft mouths. I had my mother's admiration of the penis. I
loved the way it rolled shyly and then rose up till standing
against gravity, toward warmth and comfort, the way it
could betray a man's coyness, so flushed and ready. But I'd
gotten tired of dating twenty-three-year-olds who didn't
know what they wanted to be when they grew up, who
wanted me to hold their hands, wipe their runny noses. I
fell for Peter because he was a grown-up, married, happily.
He came with excellent references, the best. He had two
kids and a wife and a dog named Lu, short for *lugubrious,*
which is to say sad, a moping long-eared basset hound.
Like my father, he was the last person you'd expect to have
an affair, which is one of the things that made him so
attractive. He'd proven his stability and his loyalty,
albeit—and this was a sticking point—not very well, but
it seemed that he was at least capable of some kind of commitment. I wasn't thinking clearly. I fooled myself into
believing I wanted him to marry me, but really I was
choosing a safely doomed relationship, my favorite kind.

I don't want to rehash every minute of my love affair

with Peter Kinney. The quick version: I'd been flirting
with Peter for weeks, watching him sketch out happy
lemons and spread different lemon faces on my desk, and
then I had a minibreakdown in my office. As a copy writer
at an advertising agency, I'm an idea woman. I come up
with concepts and write schlocky copy. My main project at
that time was the Love-That-Lemon dish detergent campaign, and I was panicked, sure we wouldn't pull it off,
furious at my boss's insane deadlines. I was crying, maybe
most of all because I knew that what I do for a living is
bullshit. I knew it well before all of those articles on
American stupidity so popular in the '90s, books that I
barely skimmed, like *Dumbing Down: Essays on the Strip
Mining of American Culture,* before Fussell came out with his
unenlightened book *BAD, or, The Dumbing of America,*
before all that American culture bashing, as if our stupidity were something new, as if our stupidity weren't something of a national treasure. I was rambling, giving Peter a
stream-of-consciousness speech that, if it had been coher-
ent, would have been brilliant.

I told him that it was clear to me that I'd been raised by
the ultimate hype machine, my mother. She was an ad
woman for the golden life, really. She omitted the unseemly—
like the fact that I was the illegitimate child of Anthony
Pantuliano (all of this quite new to Peter, who'd known me
for only a few weeks)—and played up the positive. But she
couldn't always distinguish what she *wanted* to be the truth
from the *truth.* She raised me as best she could, in her tradition of deceit and omission, and I went into advertising.
It was absolutely instinctive. It was one of the few things
that made sense to me. It makes sense to me that advertising is an essential part of life, that it shapes perception,

realigns neurons, that without advertising, people would
smell a lemon and think of lemons, not clean plates, shine,
and the vague subconscious sense that their mothers loved
them. I said this part clearly, about the subconscious link
between lemons and mother love. I think he understood.

I was clear enough to admit that it wouldn't be completely honest if I said that I went into advertising because
of the education that my mother passed down to me. I
could have said I chose my job because it's creative or for
the money—it's not bad—or I could have been profane and
said it was because I wanted to restore hope through hype.
But the truth is I chose my career out of fear. I didn't want
the machine to eat me, and yet it was eating me all the
same. The subtle infiltration: my dresser lined with bottles, Kiehl's treatment line formula, organic beeswax for
my hair, Laura Mercier's foundation primer cream as if my
face were a wall in need of a paint job, and in my closet, a
pair of mannish oxfords by Miu Miu, a red-lined black
Tahari dress I remember singling out a few items: "My
sunglasses are Black Flys. I bought a hair straightener even
though my hair is straight. If I were to ever get married,
I'd buy a Vera Wang dress, regardless of markup." I made
the point, I think, that in little ways, I cave in to the
machine, I fall for it.

I said, "I don't want to be my mother, to believe that
bullshit promise that each little item, if cared for deeply
enough, will amount to the golden life. I thought I was in
control, helping to drive the machine, that I was behind
the wheel. I voted for Clinton, twice!" Here, I'm not sure
he understood what Clinton had to do with anything. I
could have explained that it was the same kind of duping.
I signed on to a pot-smoking, draft-dodging philanderer,

my eyes wide open. I was sucked in by Clinton's dented armor and because I wasn't getting sucked in by shiny armor, I didn't realize I was getting sucked in all the same.

I said, "My mother's generation had faith in the golden life, in virtue, pride, the American dream. I can't. Nixon resigned when I was four years old. My earliest word association with *president* is *crook*. Any shine left over from World War II was completely muddied by Vietnam. I missed seeing Neil and Buzz moon-walk, but I was watching television my sophomore year with my entire Catholic high school—televisions set up in classrooms, the cafeteria—when the spaceship *Challenger* exploded. And as soon as my hormones started to kick in, AIDS showed up and that party was called off. No sex, no drugs. Even rock and roll turned into fucking 'Wake Me Up Before You Go-go' and 'Abracadabra.' I'm my mother, but I can't be. See?"

I sat down on my desk, which was strewn with Peter's lemon sketches. I ran my hands through my hair. I hiccupped, wiping the tears from my cheeks. "I'm not married. I have no kids. I'm almost thirty. And what I care about most is a fucking lemon that either does or does not wink, and, if so, with the left or right eye?"

He walked up close, then kissed my cheek and then my mouth, and I kissed back. It was a year of office quickies and an occasional overnight at my place, lots of late-night phone calls with long, hot silences. I was always waiting for him to confide in me, to tell me his secrets, the way maybe my father told his secrets to Vivian. I told him mine. But he didn't reciprocate; perhaps he had no secrets or he'd already let his go, to his wife. We didn't have the advantage of running off together, like Vivian and my father. Peter had to bounce back and forth between his wife and me, two very different realities of himself, which made it tough. And then his wife was pregnant with their third. I was pissed. He'd never mentioned that he was sleeping with his wife. I felt cheated on, although that isn't logical. Of course he was sleeping with his wife! And the third child was a deal breaker for him; there was no getting out. Slowly I started to feel like another burden, a responsibility.

I loved Peter Kinney because he loved people easily, intensely. He walked through the city falling in love with people: the Chinese grocer angrily spraying rowed tangerines, the girl crying into the pay phone, the cabbie singing along happily to the Muslim station. Peter would sit in the back of the cab and sing, too, in Arabic, the best he could. He was the type of man who, when passing a field of cows—we once went to the Jersey shore together—rapped his fist on the car door, stuck his body out the window, and mooed at the top of his lungs. He felt he had something in common with everyone.

He broke up with me on a Saturday at a laundromat, cleverly named Laundromat, on MacDougal Street. It was one of our favorite spots. We liked to whisper in a back corner over the noisy churning machines. But things were winding down. Ours was obviously a crumbling relationship. I had just taken my first few pregnancy tests. I had one in a Ziploc bag in my pocketbook.

Peter, not a big guy, had sandy hair and blue eyes with heavy lashes. I was already crying and he was choked up, too. He said, "You know, I envy those guys on talk shows, pilots and traveling salesmen, who have one wife in Duluth and one in Ho-Ho-Kus and another in Baltimore. I don't want to have an affair. I love my wife, and I want to marry you. I want to lead a bunch of lives, a kind of compressed reincarnation without the uncertainty of death. Do you know what I mean?"

A lot of the time I didn't know what he meant. He spoke in hypotheses that jumped over important points. But this time I did; hadn't I been borrowing other people's lives, my mother's, Vivian's, and now, pregnant with no husband, my mother's life again? But I was too angry to agree with him. "You know, when the guy dies of a heart attack, everyone comes to claim the body," I said. "It's a reunion to some fucked-up family no one wants an invitation to. You're an egomaniac. You want everybody to love you."

"Don't you?"

"No," I said, confused, angry. "No, just you, only you," I said, sounding like some soap opera diva. I thought of Vivian and my father, how she must have felt when it unraveled. She had so much to lose, not just a man, but a way of life. If he loved her, if she could keep him, she wouldn't have to go back to her crazy mother and her possibly incestuous father (I'd inflated Ruth Spivy's comment in my mother's foyer that Vivian's father loved his daughter too much), to concrete-pouring brothers and dog racing. And what did I get if I could win over Peter Kinney? A way out of smoky bars, blind dates, orgiastic failures of love. I was so tired of having to hear strangers' life stories, to nurse them through memories of their fat childhoods, their evil mothers sending them off to athletic camps, cowering in the shadows of their fathers who hid behind newspapers and in basements tinkering with boats in bottles, of understanding men's weird quirks—waking up to find them masturbating in the middle of the night, clutching my panties, for example. I was tired of handing over my

own life story, only to have to repackage it for the next
fucking weirdo. I was tired of get-togethers with girlfriends where I always felt forced to spill my loveless life on
the table like dumping out my pocketbook—tampons, lipsticks, a circular diaphragm case, everything rolling off in
every direction.

Sitting there in the laundromat, I started to feel that
heaviness, my uterus just pouching enough to make my
pants instantly tight, the button strings taut. I held my
pocketbook in close to my ribs and glanced around at the
people folding and sorting. I thought about slapping the
test down on the table, asking him to choose. But I didn't
do it. I couldn't do it to his wife, his two kids, the one just
on the way. I decided then that it would be like a virgin
birth, that my child would have no father—though I was
by no means a virgin. Everyone knows the precedents for
this virgin birth: Mary's conception of Jesus and, if you can
allow yourself Bob Jablonski's willful suspension of disbelief, my mother's conception of me. But it was not a calm
decision. I was panicked inside, shaking. I stood up, rumpled his hair like he was just some kid on the street, and
then I walked out of the place. He didn't follow me. He
just sat there and watched me go. And I felt a strange
relief, thinking maybe I'd begun to believe in the golden
life too much, that I'd begun to rely on hope—the most
dangerous emotion—through Peter Kinney. Wasn't this
the best outcome, the only outcome, finally arrived?

5

The Fiskes' house was enormous, three stories, and old. In the front yard there stood two towering oak trees and a row of rhododendrons in full bloom. We drove up a rock driveway to the back of the house and parked next to a silver Saab in front of a garage, built, judging by the small size, with horse carriages in mind, not wide-bodied cars like my father's Corolla. The garage was used by Mrs. Fiske for painting miniature portraits of her dogs, Chelsea and Spencer—named before these were common names for children—and her cat, Kit Kit. This artistic hobby Juniper had let slip in the phone conversation with my mother, who'd related it to me as if it was the key to understanding the delicate psyche of Juniper Fiske.

We used the back door and lugged suitcases into the kitchen, a large, high-ceilinged room with oversize sky-lights that made it greenhouse-stuffy even with the cranked-up air conditioning. Piper Fiske was only a few months younger than I was, but she seemed much older, at least a year or two. She skulked down the servants' stairs and slouched into the room, holding a copy of *Naked Lunch* close to her chest. She smiled at me in a practiced way that made me embarrassed about my socks, navy blue cable knit that my mother bought for me in three-packs packaged with sticky labels and little black hangers, as if anyone would ever hang them up. It was too hot for socks, and even I knew that I shouldn't be wearing cable knit with sneakers. I was also embarrassed by my hair, too neatly clipped back in silver barrettes, my flowered shorts matching my top in a childlike way, obviously bought together as an outfit. Piper had curly brown hair and wore beat-up, untied L.L. Bean moccasins with crushed heels and braided anklets, three or four per ankle. She had braces and faint freckles on a perfect nose.

Juniper was breezy and gaunt, draped in gauzy clothes, and I thought, *Oh, so she* is *an artist,* because at fifteen I associated artists with loose-fitting clothes rather than with art. Her hands were white with flour—we'd caught her baking—and she squeezed my mother's shoulders with her inner forearms, wrists bent, so as not to powder my mother's pale yellow oxford shirt. My mother and Juniper both gushed the normal pleasantries. The dogs, hunters turned indoor pets, nosed my privates and my mother's, slobbering on our shorts and bare legs. Juniper swatted their wide rumps, leaving white handprints on them, and offered my mother a stool at the kitchen island while they fawned over each other's youthful appearances.

Piper snorted and rolled her eyes. We were asked to take the suitcases back up through the narrow servants' stairway to the guest bedroom, which my mother and I would share.

It was immense and pristine with an assortment of variously sized towels on a chrome-metal standing rack. Then Piper led me to her bedroom. There was no mention of her brother, Church.

Her room had none of the frilliness of girlhood, and unlike the rest of the house, it was a mess. The floor was littered with tennis skirts and rackets and sneakers and small piles of paperbacks. Her chest of drawers was covered with perfumes, lip glosses, a lid-flipped box of tampons, and wax and tiny multicolored rubber bands for her braces. I assumed that her mother had insisted on the watercolors of sailboats—originals, no doubt—that hung on the walls. She had a light comforter with preppie blue-and-purple stripes, thrown on an unmade double bed. She watched me as I glanced quickly around her room.

"I don't believe in exploiting the lower class by making them clean up our crap," she said, slumping onto the bed and scooping up Kit Kit, who'd been sleeping there.

I'd never thought of Mrs. Shepherd, our maid, as being lower class. She'd always seemed so superior, cleaning the house with her *tsk, tsk* and solemn head shaking.

"So, are you seeing anybody?" Piper asked, bored by my answer before she got it.

"No," I said, making my way across the room. "Not at the moment."

"So, how far have you gone?"

"I don't know," I said, standing in the middle of the room, arms crossed. "Far enough."

In actuality, I hadn't gone very far. I had the impression that a lot of the boys in my school knew that my father was a gynecologist and that that intimidated them somehow, made me too dangerous to date, like being a cop's daughter. In reality, there was really nothing dangerous about me. The only effect my father's profession had on me was that I was very comfortable saying the word *vagina,* having learned, however, well before this point, that other people were not as comfortable with the clinical term. To answer Piper truthfully, I'd attended a school homecoming dance with Eric Banter, a piggish boy with pimples and a spitting habit, and I'd kissed Jimmy Owens, whom I'd met on one of our family vacations to Lake Winnipesaukee, someone I'd never see again.

At this point, the door creaked open, a heavy paneled door with a metal handle, and Church sauntered into the room. He, too, was slouchy, with rumpled hair and a wide grin.

"I know a girl with a studded tongue," he said. "They do that, you know."

I'd never heard of it—it was something that really wouldn't catch on for years to come. "Why do they do that?" I asked.

Piper rolled her eyes and tossed Kit Kit to the floor, where the cat padded off. "To give better fellatio," she said.

I looked at her, confused. Church kind of smiled and offered, "She means sucking cock." I thought at that moment that they were really rich, that only a really rich person would have such a long, flowing word for something like that and be able to say it so breezily. Church's translation was a little off: "Sucking cock" was really lower class; I was middle class—I would have said "giving head," not that I went around saying it. In any case, I understood Church's translation.

"Doesn't it make it hard to talk?" I asked.

"You can't talk while giving fellatio," Piper said.

"No, I mean with a studded tongue. Don't they"—and I still didn't know who they were—"talk funny?"

"She . . . kind of . . . lisps," Church said. "And she's always fiddling with it—you know, with her tongue. It's distracting."

Piper wheeled around, looking at her brother for the first time. "You don't know anybody with a studded tongue. You read that in one of those sick misogynistic pervie magazines."

He shrugged and smiled as if to say, *So?*

"Oh, God," Piper yelled out, flopping around on her bed.

"And *Naked Lunch* is a piece of art?" he questioned.

Piper screamed into her pillow, "Fuck you, Church. Fuck you!"

He ignored her. "You want to play badminton? We've got a net set up in the backyard."

"Sure," I said, and I followed him out of the room.

And so this is how I first came to adore Church Fiske. He was so cocky and relaxed, the opposite of how I felt, that he was exactly what I wanted, what I wanted to be. From this very first time I met him, his life seemed to afford him this confidence, this ability to say whatever he wanted to say. I was envious. And, also, now thinking about it, that might have been the moment I first linked him to my father. Having just misplaced my father, however temporary I thought that might be, I needed to imprint on someone, someone sturdy and confident. Church was a role model, not a fatherly one, but the only male stand-in I had handy. However, if I allow myself to link Church with Bob Jablonski, I have to admit that he'd also be equally, if not more strongly, linked to Anthony Pantuliano, my biological father. Church would become my young romance, and although he'd fall far short of my mother's mythological lover, once again he was all I had. I wouldn't be aware of this

odd linking, on a conscious level, until college, during my
affair with Joey Pedesto, but it might have started that far
back, that immediately. In any case, I'd begun to think
maybe my mom was right in bringing us here, that it was,
in fact, a crash course of sorts—but in what subject, exactly, I still have never quite figured out.

Church, as it turned out, was horrible at badminton. I
told him he might play better if he removed his hand
from his pocket, but this seemed out of the question and so
instead we sat on the side of the garage not facing the house.
Even though he was a year younger than I was, a fact that
at that age was very important, he seemed so much older,
so much more worldly, that I forgot he was only fourteen.

After a minute, Church walked to his mother's Saab and
pulled a pack of cigarettes out of her glove compartment.
He offered me one, but I shook my head. He lit up and sat
down next to me.

"So, your parents are divorced," I said after a few minutes.

"Yeah, my dad lives in Annapolis. That's in Maryland."

"My dad kind of split," I said, acting bent up and hard-
luck but not really feeling it.

"And does your mom have a case of nerves? Juniper is
wound up tight! She pecks around like a cat in snow. Ever
seen a cat in snow? It sucks." He put his arm around me
and took a drag off his cigarette. "They've got a pill,
though, that can knock them out. My mom will definitely
lend some to your mom. It's good stuff. It's how I learned
to drive the Saab." He grinned.

"You know how to drive?"

"Well, Juniper can't drive when she's gassed. And Piper's

too high strung. She freaks just backing out of the driveway and ends up in between the oak trees. She flattened
some bushes last month." He stubbed out his cigarette
with the heel of his L.L. Bean moccasin.

"Oh," I said.

"Hey, if our moms get looped together, I'll take you for
a ride." He grinned again, as if the ride meant more than
just a ride.

I shrugged and said, "Okay," and then Church Fiske
kissed me full on the mouth and put a hand on my tiny
breast. He tasted like the cigarette. He held still just like
that, and then after about five seconds, he stopped, as if
that was the end of his repertoire.

"Let's eat," he said. And we got up and went inside.

At dinner, Church announced that Piper wanted to get
her tongue studded.

"Why, dear?" said Juniper, who looked pale and a bit
shaky.

"I do not," Piper whined with exhaustion.

"Oh," said Juniper. "Okay, then."

Juniper had prepared dinner herself, which, I took it,
was a rare event. Church and Piper seemed suspicious of
the food, smelling the vegetables in white sauce and picking at the chicken before putting it in their mouths. My
mother mentioned her little Weight Watchers scale, but
said she was ready to splurge. We ate informally at a big
table in the kitchen. The dogs circled our chairs, looking
for scraps and handouts, and the kids kept glancing around
as if looking for the regular help, a woman named Dinah.
Finally, Piper asked casually where Dinah was.

"Oh, Dinah is wonderful, but I love to cook and sometimes I've just got to shoo her away so I can whip something up," Juniper said in a high voice, her eyebrows hitched and the wrinkled skin between them pink.

She'd made chicken Dijon and, unfortunately, had persisted in making homemade bread—not French bread but a shorter, rounder loaf. It was awkward just the same. When I saw it, I glanced at my mother furtively, and it was obvious she'd seen it, too, and had thought of the erect penis of Anthony Pantuliano. I refused to eat any, but she couldn't, for reasons of politeness, and it was a terrible sight to watch Juniper slice the bread, to watch my mother butter it with two pats, shyly bend her head and take a measured bite. And then she had to praise Juniper, the bread, the taste, and texture. It was unseemly and awful.

"Piper would like to be a tennis pro," said Juniper. "She's quite good."

"Oh, Mother," Piper protested. "That was when I was ten years old and an idiot."

Church said, "Now she'd like to become a lesbian."

Piper glared at him in such a way that made me believe that Piper had admitted lesbian aspirations.

"If you want to be a lesbian, that's fine. Just be the best lesbian you can be," Juniper said with an odd smile and wink.

"I wish I'd thought to become a lesbian," my mother said, as if it were the fault of a guidance counselor who hadn't helped her find the proper college major. "It's such a nice lifestyle."

"And there'd be no reason for you to stud your tongue," Church added, and then he reconsidered, thoughtfully, "but, then again, I guess it could still come in handy."

My mother eyed him with suspicion. Juniper seemed oblivious and quite accustomed to such talk. She said, "Oh, but we didn't know those opportunities existed back then."

Piper said, "Oh, please, gag me," and made a gagging gesture with her finger in her mouth and a coughing sound. Juniper, looking even paler and more frazzled, abruptly pushed her chair away from the table and scampered to a nearby bathroom. Piper and Church went on picking at their food, as if nothing had happened. My mother and I sat in a respectful silence while we listened to Juniper throw up.

That night Juniper took a couple of her little pills and passed out, and my mother drank a bottle of red wine, smoked cigarettes—which I'm sure Juniper wouldn't have allowed had she been conscious—and listened to records from the Fiske collection, throwbacks to the '60s, but the tame, stiff-coifed '60s, nothing revolutionary, no Baez or Dylan. My mother sat on the sofa in the living room and looked through photo albums that Juniper had pulled out for the occasion, while Juniper slept soundly in her bedroom. Despite the fact that both of our mothers got looped, Church didn't take me out for a joyride in his mother's Saab. Instead, we hung out in his bedroom. Piper found my interest in Church to be wholly despicable, and she wouldn't look at or speak to us. I could hear her in the house, though, talking on the phone in her bedroom and blaring the TV in the upstairs study. Church and I played Bob Marley tapes and talked about getting stoned, although I was pretty sure he'd never done it, just as he'd never really met someone with a studded tongue. Unlike me, Church was a natural liar—I would have to work at it—and he was one who didn't really mind getting caught. When I questioned him on the term *roach clip,* what one exactly looked like and how it was used (I'd seen them only as hair clips with long feathers worn by high school druggy types in fringed suede lace-up boots and black eyeliner raccooning their eyes), he hemmed and hawed and finally gave that smile and shrug. He seemed to like lying for the sport of it. It was not a way of life, as it had become for my mother, nor was it used for malice. He was a purist in the field of deceit. He simply enjoyed a good lie well told.

His bedroom was more typical for a kid his age than was Piper's. It was smaller and neater, complete with a Kathy Ireland poster taped to the back of the door. Evidently he didn't share his sister's distaste for exploitation. Although we were propped up in his bed, he didn't kiss me that night. I thought he would, but he never did. I think the fact that I hadn't fought him earlier that day scared him. I had the feeling he was the type of kid who'd already been slapped by a girl at fourteen, and that maybe I was the first girl who'd ever kissed him back. In any case, I found myself wishing he would kiss me. I loved his slouched cockiness, his messy hair and baggy clothes.

It got late. Eventually, I heard my mother's feet on the stairs. She called my name in a whisper, "Lissy? Lissy?"

I said, "I gotta go," expecting Church to at least kiss me then, just a peck or something. But he didn't. He just flipped up his hand in a little "bye-bye" wave. I slid off his bed and popped out the door.

My mother stood almost on the top step of the stairs, leaning into one stiff arm, which was propped by the rail, her body slouching into the arm like it was a crutch, the only thing holding her up. She said, "C'mere." She wrapped her arm around me and we staggered to the guest bedroom, where she fell back into the bed, a dead weight.

"I missed everything," she said. "Listening to Juniper Fiske and which fork to use and the last acceptable day to wear white shoes and the dirty sin of panty lines. I was listening to Pat Boone, for Chrissakes." She went on for a while about Pat Boone, his perfect hair, glossy teeth. She accused him of putting Vaseline on them before album cover photo shoots. She also seemed to hold Ray Conniff personally responsible for her missed opportunities, the song "I Love How You Love Me," in particular. Petula Clark also shouldered some of the blame. She lay on her back and stared up at the ceiling.

She said, "The fifties made promises they couldn't keep. They dressed me up, Dotty Verbitski, like I wanted to get voted prom queen. They said, *C'mon in. There's no end to the golden life.* But they were Indian givers. My mother's kitchen wasn't pink. We didn't drink out of polka-dotted glasses, and there was no Chevy Bel Air in our garage. There was no garage! They said, *But you, Dotty, you can have it all.* But they took everything back. One massive product recall," she said, "and I've never said this to anyone, Lissy, not anyone: My mother couldn't love me, and that was what I wanted, the mistake I wanted to unmake." She turned and hissed in my ear, "They promised. But none of it was true."

For the first time, I thought of my mother as a girl like

me, as still being that girl, only older, that I would age
but be the same person that I was right then lying next to
my drunk mother. I felt that we were completely alone in
the world, cut loose and spiraling farther and farther from
what we knew. I laid my head on her chest, something I
hadn't done since I was a little kid, and she stroked my
hair. We were quiet for a long time and then I noticed
that her breathing had grown suddenly deep. She was
asleep. I took off her Keds and then hoisted her legs onto
the bed, and she curled into a knot by the foot of the bed.
I pulled a T-shirt from my suitcase and slept horizontally
up by the pillows. It took me a long time to fall asleep,
the day buzzing through my head. But finally I drifted off
to the rhythm of her deep breaths, and I dreamed of my
mother as a young girl, quite happy, riding the parade-
float penis of Anthony Pantuliano like a prom queen. She
was throwing Dum-Dum lollipops to the crowd, where
my father carried Vivian on his shoulders like she was a
little girl. I was desperately picking up lollipops to give
them back to my mother, as if she were throwing away
something precious.

The original plan was to sightsee on Cape Cod, to hit
vacation spots, cranberry bogs, and whatnot. But we
ended up leaving the next morning. Juniper claimed to
have the flu. She said she'd just feel terrible if we caught it.
My mother offered to help out until she was back on her
feet, but Dinah had already showed up to take care of her
and take over the house. We'd never really unpacked, so my
mother and I zipped our suitcases and walked back down
the servants' stairs into the kitchen.

Dinah was a tall, slender black woman with a thin gap between her front teeth, so unlike Mrs. Shepherd that I was shocked. She was my mother's age and wore a blue shirt with puffed sleeves and a tan skirt. She stood at the sink cleaning dishes from dinner the night before. It was a Monday, and when my mother and I came down for breakfast, the two kids were hunched over cereal bowls, dressed in tennis whites for a morning lesson. They looked completely different. Their clothes fit, sneakers were laced. Their tattered braided anklets were hidden in their short socks. Church's hair was slick from a shower and Piper's was back in a tight ponytail. The remains of Juniper's breakfast sat on a small silver tray on the counter.

"This is Dinah," Piper said, introducing us. "And this is my mom's friend from college, Dotty, and her daughter Lissy."

"Hi," Dinah said, nodding from the sink. "Breakfast isn't anything fancy today. Help yourselves to cereal."

And so we did. Piper and Church were finishing up breakfast, and Dinah grabbed the keys off a silver hook on the wall.

"I've got to run the kids to tennis," she said.

"Don't worry. We're leaving. We'll show ourselves out," my mother said.

Church jerked around and then slouched, his hand in the pocket of his tight white tennis shorts. He smiled sheepishly, and I wondered what lies he was concocting. We ate whole-grain cereal with Juniper's low-fat milk. My mother didn't weigh her portions. She was groggy and hungover, and I was imagining Church sitting next to Piper in the backseat of the Saab, whispering, "We did it. Me and that girl Lissy. She was good, like a pro." I didn't care. If Piper believed Church at all, she might think I was wild, and that was okay by me. I was tired of my dull, predictable life. I even thought maybe we would have done it if one thing had led to another. I wanted drama, my own drama. I was beginning to think that anything was possible.

6

My gynecologist is a woman, Dr. Jennifer, a young, sure-handed petite blonde with bobbed hair and straight teeth. I chose her because she's nothing like my father and should not in any way remind me of him. Still, her office brings him back to mind. The instruments have changed—the wide bulb lamp is a sleek-lined Welch Allyn; now there's Aquasonic gel for sonograms, the German-made colopyscope, an evacuation air filtration system, and an unlimited supply of ambidextrous Sterigard gloves. But essentially things haven't changed: the whiteness, the clean, empty counters, the little shiny tools hidden in drawers, the strange and sterile intimacy. I can't help but think of my father, how it must have been to have him as a gynecologist, this shy, awkward man, flustered and astonished each time he surfaced from the white tent covering his patients' legs. It's the way I have always imagined myself giving birth—the icky image, not at all sexual, of my father's pink-flushed face rising up from between my stir-ruped legs as if I'd given birth to this full-grown man. *It's a boy*, the nurse squeals. And he shyly nods, straightening the eyeglasses that have slipped down his tilted nose.

Of course, it makes no sense that Dr. Bob Jablonski should be the one I'm giving birth to. For genetic reasons, I should be giving birth to a little Anthony Pantuliano, my real father. It's Pantuliano's recessives and dominants that my eggs haul around. But I've never really been able to see myself as his daughter. He is a part of my personal myth-ology, as if my mother were a Bayonne maiden who had caught the eye of a strange big-headed, big-cocked god, a Cyclops, no less—like the seduction of Europa, riding the bull, or Leda being struck by a giant swan's beak—and I was the product of their union.

I have been a regular at Dr. Jennifer's for years. I go to the gynecologist more often than most women do. In addi-tion to the fact that I'm prone to urinary tract infections, irregular periods, and murky Pap smears, I've gone most often for a heaviness in my pelvis, an expanded uterus, and nausea. I have convinced myself again and again in the weakest of moments that I was pregnant. I've bought preg-nancy tests in bulk. I've peed on hundreds of test strips. After the tests came back negative, I became convinced that I was dying, rotting, that my tumorous uterus was going to fall out of me, that I would be stripped of what was essentially mine. It was an issue of control, dating back to my earliest notions of pregnancy, my mother's stories of Anthony Pantuliano, the idea that pregnancy is something that can happen to you without your stamped approval.

I went to Dr. Jennifer for reassurance. She would take a look and smile and say, "Once again, I pronounce you unpregnant and healthy." And I would walk out of the office thankful, relieved, renewed. I could believe for a short time that I was not dying from the vagina out, that I was fine, the way I imagine someone truly Catholic must feel after confession, knowing that if a bus hit her right at that minute she'd be going to heaven.

Shortly after my breakup with Peter Kinney, shortly after Church fell in love with Kitty Hawk, I wrangled an appointment from Dr. Jennifer's receptionist, a stingy woman who always implies, with her typed-up set of questions and little annoyed sighs at my responses, that mine is not an authentic emergency. I had convinced her this time that I'd taken tests that actually proved positive. I walked into the back wood-paneled office defiantly and pulled a bouquet of pregnancy tests, all positive, out of my pocketbook. I was proud almost, finally demonstrating that I am not absolutely insane after all. But I was like a crazy person in a storm that she had predicted, not really aware of the storm itself, the high winds and gusty rain, but finally ecstatic to be proved right, the way Noah must have felt after having been called an old, addlepated drunk, except of course I had no ark. I hadn't thought that far ahead.

She was startled. "Oh my!" she said, like a little old lady at a church bazaar who's just won a raffle.

"What's that supposed to mean?" I asked.

"I think it means you're pregnant," she said.

I thought of the names *Megan* and *Todd*, although I'd never name a child Megan or Todd, names that brought to mind a sunshiny kid raising a hand in math class. I realized that I could become a mother, that I could swell up and give birth and go to PTA meetings. I was shocked. The diaphragm had failed. It suddenly seemed a ridiculous

thing to have put faith in, jelly coated and slippery. I felt
betrayed and overwhelmed, stupid, realizing that thinking
you're pregnant and knowing you're pregnant are two completely different things.

I felt for the first time in my life really and truly alone.
I had the keenest sense of panic. I wasn't thinking con-
sciously of my mother, her instinct to find someone, to find
a husband for herself, a father for me. But it was there, the
lurking fear. My mother was raised in the artificial neon
glow of the '50s, and I was raised in its psychedelically
altered afterglow. It is one of the most obvious reasons that
I cannot live my mother's life. The '50s, my mother's
youth, marked the golden age, the coming of age of the
golden age of the golden life. The American dream became
a machine that everyone drove together, willingness to
believe at an all-time record high, hope for the masses. In
the '60s, the disparity between hope and reality started to
become more obvious, a string in the seam that some people tugged at and others ignored. It tore straight up the
middle of the country, and by '69, my mother was only
twenty. She didn't have a chance. But I couldn't believe in
the golden life—it no longer existed as a concept. I was
twenty-nine, a single working woman of the nineties. I
couldn't believe that I needed a man to complete my life,
and yet I did; it seemed a cruel paradox, that I was raised
to believe something that I would find appalling. And so,
when my mind flipped to Church, the idea wasn't blatant.
It couldn't be. I wouldn't have allowed it. I was telling
myself that I was not envisioning Church heroically swooping in to save the day. I was thinking only that maybe I
could confide in him. I decided that I would tell Church
that I was pregnant. I wasn't allowed to think of it out-

right, to admit it even to myself, but my hope was that Church, despite being temporarily sidetracked by Kitty Hawk, had come to rescue me.

I lay there on my back, looking at the white sheet, my red knees. Nothing was real to me, not the pregnancy, not the child taking root. I felt as if I were lying not within myself but next to myself. I was detached, separate. I imagined my father, Dr. Jablonski, emerging in his white coat, his thick glasses sitting crooked on his bent nose, saying, in a reverent, perplexed voice, "It's happened again. A miracle."

Church and Kitty were inseparable. I couldn't find a moment alone with him. They slept together in my guest room, Kitty's old room, where Church had taken up residence. They showered together, brushed their teeth together, fed each other. Church tagged along after her when she worked, hanging out in the dressing room while she strapped on her Velcro-fastened gear—lily bras and panties, leather G-strings—and then while she danced, he was belly-up at the bar.

The relationship was typical Kitty. She loved intense romances, to be the star of her own feature film, a passionate love story, strutting and glaring, the queen of the Bette Davis moment. And when she looked up at Church, even when they were just hanging out on the sofa watching TV, their fingers stained orange from cheese curls, there was a *From Here to Eternity* intensity in her gaze. She was beautiful, too, and fairly young, midtwenties, smooth skin, upturned eyes, white-white teeth, and that shiny hair halfway down her back.

Kitty liked to focus in and wring someone out. I'd seen

her do it to boyfriends, to a few of her coworkers at the
Fruit, Cock, Tail Strip Club. She'd done it to me, too, in a
way, although not with as much ferocity. I wasn't worth as
much to her as Church, a rich American man. She'd pri-
marily asked me questions about my childhood. She wanted nothing to do with the summer in Bayonne—didn't
know that Church and I had lost our virginity together. She
stuck to life in Keene, New Hampshire—sprinklers, ice
cream trucks, streamers on the handlebars of my bike. She
wanted to know if I gave apples to my teachers. I thought
she was sweet and in a strange way naïve, even her ability
to dance naked in front of men a kind of innocence. I
taught her the doo-wop hand gestures to "Stop in the
Name of Love." We sang into hairbrushes.

But when I asked her questions about growing up in
Korea, she'd say, "Oh, Korea is a dirty, ugly place. No one
want to live there. I always want to live in America with
superstars!"

In the end, I didn't like Kitty Hawk because she was the
worst kind of liar, no sport to it, no art. She lied to get what
she wanted. She was a slut, too, not because she loved
men—it's perfectly acceptable to be a slut if you truly love
men, even in a whimsical way, as I once did—but because
she despised them. She wanted power, which is what she
got onstage, an audience. She hid behind the broken
English, the girlish giggle, the mincing steps. And she was
a thief, too, which is why I'd finally kicked her out. When
I realized she'd stolen my mint sweater, she broke down
and cried, "My parents never love me." When she'd taken
my alarm clock—as if I wouldn't notice or call her on it—
she said, "Mine not working." She started to sob. "And
everything work for you, you so perfect." She stole money

and jewelry, not to mention bits and pieces of my childhood, a glued-together assortment of details that I've
decided she'll try to pass off one day as her own.

Kitty was all façade. Once, when we were still roommates, I saw her out with a group of other Koreans at
Beauty Bar. It's an old salon-gone-bar, complete with sixties-
style dome hair-drying chairs. It has a velvet-curtained
glass-enclosed counter case with vintage knickknacks, Kew-
pie dolls, and soap bars. The whole place has a carnival/
funeral parlor feel. Kitty sat at the head of one of the
lounge-style tables with their mismatched, circa 1969
chairs. She was loud and tough. I said hi to her, and she
stopped and just gave me a look, her nostrils flared, a look
that implied that I had no right to talk to her in public,
that we were not friends. She was wearing her mirrored
sunglasses, and all I could see in them were two warped
reflected versions of myself, confused and uncomfortable in
front of her group's table. She said nothing, turned away,
and whistled through her teeth to get the bartender's attention. Kitty was untrustworthy and sad. I had the feeling,
although she never talked about her childhood, really, that
she'd been through awful things, that she'd learned at a
very young age to take care of herself first, to survive.

When I told Church all of this a couple days after they'd
met, catching him alone for a minute in the kitchen, where
he was scraping black off his toast, he said, "She's complex.
You don't get her. She's really honest. She has nothing to
hide. You should see her strip. It's nothing to her. She is
who she is. I love that."

And I looked at him and it struck me that Kitty fit
into his definition of "real people," was essential to the
"authentic experience" he'd come to the city looking for.

She was another shot at lowering his class. He was bur-
dened by the notion that he'd missed something, something real, possibly dirty, that the rich had rinsed from
their bleached lives—something like Kitty. It was an outdated notion, something political advertisers played up in
times of depression and war, all of those poor-little-rich-
girl movies of the *Roman Holiday* variety, the idea that the
rich were unhappy and unloved, that the poor were dirt
poor but singing-and-dancing happy. They were coming
at it from different ends, but both Church and Kitty were
desperate for different lives, for American middle-class
existences—no different from my mother. They were in
many ways a pathetic couple, but not one you could really feel too sorry for, because they were so sexually charged.
It's hard to feel sorry for sexy, in-love people, especially
when you're dejected.

I said, "You know the American middle class isn't a religion. You can't convert."

Church stopped. "I disagree. I wholeheartedly object. I
could be pope, actually, of the Church of the American
Middle Class. We'll worship power lawnmowers and try to
conceive children to get optimal tax advantage." Then he
quickly changed the subject. "I think I'd like to be a
columnist. Not that I'd enjoy actually writing, but I'd be
great at riding the camels and eating soup with the homeless, test-flying jets, or just, you know, making fun of pota-
toes. You know that kind of stupid banter. Or I could be a
poet. Nowadays, I hear, even these cat hair–covered profes-
sors at Ivy League schools are writing shoot-up-heroin and
tough-times-in-prison stuff. The critics love it. It's a rip-
off—don't get me wrong. Like M.C. Hammer's attempt at
gangsta rap. But it's a bandwagon that anyone can get on."

And then he strode off into the other room, shouting out his new ideas to Kitty.

Yes, Church was crazy, but I wasn't really in any position to point this out. I was pretty crazy myself, having sunk a small fortune into pregnancy tests.

In any case, I felt immensely more stable than Kitty Hawk and decided that maybe I should target her. I caught her one morning, shuffling out of the bathroom in Church's boxers, her little tan boobs jiggling. I said, "Look, don't fuck with him."

"I'm going be his wife. I fuck with him all time." And she smiled sweetly.

It was quintessential Kitty. She wanted to leave me wondering if she knew the difference between *fuck with* and *fuck*. But I knew she did know the difference. She contorted the language, was a master of the nuances of mangled English and how to use miscommunication to her advantage.

The next Saturday afternoon I was sitting at the kitchen table eating buttered toast and drinking orange juice, something I'd begun to crave, and thinking vaguely about issues of maternity leave, clothing, child care, but still these weren't real issues. I realized that many people in my situation would have considered abortion. I'd had a number of friends who'd had them. But I couldn't think of it as a real option, not because I'm kind of still Catholic—I'm also pro-choice—but because I was an accident myself; an abortion would have been a suicidal thought.

I had been given a Peter Rabbit diaper bag at Dr. Jennifer's office. It was filled with pamphlets and formula, a book of children's names and a week-by-week breakdown of the events of pregnancy with pencil drawings of the eventually enormous uterus, but I didn't dwell on these pictures. I preferred the notion of a Megan or Todd, someone else's eight-year-old. But that, too, was uncomfortable, as if I were being forced to fall in love with a stranger. Really, your child is a complete stranger; everyone seems to overlook that—a stranger who will never go away, unlike my favorite kinds of relationships, which end before really beginning. Having a child is a giant act of hope. I've come to deeply mistrust hope.

I was flashing to my parents. This was before my father had had his first heart attack, and both seemed very healthy, like they would live forever. I was wondering how I would tell them, wondering what they would say, especially my mother. They'd recently gotten to that age when their friends were bragging about grandkids, and I was, after all, nearly thirty, with no prospects. I thought they'd probably be a little relieved. But there would be no way around the obvious question, the father. Perhaps my father could overlook it—he had experience in that area—but my mother would want to know. She had, after all, told me her secrets, in great detail. I thought how much easier it would be to arrive with Church, already three or four months' pregnant, and have him announce the news, how I'd never have to mention Peter Kinney, his wife and kids. Still it wasn't real to me, the pregnancy, even the nausea that took hold every once in a while and sent me reeling, the fatigue settling in.

And then Church unlocked the door, kicked it open with his boot, and carried Kitty Hawk over the threshold of my apartment, la-la-ing "Here Comes the Bride." He plopped Kitty down on the sofa. A little champagne from a bottle she was holding spilled onto her dress. She threw out her hand to show me a diamond ring.

"Nice rock," she said. "Right?" She was all legs in a white minidress, her pillbox hat cockeyed on her head. She had a cheap little nosegay.

Church said, "Well, we did it. We're officially Church and Kitty Fiske." The name conjured up an old golfing couple in matching shirts. Church was breathless. I wondered if he'd carried her up two flights of stairs. He wasn't in tip-top shape, had never been much of an athlete despite all the tennis lessons. "What was the witness's name?" he asked Kitty, a leading question that they both obviously knew the answer to.

Kitty said, "Mr. Nixon! The president of the United State!"

States, I said in my head, correcting her. And then aloud: "For God's sake, United *States*."

"An inventive street person," Church said, "a top-notch citizen." He turned to me. "We've come to collect you," he said. "You've been invited to the reception."

I was not impressed. "Where?" I asked dryly.

"The Fruit, Cock, Tail, of course."

"Who else is invited?"

"Giggy and his girlfriend, Elsbeth, and Matt, of course."

I'd never heard of Giggy and Elsbeth, but Matt was one of Church's college buddies who lived with his parents on Long Island and sold Italian water ice seasonally. I'd heard stories of him. Once, visiting Piper at Harvard, he and Church had jumped off a bridge into the Charles.

"Matt's girlfriend might come, too, but they're kind of on the rocks," Church said. "She wanted to go halvsies on an ab roller and he's not into that kind of commitment."

"I'm not dressed," I said.

"Look," Church said, walking up to me, lowering his voice, "this is important to me."

"Okay, okay," I said, sighing loudly. The thought crossed my mind quickly, *Mothers don't go to strip clubs. See, I'm not a mother.*

Kitty squealed and tossed the little bouquet with too much force; she was used to throwing things into a deep audience of hungry men, but also I read the force as a little brewed anger. I ducked, and the bouquet landed in the kitchen sink.

S hahid, the doorman at the Fruit, Cock, Tail Strip Club, had already heard the news. He had long black hair, slicked back over his ears into a ponytail, and huge biceps that stretched his T-shirt sleeves. He clapped Church on the shoulder in congratulations and shook him a bit, and then Shahid saw Kitty. He lifted her up off her feet and kissed her cheek.

"Thanks, thanks," Church said, laughing. "Okay, okay. That's enough now. Enough of the whole touchy-feely. Okay, great."

Shahid raised his eyebrows at me. "Who's the redhead?" he asked, and it was still strange to hear myself referred to as a redhead, the hair dye being pretty recent.

"Lissy," Church said, introducing us with little energy, "Shahid." It was obvious he wasn't a big Shahid fan. We shook hands and Church hustled us into the club.

Kitty said, "You like Shahid, I can fix you up. He's available. Not like Peter, but a real man. You know?" Her face was so close, she looked cross-eyed, staring at me so earnestly. It was meant as a goodwill insult.

"No, thanks. That's sweet, but no, really. Shahid's not my type."

"Too bad no Churchie for you," she said with a smile.

"I had him," I said. "Didn't you know we lost our virginity together?"

It made her pause, but only momentarily. "You got the boy. I got the man!"

"I have trouble thinking of Church as anything more than a big boy," I said.

"Whatever!" Kitty said, cheerfully. It sounded like something I'd taught her.

The Fruit, Cock, Tail was typical strip club, a steep cover for overpriced, watered-down drinks and tits galore. Shahid waived the cover, and the drinks were on Church. I was going to drink only lemonade anyway. I'd been there before with Peter when Kitty and I had been friends and she had wanted me to see what she did for a living. It was a dark, hot place with little tables and lots of seats. Peter and I sat right next to the stage because Kitty wanted us to have good seats. And she danced in front of us, in front of Peter mostly. I told him to give her a twenty, because I didn't want to insult her. And so he awkwardly tucked it into her G-string. I was thankful she was off tonight.

Giggy and Elsbeth were obvious in the Fruit, Cock, Tail Strip Club. I didn't need to have them pointed out. They sat rigidly in the corner, as far from the greased poles on stage as possible. Giggy sat with his legs crossed, staring at his loafers, while Elsbeth watched the women writhing on stage, her back straight, keenly observant, unmoved. Giggy and Elsbeth were both still tan, their hair sun-streaked. Elsbeth wore a V-neck sweater, a small scarf knotted around her long neck, and a slim skirt, and Giggy wore a linen shirt and unpleated khakis. Matt showed up just as Kitty, Church, and I got to the table. He was slouchy, tucking in a baggy shirt. He'd been in the bathroom—his eyes red, lids puffed—where I figured he'd gotten stoned.

"Giggy, Elsbeth, Matt," Church said. "This is Lissy." I nodded. "And this, this is Kitty Fiske, my wife."

I moved to the side, and Kitty appeared in her white minidress, her boobs pushed up, jiggling, on the verge of popping out. She did a little turn, spinning around. She curtsied, and then held out her hand to show everyone the fat ring.

Matt congratulated Church with claps on the shoulder and winks and whatnot. Giggy and Elsbeth applauded lightly from their seats, and we settled down at the table.

"We need to drink," Elsbeth said. "Heavily." She spoke like a newscaster, but I liked her sentiments, even though I'd be having lemonade.

Church got our beverages and we all started talking at once, the group straining to keep one fluid train of thought. Elsbeth asked Kitty about the details of the wedding, but there were so few details, aside from Nixon, that Matt ended up picking up the slack, filling in with chatter about hashish he planned to score out of Miami and lamenting the loss of his girlfriend, Sue—evidently the ab roller had in fact proved a final straw. Kitty got bored quickly and went backstage to talk to her girlfriends, to show off her new ring, no doubt. Giggy and Church were in serious debate, as far as I could hear, about marrying Kitty, the absurdity of it.

"Are you really sure about this one?" I heard Giggy ask. "Is this for some sort of effect?"

"Don't be a dick about it, Giggy."

But Giggy persisted. Elsbeth let it slip that Giggy's father had been the Fiskes' accountant for years, and Giggy, an accountant now, too, was planning on taking over the account. "He's being selfish," the monotone Elsbeth told me. "He doesn't want her to take half of everything. He's come to think of the Fiskes' money as his own." I understood. Even though I hadn't actually laid eyes on Church in fifteen years, I still thought of him as my own. I had, after all, mistaken him, once upon a time at the Fiskes' house in Cape Cod, for a father figure and for my own Anthony Pantuliano. And even though he proved to be neither of these, I'd claimed him in a way that I couldn't undo.

Finally tired of Giggy's nagging, Church stood up and said, "Dead people. That's the topic. What did they last eat?" It became silent.

At last, Giggy gave in. "Jimi Hendrix?" he asked weakly.

"Tuna fish and wine," Church answered. "Buddy Holly?"

"A hot dog," Giggy replied.

"It's a game of theirs," Elsbeth said. "Church and Giggy, at one time, were going to write a morbid cookbook."

"Church is always on the verge of doing something."

"Well, he's done something this time," Elsbeth said, nodding toward where Kitty had been. "This is all so fucked up. Don't you think?"

"It won't last," I said.

"Oh, God, it could go on forever."

"The marriage?" I said. "You think so?"

"Oh, I thought you meant the night! The marriage is a joke."

"Yes! Someone who agrees with me," I said loudly. "Jesus!"

Church, hearing only the last word, thought I was playing the game of famous dead people. "The Last Supper, unleavened shit," Church shouted. "C'mon, that's common knowledge. Give me something a little more challenging!"

Everyone drank until they were all quite drunk, except for me. Alliances turned. Matt and Elsbeth ended up in a sour discussion about relationships.

"She's a bitch, really, pushing an ultimatum on me," Matt said. "I'm in no position to move into that kind of relationship. Italian water ice is only seasonal."

"She was holding you hostage emotionally," Elsbeth said. Church told me later that she was a counselor of some sort. "She had you by the balls. Sometimes it's all you've got."

Kitty had wandered back to the table and had turned to Giggy for attention. She was now sitting on his lap. Elsbeth seemed vaguely aware. She rolled her eyes and went on counseling Matt. Kitty was listening to Giggy talk about his favorite childhood nanny. It looked to me like a recipe for disaster. Kitty fawning, trying on Giggy's glasses and then rearranging them on his face, at the tip of his nose and then higher and higher.

Church was now leaning up against me, still shouting out dead people's last meals. "Cleopatra? Anyone? Anyone? Figs! Asp-wrapped figs. Karen Carpenter? Anyone? Anyone? Trick question! How about James Dean? Anyone?" He was bombed, the words slurring off his tongue. I was exhausted, ready to go home, eat some toast, and go to sleep for days.

The crowd had started to get a little rowdy and it was harder and harder to hear above the throbbing bass line and hooting men. Giggy started to bounce Kitty on his knees, and I could barely hear him mimic his nanny in a Cockney

accent. "This is the way the lady rides: *trit, trot, trit, trot.*
This is the way the gentleman rides: *trit, trot, trit, trot.* This
is the way the farmer rides: *galopy gee, galopy gee, galopy gee*
and down in the ditch." With this, Giggy tipped Kitty
backward, sending both tits popping out of her dress. She
landed on the floor, laughing.

But no one else was laughing. Elsbeth was fuming, Giggy
fumbling, Matt and Church dumbfounded, but not any
more dumbfounded than they'd looked moments before.

"I'm okay. Okay," Kitty said, as if we'd been concerned
that she'd hurt herself in the fall. She looked around the
table. She was embarrassed, I could tell, confused by the
scene, why everyone was gawking at her. Everything had
turned so quickly. She looked at me, too, and Church leaning on my shoulder. I thought she might cry. She shoved
her boobs back into her dress and walked quickly away. I
felt bad for her, actually. I nudged Church. "Are you going
to go after her?"

"After who?" he asked. He was blind drunk. He couldn't
have gone after her if he'd tried. But it was further indi-
cation to me that although he might love Kitty on some
level, for some reason, he didn't love her as a wife, not in
that deep way.

Elsbeth stood up. "Give me the keys, you fucking stupid
asshole."

Giggy straightened, indignant. "I didn't grab her tits,
you know." He gave her the keys and she gave him the finger, the longest, most elegant, and well-manicured finger
I'd ever seen.

Matt looked at Church, whose eyes were sagging, chin
dropped. Matt said, "Now, see, I just have to find the right
girl and then I'll settle down, like Church here."

Church piped up. "I could kick your ass, Matt—you, too, Giggy." His head fell into my lap. He said, "James Dean had an apple and Coca-cola. Isn't that a beautiful thing? Isn't it? So beautifully American."

I patted his hair. "You'd make a good pope of the Church of the American Middle Class, Church, really. I could think of no one better." A terrible husband, most likely, I thought, probably a lousy father, but irrepressible, lovable, and that must be worth something.

He smiled and closed his eyes.

7

Just outside of Bayonne, we pulled up to a Gino's drive
through. The hot wind had been beating on us for five
hours. I'd fallen asleep, and when I awoke, it seemed everything had changed. We were no longer surrounded by the
pristine landscape of Cape Cod but by buildings, cement,
tar. The air was hotter and thicker. My legs were stuck to
the vinyl seat. I'd never been to New York City—I would
not visit even during this trip, although I'd gotten so
close—but I could sense its pulse, its tension. And even
though we were obviously in a bad part of Bayonne, I liked
it, the grimy city feel. In the parking lot, a couple of boys
my age were pulling bottles from a 7-Eleven Dumpster in
clear view and breaking them on the street. My mother
looked a little bloated and pale. We ordered hamburgers
and orange sodas, nothing diet.

My mother said that she didn't know where else to go.
"If you're going to hear the whole story, you might as well

hear it right where it all happened," she said. "And this is where it all happened." She spread her arms wide in mock grandeur.

We ate our food in the car parked in the lot. I had to pee. My mother sighed heavily, handed me a Wetnap package, and said, "Hover, for God's sake; don't sit."

I rolled my eyes. "I'm fifteen, you know."

The bathroom was filthy, both toilets clogged. I peed anyway on top of the heavy paper, unwrapped the tightly folded Wetnap and wiped with it. I didn't attempt to flush.

My mother drove down the road to an orange-roofed Howard Johnson and parked at the front door under the tacky orange awning. "Does it have a pool?" I asked. I wasn't much of a swimmer, having mastered only my mother's gliding frog kick, but it was stinking hot and I was dying to cool off.

"We're staying here only if we have to. I still have connections, I think." She was wearing a yellow Izod shirt, stained a darker yellow under the arms, and as she got out of the car, I could see the stain across her shirt's wrinkled back. I hung out the window and watched her flip through the pages of a phone book at the front desk in the lobby. The receptionist pointed her to a pay phone, and I watched her chat, chat, chat, pull a napkin from the endless supply in her pocketbook, and jot down directions; I couldn't imagine where to. She hung up and half jogged to the car.

"Did you ask if it has a pool?"

"We're staying with friends." She did a U-turn into a parking space and started rummaging in her suitcase in the backseat. She pulled out a teal dress and shimmied into it, lying down in the back seat.

"With who?" I asked, impatiently.

She was applying a fresh coat of makeup, rubbing the lipstick from her teeth. "We're going to Dino Pantuliano's. The old bastard's still alive."

On the way to Dino Pantuliano's house, we hit traffic and my mother gave me the first installment of her love affair with Anthony. She told most of the story while yanking the wheel this way and that, weaving in and out of slow lanes. The story went something like this: At sixteen, Anthony Pantuliano had a Nikon camera, and he would wander the streets of Bayonne taking pictures of the gray steepled sky, the bulk of hard labor in people's arms, the deeply lined faces with that expression of new freedom, of coming up in the world, immigrants with that we-aren't-dirty–New Yorkers kind of pride, as he gazed through the lens with his one good eye. One afternoon in February of 1965, he took a picture of a crowd roped off from a fire on Avenue C. It was a small fire confined to one apartment above Verbitski's Fish Shop. He snapped a few shots hurriedly before a policeman grabbed him by one of his short arms and pushed him back behind the ropes. When he developed the pictures in the basement of the apartment building on Avenue E where he lived with his Uncle Dino and had converted a corner into a darkroom, the blurred image of my mother at sixteen appeared at the edge of the rope—her dark eyebrows raised, her face wet with tears, her mouth open, sobbing, releasing a white ghost of hot breath into the cold air. Her face grew clearer and clearer as if he were creating her, as if she hadn't existed until he'd taken this picture. He fell in love with her. He cropped the picture and kept it in his wallet.

Three months later when he saw my mother on the Avenue C bus in downtown Bayonne, he walked up to her, smelling of the Bayonne Rendering Plant where he worked. He walked up to her as if they were already lovers separated by something like war. He said, "God, it's you."

My mother snatched her purse in close to her body as he reached into his back pocket for his wallet. He showed her the cut-out picture. He placed his wide hand on his chest. "I am Anthony Pantuliano."

She recognized the picture immediately and glanced around the bus. "My mother didn't start that fire," she said. "It almost killed her."

Of course, my mother was lying to Anthony Pantuliano. My grandmother hadn't technically started that fire, but she was responsible, and my mother would end up telling him so that first day, because she trusted him, because she was already in love with him.

I have to admit, though, before I go on that all of the stories that would come from my mother in bits and pieces during the summer my father disappeared with the red-headed bank teller have also passed through me; my mind has turned these stories over and over, rubbed them so clean, a hat to the bare band, that I'm not sure what came from her and what comes from my imagination. When I think of my fifteenth summer and, therefore, my mother's youthful romance, I remember it as if I am still fifteen.

I will say, however, that the way my mother laid the stories out—not just this one told in downtown Bayonne traffic, but all of the stories from that summer—her life was nearly tangible. It was so real that I almost felt as if I could step in and alter history. Perhaps it's why I've worked so hard to get these stories right, in hopes that if I replay them enough it will seem as if I am standing there, present in my mother's life, and I will be close enough to be able to step into her world to comfort her, to fix things. In any case, these are the facts as good as they get.

I remember distinctly that she loved Anthony because he was pure. "Pure," she'd say, "pure." And then she would shrug, because she knew no other way to put it. The day they met she'd been on her way to meet a group of friends at the DeWitt on 24th Street, showing the musical *Gigi*, a movie she still has never seen, and Anthony had just gotten off his shift at the rendering plant. It was February and a cold, clear day. They stepped off the bus together and walked through Hudson County Park to the edge of Newark Bay, where they looked across the water to the tankers in Elizabeth's seaport. They talked for hours, their feet freezing in their shoes.

Anthony told her the story of his childhood. His family was in the olive business in rural southern Italy along the Mediterranean. He came to America with his Uncle Dino when he was ten years old, after the death of his mother. He was the youngest of eight sons, the baby, and his mother loved him best. It was plain. One day when he was about five years old, he was trying to untie a knot in his shoelaces with a fork. The fork jerked from the lace, flew into his face, and poked his eye out. Anthony's mother was heartbroken. For days she held him to her breast, rocking him in a wooden rocking chair. She blamed herself for not having watched him carefully enough. And so he laid there, one eye bandaged up, gauze wound around his head, and the other eye pressed to his mother's breast.

Finally, the second-youngest son, the one that Anthony displaced as the baby of the family, took him aside while his

mother was making soup and told him that he was a freak
from the circus that they'd taken in out of pity. He told him
the story of one night when their father had been out walking the hogs. It was a drought and he went out in search of
mud for them to roll around in. And it was hot, so hot the
birds were falling from the trees, already dead. Their father
had picked up one of the dead birds in his hand when an airplane appeared in the sky, its two dim wing lamps spot-
lighting him. Anthony had envisioned it clearly: The nervous hogs pulled at the ends of their tethers, burning his
father's palm. The lights lifted to the trees, leafy and full of
fruit. The engine coughed to a sputter; the light flickered
and snapped out. The airplane lowered, gliding down,
crashing through the orchard, stuttering through the trees
until, finally, it stopped. Olives fell, plopping against the
roof and on the ground. Their father ran to the crashed
plane. On its side were the words FETUCCI FLYING CIRCUS
in bright red letters. He peered in its shattered windows
and saw a contortionist folded like a foldable measuring
stick and a giant lady and a poodle with a tiny umbrella, all
dead and gone. The boys' mother, fat now even when not
pregnant, waddled from the house as if strapped to a big
bass drum, and her boys shot off in front of her. The hogs
rooted through dented metal. The family circled the plane,
awestruck. And then it rocked on its belly; the door swung
open on its loose hinges. And a strange figure appeared. At
first they thought it was a little bear in a suit with a little
top hat and then they thought it was a little man, but then
someone said, "It's just a baby!" And it was a baby with a
man-size head and a man-size top hat. The baby walked
down the stairs, tapped his pointy shoes, and popped open
his little hat and said, "Ta da!"

Anthony Pantuliano was a smart little boy, though, and he asked his brother, "What did you do with all of the people in the crash?"

"We buried them," he said. "It was very sad. We all cried because no one could cry for them. You were just a baby; you didn't know better."

"And the plane," little Anthony insisted. "Where is it now?"

The brother looked around suspiciously. "This," he said, "this is why you must never speak of it. You were Mother's favorite. She doted on you from the first day, because, she said, how sad a boy with no one in the world. But Father became jealous. One day while you were still a baby, he ranted through the house, slamming doors. He threatened to take you back to the circus. But Mama refused to let him. He ran to the orchard and dragged the plane with his bare hands, scrap by heavy scrap, into the sea. It took him forty days and forty nights and the fruit turned bitter and we almost died with no fruit to sell or eat." The brother shook his head in shame.

"And so I'm a . . ."

"Fetucci. Yes, I'm afraid so. A circus freak—and lucky you're not a dead one."

Anthony couldn't think of another question. He believed that he was not one of his brothers. None of them was afflicted with his disproportionate body. His mother adored him, and his father called him a mule-headed runt. It was a logical explanation, and even though as he grew up he learned that it was ridiculous, there was some part of him that had believed it too deeply to ever unlearn. Once, when he was about eight, he was out walking along the shore and he found a rusted piece of metal washed up, half buried in the sand. He cried and ran back to his house and his mother. But when she pulled him to her chest, he shrugged away and ran to shut himself in a bedroom.

When he was ten, his mother died, and a month later his uncle decided to emigrate to America. His father asked Dino to take the two youngest boys, because he couldn't raise so many kids alone. They compromised and Uncle Dino took Anthony with him, and so Anthony became an orphan of sorts, and an American. "And that is why," he ended, "I feel at home among sawdust and peanuts and circus freaks, the poor, sick, and deserted." That's the way Anthony told the story. My mother loved it.

She laughed, although she wasn't sure he was kidding. She said, "I'm just Dotty Verbitski from Bayonne. There's nothing to know about me."

He disagreed. "Every day I look into the eyes of those animals in the slaughterhouse. I walk through their stalls. I run my hands down their bony backs. Horses, pigs, sheep. I whisper, 'One day I will set you free.' They are no different from me," he said. "My fence only stretches a little bit wider to include an apartment, a store, a church. But inside, it's a vast landscape." Anthony's one good eye flared. His teeth shone bright. She could smell the stench of the animals on him. "It's countries and mountains, because I saw your face. You, Dotty Verbitski, you set me free."

By this point we were in front of Dino's house. My mother parked the car by the curb, but the engine was still running. She sat there with both hands on the wheel, smiling sadly. She told me that her eyes had filled with tears when Anthony said that she set him free, that the tankers' lights in the seaport had flickered on and each glow teetered and rose up in her teary eyes. She said that she looked up at the sky and wiped the tears back into her hair. "That fire *was* my mother's fault," she'd told Anthony, but it seemed like she was confessing to me there in the car in front of Dino Pantuliano's house at the same time, that she was trying to prepare me for something. "She's crazy," my mother had told Anthony, "and I am, too."

When my mother, standing on Dino Pantuliano's out-door poolside patio in a nice section of Bayonne, asked Dino what he was doing for a living these days, he said, "Vitamins."

The house was really two row houses—typical of Bayonne—made into one, a version of the double-wide trailer like the ones in the Ashuelot Estates Trailer Park in Keene, but upscale with nice Persian carpets, leather furniture, Jesus statues and crosses, the ceramic face of Mary and her praying hands hung on the wall. Dino was wiry, his bronze-colored running pants, hitched up a couple inches above his waistline, swishing as he got drinks at an outside bar under a lavender awning. And his chest, bare and tan, wasn't bad for a man of his age—sixty-odd years.

His wife, Ruby, maybe ten years younger, was followed around by a little Chihuahua named Jacko with his head in one of those white plastic funnels as if everything had slid through but his fat face. I found out later he had a skin condition and he couldn't stop chewing on himself. He looked like a dog caught in a Victrola, and I had to keep myself from laughing. Typical of the similarity in looks between dogs and their owners, Ruby had Jacko's popping eyes and underbite and quick little steps. She added to Dino's vitamin comment, saying, "Yeah, he wakes up at the crack of ass . . . pardon my Fran-says . . ."—here, she smiled at me—"every morning. Work, work, work. Vitamins are his life." She laid a tray of Cheez Whiz-ed crackers on a little glass-topped table. She smiled with her red lips and squinted through her popped eyes, turned, wrestled the sliding door, and waddled back inside, teetering precariously on a pair of silver open-toed high heels that my mother later referred to as "those shoes she must have stolen from Charo."

"So what do you do with vitamins? Manufacturing? Sales?" my mother asked.

Dino brushed his hands in front of his face as if lazily shooing a bee. "Import, export. Nothing. You know."

He handed my mother a Bloody Mary with a stick of celery poking out of it and me a fresh-squeezed orange juice with bits of pulp so big I had to drink and chew. We were sitting on lawn chairs and it was hot. He stirred his drink with the celery stalk and said, "So, the *punske* girl is back in town. You remind me of the good old days when life was sweet and simple. You still look like an angel."

My mother looked down at her hands. "Oh, please," she said, rolling her eyes.

"I thought you were married to a northerner. A doctor, of the down-there variety."

"Yes," my mother said. "This is a vacation."

"A vacation from him?" He laughed and then leaned forward and whispered, "Those vacations are the best kind." He sat back and popped a Cheez Whiz-ed cracker in his mouth, and, chewing, said, "You will stay with us, then, until your 'vacation' is over."

"Oh, Dino, that's very nice, but—"

"No, not another word." He said it so strongly that a

tiny spray of cracker flew from his mouth and I was scared
of him for a moment. But then he quickly softened. He
gazed at my mother, lovingly. "Anthony would be pleased
to see you like this, so radiant. Not like the last time I saw
you. I've always felt terrible about that last time. I didn't
take things seriously. I didn't realize that it was the end,
you know? You were such a sweet kid, like my own, if I'd
had any." His eyes were misty, and I could see his eyes lock
on hers, for a moment guilty as if he owed her something.

"Forget it," she said. "Ancient history."

I didn't really understand the communication between
them. I was still in shock from hearing Dino say his name,
that Anthony Pantuliano was real, verifiable, that he'd
walked through other people's lives and could be mentioned so offhandedly. It dawned on me then that Anthony
had probably been in that house, that he had wiped his feet
on that mat, sat on those sofas, stared at their crucifixes,
that he'd touched things and held things. It dawned on me
that I could find bits of Anthony in that house, in the trinkets and drawers, maybe even pictures of him.

"And what's he up to these days?" my mother said, trying to sound casual.

"He doesn't speak to me. I haven't seen his face in what?
Ten, fifteen years," Dino said, and then he smiled broadly,
his mouth so wide I could see a bunch of shiny gold teeth
way in the back. "He finds me immoral. Anyone can
believe in America when times are good, but I never aban-
doned my country. I stuck with my country. If being an
American is immoral, believing your president, if living
the good life and all of this is immoral? This," he said,
putting his hands in front of his chest, making a circular
motion and expanding his arms to show us the pool, the

yard, "then I am immoral." He crossed his hands on his chest. "And God can do with me what He wants. Am I right?"

And I thought, *Of course you're right. How could you not be right?* But I wondered what Anthony Pantuliano had really been talking about. Certainly he wasn't objecting to a sixty-year-old man in swishy running pants drinking a Bloody Mary on his patio. Dino popped another Cheez Whiz-ed cracker into his mouth, chewed a bit, and said, "The last time I saw him in person he was an angry little god, set out, I suppose, to save the world or damn it."

My mother switched gears and said brightly, "It's a nice place you've got here. A far cry from the back room at Ferry's where you used to beat my father at poker."

Uncle Dino said, "But he gave up on the game. Soon he came into Ferry's in his fish-stained apron only to fill his silver pail with tap beer. Was it for your mother? He never drank. I always wondered about your mother. A serious woman. Is she still living?"

My mother shook her head.

"Sorry," Dino replied.

She changed the subject. "I'd think Anthony would want to see you."

"Ah," he said, "one day, he will regret it. That's what growing old allows you. More and more regret."

8

I don't want you to get the impression that I wasn't thinking about Bob Jablonski, my missing father, and Vivian
Spivy. I was. Dino and Ruby put us up in one of their guest
bedrooms with two single beds, draped in red-fringed vel-
vety blankets that matched the drapes. There was a formal
chair with a red silk pattern covered in plastic in one corner; we didn't sit on it. I spent a lot of time in that bedroom lounging around, trying to picture my father in his
new surroundings. Oddly, I still think I felt more bitter
envy than bitterness. I envisioned him at a Howard Johnson's like the one we'd left behind, the orange roof reflected in the pool in front of him as he lounged in a
deck chair, his real leg sunning up nicely and the fake staying forever pale and permanently laced-up in that shiny
black shoe and sock; the maid in their room changing the
white sheets, the trash can liner, the white towels; and
Vivian floating on a neon-pink raft in a modest one-piece

swimsuit—I had decided she was modest. But my father wasn't relaxed. I imagined him fretting over not being with me and my mother, of course, missing us. I believe he loved both of us, but, moreover, I pictured him antsy about his clients' appointments, made sometimes an entire year in advance; his car, knowing my mother would forget to take it in for its scheduled oil changes; the lawn, which was surely getting overgrown or burned out with brown bald spots. I tried to think of him as Vivian's free-and-easy Bobby, but it was impossible.

It was certainly within my imagination that my parents could divorce. It was 1985; the divorce statistics were staggering. To me, divorce wasn't particularly ominous, probably because I never really believed it possible, and I was right. In the end, my parents would stick it out. Anyway it seemed that the coolest kids' parents were divorcing. There was travel involved, back and forth between parents, and I liked traveling, anything to get me out of dull, foot-dragging summer afternoons practicing clarinet with the insatiably boring Louisa Eppitt, our lofty scales pitching and rising over the chatter of her father's television set. Divorced kids seemed spoiled, caught in an attention war. Their mothers got jobs. The kids were often on their own without any adult supervision. I'd heard of after-school basement parties, although I'd never been invited to one. It didn't sound too bad.

The sticking point for my mother would be Catholicism. For some reason, she cared particularly what a handful of nuns in her convent school thought of her—even though she didn't really keep in touch with them. But it wasn't only Catholicism that made my mother certain that she and my father would be reunited. I asked her one of those early nights in Dino and Ruby Pantuliano's guest bedroom, lying in our beds, which were side by side the way I'd seen them in the rooms of girls with sisters, "Do you think he'll come back?"

"He'll come back," she said.

"How do you know?"

"We have an agreement," she said.

"What kind of agreement?"

"Well, in addition to our marriage, an unspoken agreement."

"What are you agreeing to?"

"We've agreed to overlook things, as a courtesy."

"Like what? The fact that I'm not really Bob Jablonski's daughter?"

"Yes," she said. "I owe him a favor."

It sounded very bizarre to me, not at all the way I pictured marriages working. "A courtesy," I said.

"Exactly."

One Monday morning she called Mrs. Shepherd on the Pantulianos' sleek red wall-hung kitchen phone during her regular cleaning hours in our house, and the old battle-ax answered. My mother asked her if she had run into Dr. Jablonski while cleaning. But she must have said no, because my mother went on: "I apologize if his golf socks have been left out or if his clubs are cluttering the hallway closet." Again, she must have said that they weren't. "Did he get to the lawn?" Once more, no, and then Mrs. Shepherd must have scolded my mother for sour, week-old garbage left in the kitchen; my mother apologized with little energy and asked her to send along the mail. I could tell that Mrs. Shepherd was hemming and hawing. My mother said she'd pay her extra, and Mrs. Shepherd complied. She gave her Dino Pantuliano's address in Bayonne.

The mail arrived on Thursday, which would become a

habit. There were no personal letters the first week. But the next Thursday there were three: one from Grandma Tati and Aunt Bobo in Boston and one with no return address but rubber-stamped as being from Tucson, Arizona, and one, to my surprise, from Church Fiske, who must have gotten the address from the envelope in which my mother had sent her thank-you to Juniper.

The letter from Arizona was from Vivian Spivy. My mother read it aloud one time. We sat knees to knees on the edge of our single beds in Dino Pantuliano's guest bedroom. She warned that she would read it through once and that was to be that, that we weren't to dwell on it, for God's sake. It read something like this:

Dear Mrs. Jablonski,
    ("Again with the Mrs. Jablonski?" my mother said. "You'd think sleeping with my husband would make our relationship a little less formal.")
    Hello. How are you? I'm surprised to find myself writing you. Bobby (my mother rolled her eyes) *doesn't know I'm writing this. I want you to know that he is fine. And we are in Arizona, but I can't say where. Not because I don't know but because I don't think I should tell. We may open a small business here. I've always wanted to write for a newspaper.* (My mother said, "Please—she can't even write a letter!")
    Anyway, we will not be needing any more money. I'm sorry about that. And Bobby misses Lissy terribly. It's hard for him sometimes. There's a lot to consider. I may write again.

                                        Sincerely,
                                        Vivian S. Spivy

"Oh, for God's sake," my mother said. "They've got the name of the town right on the envelope—Tucson, they're in Tucson."

I imagined Vivian in the post office, having driven my mother's station wagon—complete with my mother's box of Wetnaps and lipstick and coffee mug—into town for the day. I guess she didn't expect the clerk to stamp the envelope. I imagined she felt a little panic as she saw the stamp and then the letter swooshed away into a canvas bin on wheels, and, being shy, she didn't ask for the letter back but half jogged, shifty eyed and flustered, to the car. It was a mistake my mother never would have made. The letter was nice, though, thoughtful, with graceful simplicity, childlike sincerity. I found Vivian Spivy touching and sweet and sad.

Grandma Tati and Aunt Bobo's letter was much more ominous. They wanted to know why my father wasn't there when they made their regular Sunday night phone call, why no one was answering the phone. They stated their intentions to visit the following weekend if they heard nothing from us and possibly even if they did hear from us—which sounded like a threat. But I saw no prospect of our leaving anytime soon. There was no place else to go, really. I got the impression that my mother didn't want to be alone in Keene, her marriage failing publicly, and there was no one else that my mother felt she could be relaxed around, without their prying and gossiping about her. And the visit seemed to work well for Ruby, a terribly bored housewife who'd never had any children, because, she said, her "tubes were bad." She took my mother and me on as projects, the daughter and granddaughter she'd never had. Evidently, Jacko had been her only maternal outlet for years; the guest bedroom closet was filled with little multicolored doggie sweaters and bow ties. She had garish taste and a penchant for euchre, a card game pronounced *yooker*, that had seen its heyday in Bayonne in the 1940s, its players having since dwindled to a small core of embattled, loyal euchre pros. She was grooming us with a motherly frenzy for our euchre coming-out party at Marianne Focetti's house in downtown Bayonne—Marianne being a long-time sworn social enemy of Ruby's. By week two, my mother was wearing Ruby's leopard-print leggings, which seemed to suit her in some strange way, and there were similarly horrific outfits purchased for me. She'd convinced my mother to throw away her Weight Watchers scale, letting Ruby fatten her up. Ruby teased our hair. I was a little scared of it all and spent long hours in the pool, taking the occasional poolside instruction from my mother to put my face in, to blow bubbles—things she'd heard but never mastered. Mainly I was trying to keep a safe distance from the teasing comb and Aquanet. And on rainy days, I watched television and patted Jacko's narrow rump. I'd never had a dog, and I liked the way he appreciated my touch, arching, foot jiggling, when I hit the spot he couldn't get at with his head in its plastic cast. When Ruby watched her soaps, I practiced my clarinet. I was lonely and bored.

"Listen," I said one rainy afternoon. "Jacko sings along!" I played a few bars of "Danny Boy" and Jacko howled.

"No offense, hon," Ruby said. "I think he's in pain."

Ruby dumped the dog out the back door and plopped herself down in front of the television. It was disheartening. I was planning on asking Ruby to show me old photo albums in hopes of spotting my real father, but I hadn't quite worked up the courage. I didn't know what my mother would think of it, so I held back for the time being.

The one thing I could not escape, ever, was Ruby's daily euchre lessons. The three of us hunched over our playing cards while Ruby lectured on how to keep a man. She'd surmised early on that my father was gone. She'd guessed with a younger woman, rolling her poppy eyes. She knew little tricks of the trade, and when she wasn't endlessly chronicling the ailments of aging from which she suffered, she lectured on romance. She said, "The things they don't print in *Good Housekeeping,* if you know what I mean." I certainly didn't and didn't particularly want to hear Ruby's take on human sexuality. She believed lingerie should always be red, because it incited the appetite. "It's scientifically proven," she told us. "That's why Italian restaurants always have red booths. It makes you hungry by setting off chemicals in your brain." I imagined Ruby sashaying around the house in a teddy made of restaurant-booth vinyl. I thought about the guest bedroom my mother and I were sharing and how it was decorated all in red and felt a little squeamish, wondering if Ruby had seduced Dino in my bed. There was no escape in sight. At any mention of our departure, Ruby would stomp her Charo shoes and, in her hoarse smoker's voice, say, "Dino! Tell them they can't go!" And Dino, from the dark recesses of his study, where I think he spent most of his time watching the New York Yankees, dozing off, would say, "You can't go!"

And so I imagined my Grandmother Tati and Aunt Bobo taking the spare key from the hook in the garage, opening our side door and walking through the empty house, wandering room to room, arm in arm, Bobo frightened and Tati pissed. My mother tore up both notes and threw them in the garbage.

My mother handed Church's letter to me and said, "Don't get involved with a Fiske. They're a little fragile, don't you think?"

I said, "It's just a letter."

It went like this:

Lissy,

My Dad's got a girlfriend named Daisy, for Chrissakes, and Juniper is wigging out. She bought me a shirt with an Eton collar and wants me to actually wear it. Piper is hormonally imbalanced. I told Juniper that your mother soothed me and that you get straight A's. I just assumed that. (He was right.) *Anyway, I'm N.I.B., you know, from the boarding school in Delaware. See what I'm getting at? What do you think?*

Sincerely,
C. F.

In the P.S. he scribbled his phone number, adding, *It's Piper's private line, but I'd rather her know you're calling than Juniper. This has got to be a covert operation. No shit.*

I didn't dare ask my mother what 'N.I.B.' was. I assumed it was something perverted. The letter actually made me a little queasy. I was giddy over the fact he'd written, but I didn't know what it meant and I wanted it to mean a lot. That afternoon I excused myself from our euchre lesson on the patio to go to the bathroom, and I called Church.

Piper answered, "Yes? Piper Fiske here."

"Hi, it's Lissy. Is Church around?"

"Oh," she said. "Churchie is masturbating in his bedroom and can't talk right now."

"Look, Piper, I can't bullshit around with you." I realized as I was speaking that I was scared of Piper. My
kneecaps were jiggling. "I've only got a minute here and I
need to talk to him."

There was a puff of air and stomping feet and then
Church said, "Hello?" He sounded a little sleepy or breathless and I wondered if he had, in fact, been masturbating. I
was flustered, my cheeks hot. "What's 'N.I.B.'?"

"Lissy?"

"Yeah. What's 'N.I.B.'?"

"Oh, it means I got kicked out of my boarding school.
'N.I.B.' stands for"—he said the rest with a clenched jaw,
faking a British accent— "not invited back."

"What did you do?"

"They didn't like me. The headmaster had it in for me,
really. One time I asked the French teacher if I could eat
her velvet underwear. One time, that's it. She all but bust-
ed an egg over it."

"In French?" It seemed important.

"Of course I asked in French. Provincial French—maybe
the grammar was a little off. But, yes, in French. I thought
it was clever."

"What does your letter mean, Church? It's in, like, code.
What are you talking about, covert operation?"

"Look, I couldn't spell it out because it might have gotten intercepted. C'mon, Lissy. Add it up. My dad's got a
girlfriend. My mother's intensely neurotic, borderline
breakdown. I'm N.I.B. They've got to think of something
to do with me. Right? Why not send me to a nice, stable,
loving, middle-class environment? Like yours."

Church could be a real asshole. I was a little pissed off by
the whole middle-class *Happy Days* impression he had of

us. "We're not exactly stable, Church." And then I lowered my voice. "I think Dino's in a drug ring." I'd been suspicious of the vague import-export description of his vitamin business but was also trying to play it up to make my life sound more exotic and dangerous than it was.

"Look, nobody's stable. You know what John Lennon said about the sixties? 'Nothing happened except we got dressed up.' I'm just fucking dressed up, in an Eton collar, no less. It might as well be hooked up to a leash. Nobody knows what to do with me."

"What about Piper?"

"She's too good for everybody except maybe William Burroughs and Mahler and Eric Clapton every once in a while. She just sulks around her room. My parents think she's an angel."

"I thought you guys did tennis camp."

"I got 'nibbed' there, too. In my defense, I was doing a flawless impersonation of John McEnroe and they kicked me out. The instructor, some blond asshole named Thad, said, 'Yes, McEnroe, if McEnroe were an abysmal tennis player.' See? I'm in hell." His voice got shaky. "My dad's talking military academies. Everybody's lying to me!"

Ruby had tottered into the house, but I hadn't seen her. "Holy shit," I said about the military academies, and Ruby answered, "You'd better be praying."

I hung up the phone and looked at Ruby.

"Am I gonna see that on my long distance?" she asked.

"Yeah. I'll pay you back."

"Your boyfriend?" She squinted her pop eyes, smiling sheepishly.

"Not really," I said. "No, I don't think so."

• • •

When I finally mustered the nerve to ask about photo albums, Ruby was delighted to oblige. She loved my passion for photo albums. I sat through hours of pictures of strangers, Aunt Angela before the goiter, babies squalling through baptisms, and the young and lovely Ruby on a roller coaster, as a bride, one in Italy with her hands posed to make it look like she was holding up the Tower of Pisa.

"What about Dino before he met you?" I asked.

"Oh, yeah. There's a shoe box somewheres. But it's the old country mostly, black and whites of olive pickers scrubbed up for Sunday mass."

"I want to see everything!"

My mother was in and out. I think she knew that I was looking for a picture of Anthony, but she didn't seem interested. She paced around on the patio, smoking cigarettes, staring into the pool, up at the sky, and then back to the pool where the stars were reflected.

Ruby handed me the shoe box. "He scribbled on the backs of them," she said. "I got to fix up dinner."

She'd been right. A lot of the pictures were ancient photographs of dark-skinned farmers and farmers' wives and lots of children, their faces hard and fixed, proud. I flipped through them as quickly as I could, looking for something American, a man and a boy on a ship. And then finally I saw a picture of a young Dino and a little boy with a big head, topped by a man-size hat and a white patch taped over one eye. On the back, he'd written out: *Anthony and Dino Pantuliano, May 17,* no year. Shuffling through the stack, I watched Anthony grow up, always the smallest kid in the class picture, the baseball uniform bagging at his knees, its numbers more on his fanny than his back. He wasn't scrawny like me but short and broad. Finally there was a shot of him alone, something you'd see taken in a boardwalk booth, his thick wave of shiny black hair swooping down his forehead, the fixed gaze of his one dark eye, the eyebrow arched, the other eye hidden behind a black patch, his beautiful full lips, thick knotted nose, and tight jaw. He looked handsome and determined. I'd always thought my full lips and dark eyes and hair had come from my mother, but they could have come from him, and I'd always thought my nose came from the Jablonski side of the family, but it was plainly Anthony's. Bob Jablonski was a fairer, plain, soft-featured man with unattractive sisters, Tati and Bobo being dull, pasty women. You'd think it would have almost been a relief not to be genetically linked to them, but the reimagination of my genes felt strange, a physical achiness actually as if I were being taken out of one body and put in another. It was at this moment that I realized that I was not from my father, not half calm, half quiet, half steady, and plain, perhaps sterile—despite our unmatching anatomy. But I realized that half of me came from a giant, potent cock, that the sexuality stirring in me was not an aberration but somehow genetic, ingrained, truly me. And the other half of me, from my mother, someone whom I'd always envisioned as more New England nursing school than Bayonne fish shop, was beginning to change on me, too. I felt like I was no longer who I thought I was but something darker, sexier, more mysterious. I stole the picture, put it in my pocket, and later slipped it under the mattress of my bed.

My mother didn't sleep well at Dino and Ruby Pantuliano's. Soon enough, she was waking me up for girl talk. Of course, she couldn't bang around the house to rouse me, so, instead, she would whisper my name from her single bed, and as soon as she knew I was awake, she'd start talking. My mother seemed to tell me her story with a purposeful sense of duty. She told me everything. She didn't hold back. She was as loyal to setting forth the truth as she'd been to her lies. Sometimes I felt like a priest listening to confession, as if she thought omitting a detail were a sin. The first few nights, she told me about her courtship with Anthony Pantuliano as we lay under our thin sheets.

"I loved the way he held me in Uncle Dino's car parked in the Hudson County Park at night, overlooking the tankers on Newark Bay docked in the seaport on the other side. I loved even the smell of animals on him. No matter how much he washed, you could still smell them, a kind of death smell, not fishy like my father, but more like blood, the smell of our blood. I loved the way his one good eye bore down on me. I can't describe it . . . like . . . like the single light on a train. I came to love the sealed eye, too, a quiet place, like a calm lake or something right there on his face." She paused. "And I loved his big head with his firm jaw and wild, dark hair. I loved his enormous penis, the way it rose and grew, so tight with blood it was almost blue, shining." She admitted then that they had sex in the backseat of Uncle Dino's Pinto, her feet braced on the headrest, the seat belt bruising her ribs.

"He was magical. I loved him," she said. She seemed a little hesitant to continue, but she did continue. It helped that it was dark, that we could look at the ceiling and not each other. "He got his hands on some rubbers from a guy at the rendering plant, but they were too tight, like a tourniquet." I remember my cheeks were hot with embarrassment. I rustled nervously in my bed, twisting the sheets with my feet. But I didn't say anything. I just let her talk.

"And so we did it with nothing. We were stupid, of course; it was only a matter of time before I'd get pregnant." And she did get pregnant, eventually, but not with me. I came later, after she'd nearly left Bayonne for good. "He knew the world was turning upside down. He had dreams and the dreams came true. He dreamed about JFK, a year before it happened, and Buddy Holly. He knew where Dino was headed, too."

"And where was Dino headed?"

"Well, I don't think he's in the import/export vitamin business."

I whispered fiercely, "Do you think he's a part of a drug ring?"

"He's a nice man. You don't ask questions about a nice man."

We lay there quietly for a minute and then a question dawned on me, a question about the magical powers of Anthony. "Did he know you were going to get pregnant and have his child? Did he dream that up? Did he dream up me?"

"I don't know," she said. "I certainly never in a million years could have dreamed you up. I never could have imagined someone like you," she said. "You're a little like him, you know."

No, I didn't know. "How?"

My mother was drifting off to sleep.

"How am I like him?"

"Oh, just listen to you. The way you ask your questions. You have passion."

I was surprised to hear that I had passion and that my mother was aware of it, that it was obvious to her. Now, I'd have to agree that, yes, I do have a certain amount of passion. Back then, however, it was a surprise to me, but I liked the idea that I was like him. And if it wasn't really true and I didn't have as much passion as my mother said I did at fifteen lying in the Pantulianos' guest room, I was from then on bound to acquire passion. I could feel the spot under the mattress where I'd hidden his picture, burning up into my stomach.

9

Church talked to Juniper. Juniper talked to my mother. My mother talked to Ruby. And Church Fiske arrived on the Pantulianos' doorstep in an authentic green-striped rugby shirt three sizes too big and with real rubber buttons, khaki shorts, and a huge mountain-climber's backpack strapped over one shoulder as if he were heading into the wilderness, which in a way he was. I assume that the chain of events that led him to the Pantulianos that summer hinged on his mother's fragile mental state, my mother's difficult situation, and Ruby's new role as mother. Church capitalized on the fact that everyone was feeling a little bit weak, and he got what he wanted—an escape.

He arrived in the middle of a euchre party, a small friendly get-together of glittering old women with cotton-candy spun hair, chatting above the drone of a soap opera, *The Young and the Restless* in particular, its love-struck characters chiming from multiple TVs scattered throughout the downstairs. It was a warm-up, really, for our euchre coming-out at the infamous Marianne Focetti's. Ruby liked to tell us stories of Marianne and her husband Lenny—how Marianne made Ruby lick a frog once when they were children and how Lenny had parachuted kittens off the Bayonne Bridge. She added, "Iron-ti-cally, he was a paratrooper in World War II. See how God is on my side?" These were little pep talks meant to get us psyched up. I was less than motivated.

When Church arrived, I was wearing what Ruby called flashy leisure wear, a black sweatshirt with sequins stitched on it in the shape of a cat with a little face and emerald eyes, green sparkling leggings to match the eyes, thin black socks, and high heels. I hadn't been expecting him until the next day and felt completely humiliated. Church smiled and raised his eyebrows, pointing at me in a gesture that mocked, *Lookin' good*. Ruby pulled up a fifth chair to a folding card table in the living room and told the boy to sit and try to pick up the game. She seemed immediately suspicious of him, perhaps because the stories that had preceded him had put her on guard. He'd interrupted one of Ruby's monologues on what I had come to realize was her favorite topic: how to keep your man. I'm not sure how much of it was targeted at my mother, but my mother seemed oblivious. She was on a vacation, truly, and didn't seem to mind letting Ruby dress her up or listening to the old woman's didactic stories. This time she was giving how-to instructions on heating up holiday romance. Evidently, she'd once taped holly to her nipples and shaved and ornamented her pubic hair to resemble a Christmas tree. She loud-whispered it so that no one would accuse her of speaking inappropriately in front of "the children." I pretended not to hear her. But after she'd finished, Church piped up, "Ho, ho, ho!" and everyone stopped and stared. I let out a muffled laugh, a kind of snort. My mother stood up and quickly ushered Church to his room, which was across the hall from ours. I'm sure she was under no illusions about Church Fiske and his behavior problem. When Church emerged again from his bedroom, my mother said, "Why don't you two take a walk around the neighborhood or something?"

"And take Jacko," Ruby said. The little dog had been irritating the guests, begging for scraps, paws up, his pecker jiggling with his little panting breaths.

I was relieved, having grown weary of euchre and the loving pats of little old ladies. I said, "Hold on," and left Church standing in the room of card tables and smoke and ran to my room to change into O.P. shorts and a T-shirt. When I came downstairs, the front door was open and I could see Church standing on the stoop. I clipped on Jacko's neon leash, waved a finger-wiggling toodles, and shut the door. I was thrilled to have someone my own age to talk to, finally. I decided that minute that I was free of the soap-opera marathons, the how-to-keep-a-man lectures, and the endless conversations about falling arches, arthritis, and corns. And I was free of my clarinet, too. I hated it, really, the sappy songs, the flatulent squeaks and honks.

Church was ecstatic, too, but not for the same reasons. "A card party! I love it! It's so typical. Did you see the ladies in their huge earrings and that lipstick and all their thin dyed hair air-sprayed up on their heads? Just like I thought it would be, but better! They're so Italian! Do you think they're, you know, connected to the mob? Didn't you say he was a drug lord or something? Well, not a drug *lord*—I mean, they're so middle class. It's beautiful. Even that little dog! Look at him!"

Jacko was peeing on the foot of a mailbox, thrilled to be out of the house. He kicked behind himself politely, a well-bred instinct, although there was only the sound of his little nails scraping cement, no dirt or grass. I was pissed at Church for doling out more of this whole wonder-at-middle-class-life crap as if we were a *National Geographic* special and he was laughing at the natives. As I let him chatter on, though, his voice high and almost squeaky, more like Juniper's than I'd remembered it, I realized he wasn't laughing. He was taking it all in and he loved it; he coveted it.

We walked down to the end of the block, Jacko snorting because of his asthma, the humidity, his smushed face. "We should head back. Don't you think?" Church asked.

"No," I said.

"Look, that dog's going to bust a gasket." It was obviously an excuse. Church wanted to return to the Pantulianos' house to the euchre party. I was suspicious of his motives, but we went back inside, sat on the love seat, and watched the ladies smoke and deal and gossip, Jacko snug between us.

As time passed, I realized that Church's weird admiration for the Pantulianos made it a whole lot easier for me to be around him. I'd been nervous about his showing up, but once he was there, it was as if he looked up to me. My intimate knowledge of the middle class gave me the upper hand, in a way. And as time went on that summer, Church began to be a part of the oddly cast family. I still had a crush on Church sometimes, but because he was always around, he began to annoy me, like a brother might.

He loved going to Mass at Assumption, which we attended every Sunday with the Pantulianos. "Catholics are so gory!" he said. "Jesus hanging everywhere, bleeding and dying. It's great!" He'd been raised a Christmas-and-Easter Episcopalian in a stodgy church where parishioners, mostly ancient, sang marching hymns, their crosses always unoccupied. He loved dipping his fingers in holy water, genuflecting, all the secret hand motions, not just the sign of the cross, but forehead, lip, and heart crossing, the chest rapping.

While my mother and I were taking our daily euchre lessons with Ruby, Church was studying baseball with Dino in his study. Dino was a first-generation Italian American. He believed firmly that to be a true American, you had to love a baseball team with all your heart, and he loved the New York Yankees. Church loved them, too, and the idea of loving them. He was a quick study. He'd say, "Lissy, ask me about the greatest team ever to play the game." And before I could ask, he'd say, "Combs, Koenig, Ruth, Gehrig . . ." He'd talk about Don Larsen's perfect game against the Dodgers in the World Series in '56 as if it had just happened. He was infuriated that Yogi Berra was fired after the Yanks lost to St. Louis in '64 and he bemoaned the introduction of free agency in '65. He was crazy about Mr. October. "Tell her, Dino, about Reggie Jackson. The whole thing, play by play."

When the Yankees played well, Church and Dino were happy. When the team lost, they were irritable. They were always talking about the race between Mattingly and Winfield; spitting at the mere mention of Steinbrenner's name; sticking up for Niekro, the aging knuckleballer, and Hendersen, the base stealer; keeping an eye on the other contenders, especially the Toronto Blue Jays. Dino had a bad feeling about them.

Church also loved reruns. It wasn't that he'd never seen *Sanford and Son, Gilligan's Island, The Brady Bunch.* He had, but never with simple appreciation. There had been little time for TV in the first place. At boarding school, watching TV was made nearly impossible, what with sports and study hall and lights out. And in the summers, there were so many camps. If by chance he got to settle down in front of a TV, without someone insisting on the news, he had always had to withstand the voice-over of snobbery, laughing at, not laughing with, a criticism of the anti-intellectual nature of society. Everyone, it seemed, was well versed in the rhetoric of antitelevision. Just as he loved loving the cross-hung Jesus and the Yankees, he loved loving reruns, developed a crush on Marsha Brady, a chummy friendship with Richie Cunningham. He became irate when I questioned why Gilligan, the Skipper, and the Professor had to wear the same clothes day in and day out and the others seemed to have entire steamer trunks of wardrobe.

"How far off course could they have gotten anyway? It was only a three-hour tour!" I said.

"Who do you think you are? You don't question it. You have *faith!*"

He even loved the commercials targeted at the unemployed: an endless supply of classes on how to drive eighteen-wheelers and how to enroll in correspondence classes in medical transcription. "I could drive a rig," he'd say. "Now that's a noble calling."

Meanwhile, my mother still paced out by the swimming pool, and on Sundays at Mass, she prayed fervently. She was especially fervent after the read-aloud petitions when the priest said, "And now let us pray for all of the intentions kept in the privacy of our hearts." At this moment, my mother closed her eyes, her fingers squeezed so tightly together that her hands turned a bright red.

Once I whispered to her after I'd gone up to receive the Eucharist, "What are you praying for?"

She opened her eyes and looked around as if surprised to find herself here in church.

"Are you praying for Dad?" I asked. "To come home?"

"I'm praying for my mother's soul," she said. "And mine. And yours, too."

When my mother was drunk, she cursed us in Polish," my mother said one night. "She'd call my father a bastard, *bekart*. She'd yell out, 'Jezus Chrystus,' and refer to the two of us as idiots. *'Idióta* and *idiótka.'* "

Evelyn Verbitski, my mother's mother, married beneath herself. She was originally an Oleski; a branch of her family had immigrated in the latter part of the 1800s. Her relatives did well in the new country, not so well that they were invited to the Newark Bay Boat Club, but leagues ahead of the Bohemian immigrants who crammed into one room, forming little impoverished colonies. Eventually, more Oleskis came over. My grandmother lived in Poland until 1936 when she was twelve years old and her family joined relatives already set up in Bayonne. She'd grown up in the district of Kraków, but pretty far north of the city, amid farms that mostly yielded grain. She was a superstitious woman who taught my mother strange habits like to always put the same shoe on first—if left, always left, or if right, always right—and how to throw shoes to see what your luck would be—bad if it landed sole and heel up.

"When I did something wrong, she'd tell me the story of how she sewed on a Sunday while she was pregnant with me because my father needed a button put on for church. It was an old superstition that if you sewed on a Sunday when you were pregnant, your child was sure to be born an idiot."

And so when Evelyn (then Oleski) fell in love with Wladyslaw Verbitski one day in the fall of 1947 as he sat in his friend's front yard cutting open the stomachs of long black eels, she was taking a social step backward in the Oleski tradition, despite the fact that her own family didn't have much money and was the poorest link in that tradition, and she never forgave him for making her fall in love with him. As far as my mother could surmise, he'd done nothing at all except sit there, slightly stooped and dirty and fish-smelly, carving into the bellies of slick black eels with a kitchen knife.

Once Evelyn had married Wladyslaw, she never looked back. She cut herself off from her family. She claimed to be embarrassed by him, but it seemed really to be more her choice. Each Christmas her mother would send her *oplatek*, a piece of the family's large unleavened wafer, but she never ate it. One Christmas Eve, in the Polish tradition of Wigilia, she lit a candle in the window and set a place for the Christ child at the table, with salt and bread, a coin under the plate, and straw beneath the tablecloth. She made *pierozhki*, a clear beet soup with mushrooms and carp, grain pudding called *kutya*, poppy-seed cakes, and twelve-fruit compote. My mother was eight years old. "The light," my grandmother told her, "is to guide the Christ child here to our house." But my grandmother was always angry about something, and this was no different. In the morning, my grandmother woke my mother up early. "Look," she said, her breath steaming with alcohol. "He is not here. Nothing is true."

My mother had said every dreamy word about her love for Anthony Pantuliano, and now she began to dwell on how it all came undone, a part of the story that hinged on her mother. Of course, my mother's relationship with Anthony crossed an ethnic barrier that at that time was difficult to cross. He didn't come to the house for a date, ring the doorbell with a stiff arm extending a large and bloom-heavy bouquet, and have a chat with her father as he would have had he been Polish. My mother would tell her parents that she was out with a girlfriend—Peggy Harpes, or better yet, Elsa Pawelski from Mt. Carmel, *their* church, meaning the Polish Catholic church in town, as opposed to Assumption, the Italian church where the likes of the Pantulianos went every Sunday to pray and every Wednesday to confess. She would meet Anthony a block down and over from Verbitski's Fish Shop. Sometimes he'd have his uncle's Pinto and they'd head out to look over the tankers on Newark Bay from the Hudson County Park. Sometimes they'd walk to his apartment building and he'd show her the pictures he'd developed in his darkroom—ugly, beautiful pictures. She remembers a little girl with a burn-scarred face staring out of a car window, World War II vets playing poker at the VFW, and, of course, the picture of her at the fire. With that picture blown up, she could make out her father in the background, picking up bits of glass from the street.

"What did your mother do? What was so crazy?" I asked one night. My mother had such high standards for herself and others that I expected that her complaints about my grandmother wouldn't be so terrible. And, at first, it seemed I was right.

"She drank too much. She was always cold, her little blue hands like something iced. I never saw her undressed, not even in a slip. I hated her." My mother stopped there for a minute, surprised she'd said it, but not willing to take it back. "She told me she stepped on my father's foot after they were married, a superstition to ensure she would be the boss of the family. She loved failures. And he obliged her by failing idiotically so she could punish him and drink and curse her bitter life and in some strange way be happy."

"How did she start the fire?" I asked, tentatively.

"At first I believed her, that my father had been careless, that he'd started the fire, that he'd come home for lunch and left a lit cigar on newspapers next to the toilet where he'd been sitting. He went down to the shop. But fires— cigar fires—on newspapers catch slowly." My mother lowered her voice to the softest whisper. "I've thought about this for years. My mother was polishing silverware at the dining-room table. She must have smelled the smoke, but she did not move. Smoke must have spilled out of the bathroom and filled up the dining room. But she just sat at the table polishing spoon after spoon. I've seen her sitting there a million times." She tried to describe her mother's face squeezed tight with lines, the downward pull of her lips, shining up her own warped reflection. "I wish you could see her sitting there rubbing the spoons with her rag and polish, coughing, choking on the smoke, and then the heat. That's where the fireman found her, collapsed at the

table. He scooped her up and carried her out. She was prov-
ing that her husband was an imbecile, that he was killing
her. This is how she operated."

"And what did she say? Did she ever answer for it?"

"In the hospital bed, she said, 'You nearly killed me, you
dumb lazy man.' *Glupi*, she called him, 'stupid' in Polish,
tapping his head. *'Glupi. Idióta!'* And my father cried, tears
staining his overcoat. He said, 'I thought I put it out. I
thought I wet the tip in the sink first.' I stood in the door-
way and watched. She pulled him to her and said, 'There,
there, you stupid man. There, there.' In the end, a few years
later, his heart froze up. It seized in his chest and he died.
She killed *him*."

Some nights during the summer that never happened,
my mother would borrow Ruby's car—at Ruby's
absolute insistence. By demanding that my mother drive
her Cadillac Coup de Ville, Ruby was allowed to spoil my
mother, and Ruby loved to spoil my mother. She bought
her clothes and jewelry and often slipped her spending
money. She fed her homemade cannoli. I'd seen other
people react to my mother this way. It was as if they could
sense that she'd had a bad mother and they instinctively
wanted to make up for it. My mother must have sensed the
inverse in Ruby, who'd never had children, and so they
made a good pair.

My mother would go out driving around the city by herself. She'd come home dazed and dreamy, her hair tossed by
the hot air that beat in through the rolled-down windows.
I'd ask her where she went and she'd shrug, saying, "I don't
know." But I was pretty sure she'd driven past the spot that

used to be Verbitski's Fish Shop, Uncle Dino's old apartment building, and out to Hudson County Park. I imagined she parked the car and smelled the musty sea water and stared out across the water to Elizabeth's seaport.

On those nights she'd borrowed Ruby's car, my mother would get into bed late. She'd stretch her arms up over her head and stare at the ceiling. I was always waiting for a story to follow, another installment in the saga, even when I was still drowsy from having been awakened. But on the nights she circled Bayonne in Ruby's Cadillac, she'd sigh quietly, not saying a word. I wondered if she'd even noticed the change in things or if she was able to still see it as it had been, pristine.

I'd started to tell Church my mother's love story. He was the first person I would tell, but not the last. The versions I gave him were abbreviated summaries in the beginning, probably because I loved the way he'd beg for more details. "How did it happen?" he'd say. "Slow down. Just tell it like she told it." And I'd consent, giving more and more detail until the details rose up clearer and sharper from the things my mother had told me and from what she'd left out. One day Ruby trudged off with my mother to the Short Hills Mall, what I knew would be an all-day affair. My mother would in fact return with an entire new wardrobe of stretch pants and gold sweatshirts and accessories so metallic I'd envisioned them shopping with a metal detector like the ones those old men on the beach use. Also, my mother needed new clothes because she'd gained a few extra pounds because she'd stopped weighing her portions. Church and I took the opportunity of a free day to ride the bus all over the city. We walked through the park, now dirty and ill-kempt, the homeless parked on benches, Dino's old apartment building, laundry strung across six-

foot balconies, and, last of all, the fish shop, now a neon-lit
video store. In the apartment above it, where my mother
had once lived, a light glowed in the window. Church was
like a kid on a field trip to the nation's capital, but the
things he'd point out were not the Lincoln Memorial or the
White House but a hypodermic, a trashed rubber, a homeless woman walking without shoes. For me the trip was
disappointing. I'd expected a historic replica, I guess, little
shrines and plaques stating that Anthony Pantuliano and
Dorothy Verbitski had sex here, and if not that, at least
some respect, some upkeep, well-trimmed shrubbery and
little PLEASE KEEP OFF THE GRASS signs.

I would lie in my own twin bed on those silent nights
and try to aggrandize Church into something he wasn't. I
tried to imagine that kiss he gave me beside his garage on
Cape Cod, tried to pluck Anthony and my mother out of
their smoky love scenes and replace them with Church and
me, but Church always failed, the scene bubble-popping
because of one of his smart-ass remarks. Every once in a
while, though, when Church was upset, scuffing up in L.L.
Bean moccasins and fiddling with his string bracelets, I
thought I could love him then. He became sweet and vul-
nerable, his eyebrows slanting, more like the star-crossed
Anthony Pantuliano staring dreamy-eyed at his love, Dotty.

The day I told him that my mother's father was going to
die of a heart attack, Church was in one of his hopeless, distracted moods. He said, "She loved him. Your mom, you
know, she really loved her father." We were sitting on the
curb between two parked cars in front of Judy's Arcade two
blocks down from the Pantulianos'. The kids inside were
pale and fat, hunched over Ms. Pacman and Joust, their
faces greenish and flashing. It was abysmally hot, too hot
for Jacko to be outside. The streets were junked up with

nail salons and Cigarette Cities and liquor stores. Church had just found out that his dad had bought a 20-foot speedboat and that he and Daisy, his girlfriend, were going for a coastal cruise. "I could kick my dad's ass," he said in all seriousness.

"You could probably kick both of my dads' asses," I said. "One's got a fake leg and one's half-blind."

"I can't believe you have two dads. Jesus. One is bad enough."

"You know, my parents met at your parents' wedding."

"Well, that's how they got fucked over. That marriage was cursed."

I nodded, squinting up into the sky, just white, no color. I thought about Church kissing me and I wondered if he was going to do it again. I could feel exactly what it had been like to have his hand resting on my little breast. I even knew which one it had been. I was feeling like Anthony Pantuliano's daughter. What would Anthony do at a moment like this? I was desperate for some kind of drama. I was ready for my own romance, not my father's romance, running off with a redheaded bank teller, not my mother's romance with her first love. I glanced down at Church's knee, a bony knee etched with fine blond hairs. I put my hand on it and stared off across the street.

Church said, "So, you want to do it?"

And I said, "Do what?" But I didn't look at him and I knew what.

"Are you going to make me say it?"

"Yeah," I said. "I think I'm going to make you say it."

"Well, shit," Church said, standing up. "If you think I'm going to say it, you're crazy."

10

When my mom confided in Elsa Pawelski, her good friend from Mt. Carmel Church, what it was like to have sex in the backseat of Uncle Dino's car, the failed rubbers, the blinking lights, Anthony's shining penis blue, Elsa decided to tattle. She told her own mother that Dotty Verbitski was no longer pure and had been stained by an Italian boy from Assumption. Mrs. Pawelski delivered the news to her prayer group, which started a daily novena. In the fish shop, customers started to whisper and snicker at the Verbitskis and at Dotty, too, when she took money at the counter, which she often did now that it was summer. One Friday, the shop's busiest day of the week, Mrs. Verbitski shouted at Jimmy McMillan and his two friends standing in line, "What's so funny? You a comedian? You want to tell us what is so funny to you? You dirty little mick."

Jimmy stopped laughing. He looked up at Mrs. Verbitski and Mr. Verbitski, who now had a knife poised above a trout's head, and then at Dotty sitting on a stool behind the cash register. "Your daughter's doing time with Anthony Pantuliano," he said. "Doing hard time, if you know what I mean." And he rocked his hips and grabbed his dick. The women in line sucked in their breath, but no one said a word. His two friends started laughing hysterically and hurried out of the store. McMillan walked to the door slowly, tipped his hat. The only sound was the little ting of the door's bell and the clunk of the door as it shut tight.

Mrs. Verbitski said in a low voice, "Get out, all of you. Get out." One by one, the customers shuffled out the door. The littlest old lady asked in a loud voice, probably because she was a good bit deaf, "Will you be opening later?" It being a Friday, fish was critical.

"No," Mrs. Verbitski said. "No. Leave—now." And she walked to the front of the store and pushed the last few customers out, flipped over the OPEN sign to CLOSED, and locked the door. Mr. Verbitski lowered the knife and laid it on the block. He wiped blood from his fingers across the front of his apron.

My mother was stunned. She slid off the register stool and brushed the wrinkles out of her skirt, idly. She didn't say anything.

My grandmother banged her fist on the door, on the wall, the fat of her arm shaking loosely. She said, "Who are you? Who are you?" She looked at her daughter, Dotty, and turned away. *"Kurwa!"* she cursed, meaning "whore." "I cannot look at your face!" She screamed it. "I cannot look at your ugly, stupid face! I should have known you were not a virgin, the way you take your large marching steps! Everyone must know it. You whore. *Kurwa!* You are nothing but a *kurwa.*"

My mother stood there quietly, her eyes darting around the fish shop. She felt sick, the smell of seawater suddenly pressing in. She turned and ran out the back door, tripping over the little step. She fell on her knees and threw up on the gritty pavement. She was already pregnant, but she didn't know it. When she stood up, she could still hear my grandmother's shrill voice, now directed at her father. Dotty stood up, blood trickling down both of her red knees.

My mother knocked on Anthony's door that summer night in 1966, and Uncle Dino answered. He was taller then, but still with a thin frame. He was wearing a white T-shirt, his hair black, thick, wet. He took one look at my mother's ruddy face, her red eyes, her knees bloody from falling in the alley, and he ushered her in, helped her to a seat in the living room.

"What happened to the *punske* girl?" he asked.

And my mother started to cry harder. "Is he here?"

"No," Dino said. "He's out with his photography, always taking pictures of the street, you know. But he'll come home before he works the late shift."

"I can't stay," she said. She was afraid of what my grandmother might do to my grandfather if she was gone too long. "But I'm not going to be able to see him. My mother knows everything, and she'll keep us apart."

"Oh, well, if it's true love, nothing can come between you. Look at me and Bitsy," he said, walking quickly to the kitchen. Bitsy was a woman he'd been dating. "Her brother chased me with a crowbar, yelling, 'Fucking wetback,' and it doesn't matter. Soon we'll be married." Within a year, Bitsy would end up getting run over by a milk truck. Even though my mother didn't know that then, the idea of Bitsy—a raggedly thin, blinky librarian type—and Dino Pantuliano didn't really fit her notions of triumphant love. He came back with a wet dishtowel and handed it to my mother, and she pressed it to her knees.

"Tell him that I love him," she said. "Will you do that?"

Dino patted her shoulder. "It'll work out, kiddo. Things work out."

"Just tell him," she said.

"Okay, okay," he said.

My mother jogged home, her feet swishing out behind her, her knees now sore, bruised. She stood outside the back door and caught her breath. The alley stank of dead fish, the narrow strip of sky muddied with clouds. She walked up the stairs, took the key from above the doorjamb, and unlocked the door. The room was dark, except for a slice of light thrown from the lamp on the street. It lit my grandmother's swollen feet soaking in a tin tub of Epsom salts. Dotty could see my grandmother's shoes halfway across the room, and my mother knew that she had thrown them to test her luck. Both were lying flat on their laces, heels up. A bad omen.

My grandmother started talking from the dark, not looking at her daughter. "When I was a girl in Poland, we celebrated Dozynki. My first harvest working, I was so proud. They chose me to be taken by my feet and hands. The farmers swung me out over the harvest grain, the flax linens, with bread, salt, and copper coins beneath it, and then after, I danced with the landowner. Later at night, I fell asleep at the celebration and he woke me. I was alone. He covered my mouth. No one heard me." My grandmother was staring into the dark room at nothing, her face expressionless. "When we are babies, we are so perfect. You," she said, looking at her daughter, "were so perfect, but then you grew and grew into a woman's dirty body, *brudny, brudny,*" she said, meaning "dirty, dirty." "And you throw it in the garbage. You know nothing about anything."

"Why didn't you tell me anything?" my mother asked. "It isn't my fault that I'm stupid, that I know nothing. It isn't my fault that I'm no longer a baby."

"Tomorrow," my grandmother said, "your father will put you on a bus to the country to go to schooling with the nuns. You can pack your suitcase. We will see what they do with a *kurwa* like you."

My mother was crying, her cheeks red streaked. She started to walk to her room, but my grandmother said one more thing. "I know that you are pregnant. Do you want my advice? Walk through a hole in a fence, and you will miscarry. Step over a stick on a rope and with any luck, the baby will choke in you and come out dead. That's my advice to you."

My mother hadn't known she was pregnant, but now she was certain of it. My grandmother was always right. My mother had felt hungry and weak and sick. She walked quickly past my grandmother to her bedroom and threw up in her garbage can. Then she lay down on her narrow bed, curled up into a ball, and stared out her small window. She thought of climbing out it, down the fire escape, but then what? She'd walk to the slaughterhouse? Back to Dino's? She thought maybe Anthony would come for her. But if he did, what then? She tried to envision leaving Bayonne with Anthony, only to get a couple miles out on the highway and run out of money. And now pregnant on top of everything else.

She imagined Anthony walking through the slaughterhouse, his finger deep in the sheep's wool, running his broad hand down the bony backs of old horses. She felt something like the bones of her chest breaking, crumbling, but she stood up. She packed her bag. There was nothing else to do.

When she lay down to sleep that night and many times since, she thought of my grandmother as a young girl, flying out over the grain and flax linen, brave and careless, her skirt rippling at her legs, and then the landowner, his hand over her mouth, her small ribs pressed beneath his weight, how she became someone different, how an entire life can change on a dime. My mother wanted to believe that she could become a different person, that maybe it was possible to change who she was, not for the worse, but for the better. I remember my mother whispering to me in Dino and Ruby's guest bedroom, "I thought she was right, you know. It had felt so good, being with Anthony. I thought I was a no-good whore."

In the morning her father took her to the bus station. My grandmother was sleeping off a drunk, her deep breaths rattling from her bedroom.

He said, "I can't go in the station with you. I just can't." He lifted her suitcase out of the backseat and put it down on the sidewalk between them. He hugged her tightly, awkwardly lunging over the suitcase, lifting her slightly, throwing off her balance. He whispered in her ear, "She's wrong, you know. Dead wrong." He let go of her then and she tipped back to the ground, heavily. She hated him for being weak and yet she loved him for his small acts of love, all he felt allowed to give her. He rubbed his eyes and wiped his nose with a handkerchief pulled from his back pocket.

She picked up the suitcase and walked into the station to buy the ticket. She waited for the bus inside. The loud wall clock ticked over her head. When she finally boarded and the bus heaved away from the station, she saw her father's car still parked on the side of the building and her father inside, his eyes hidden by the shadow of his brimmed hat.

11

Juniper Fiske called her son often at the Pantulianos', always kite-high and almost singing, her chirping voice, Church said, squealing like a wineglass when you circle the rim with a wet finger. I listened to Church say, "Really?" and "That's nice" over and over.

"What?" I would mouth. "What is she saying?"

And he'd roll his eyes. He'd cover the phone with his hand and say something like, "She's in a tizzy about grapes sprayed with pesticides in Paraguay or some shit."

And then Piper would get on. Church would tell me later that she'd plod off to her room, shut the door, and give the real story, that Juniper was losing it, paranoia, that she was popping new little pills that made her do some kind of hopped-up June Cleaver impersonation. One night Piper found her clanging around the basement trying to snip wires that might in some way be monitoring her pathetic life. "As if anyone could bear to listen in on this horror show," Piper would say.

Church's dad made a rare call one day, but Church said his father seemed confused, like he couldn't remember that he hadn't sent his son to a military academy. Guy Fiske said things like, "Well, this experience will toughen you up, all right" and "I'm not going to bail you out, son; you've made your bed" and "This is for your own good. Structured environments improve young men."

Church said, "You know I'm in Bayonne, right? I'm living with the Pantulianos. They eat leftovers and watch *Barney Miller*. You know this, right?"

Guy was momentarily flustered, and in a panicked, disoriented moment he put his girlfriend Daisy on the phone. Church said, "Uh-huh. Yeah, look—I'm no fucking four-year-old. You can save your goochy-goochy-goo for some kid you see on a leash in the mall."

After the call from his dad, two things happened—I've linked them because both incidents hinged on Church's deviant behavior: (1) he started stealing things from the Pantulianos and (2) he began to think we were being followed by a little old lady in a rusted-out Chevy.

Yes, I had stolen something, too—the photo of Anthony Pantuliano as a set-jawed young man with his wash of black hair—but the things that Church stole were strange. He didn't take money, although there was cash in the house—once, I saw Dino counting out wads of bills at his little office desk to the voice-over of a baseball game and the quiet smacking of mitts. And not jewelry—Ruby's dog's-eye–size gemstone rings couldn't possibly be removed from her arthritis-swollen knuckles, not without taking off a finger. Instead Church stole, for example, a refrigerator magnet prayer card with the bleeding, thorn-pierced heart of Jesus on it, followed by one of Ruby's old bowling balls, Dino's baseball cap with two beer cans attached at the sides with straws that could reach to his mouth, and a crocheted toilet paper cover stitched in red, white, and blue, bicentennially inspired, no doubt. Everyone was eyeing Church suspiciously, but the items were such a strange assortment that a motive was hard to pin on him.

And then there was the old lady. He'd seen her only twice, he said, definitely following us, but whenever we were out walking around the neighborhood, he'd get shifty and nervous. He wasn't scared so much as exhilarated. He wanted desperately to catch the old woman, for someone to believe him. He'd tell me to dodge down alleys. He'd grab my arm and say, "See, see—it's that old lady again." But to me an old lady was an old lady, hunched and gray headed. It never seemed like the same old lady, and usually it wasn't. He'd say, "Nope, nope, not her. Next time I see her, though, next time, I'll go right up to her. I'll prove it."

I asked my mom if she thought Church was kind of crazy. I hadn't divulged all of Piper's information on Juniper, but I was beginning to think maybe it was something genetic. I'd always heard rich people were eccentric—Michael Jackson had just started wearing his face mask at public appearances and Hugh Hefner was conducting business at the Playboy Mansion in his bathrobe.

My mother was teasing her own hair by this point. When I asked the question, she reared from the skirted vanity table, took a long drag from her cigarette, and said, "We're all crazy. Haven't you noticed?" And then she kind of giggled. "Look at me! My God, I'm severely imbalanced." And she bent over laughing.

Later that day, Church and I were slamming Slurpees at the 7-Eleven to get cold-ache head rushes. Sitting against the brick wall next to the pay phone, I decided to be direct. "What are you doing with all that stuff?"

He said, "What stuff?"

"All that crap from the Pantulianos'. You're taking it. Everyone knows it's you."

"I am not. Why would I want that stuff?" And that's when he changed the subject to the little old lady in the rusted-out Chevy parked by the curb, peering at us, her beady eyes just barely visible over the giant wheel. "There she is again," he said.

"Look, just admit it."

"C'mon, let's move. Just wait. You'll see. She's tailing us."

"Why would some old lady follow us?" I asked.

"I don't know. Some biddy who gets her rocks off ogling. She's a, you know, a watcher, a voyeur. Hey," he said, like a tough guy in a movie, "the city's full of weirdos."

We headed down Broadway to Cigarette City, where they turned Church down for a pack. Sure enough, there was the old lady, lingering by the glass-cased cigars. I started to believe him. "Really, Church," I said, "that's weird." We ducked into a nail salon, where I looked at the display book. "You want preetty nai-yas?" the Asian woman asked, her teeth rusty looking and bent. "Scatch yo' boyfren's back?"

"No, thanks," I said.

When we came out, the old lady was fiddling with a parking meter. And then she followed us into the arcade, shuffling through the rows of blinking lights and buzzing, grunting, gear-shifting machines, like an extremely lost, blind, deaf, foreign tourist. She carried an enormous black pocketbook with an industrial-size buckle, hung in the crook of her elbow, her fist pointing up. It looked heavy, as if filled with lead to crack over a purse snatcher's head.

"I'm gonna ask her what she wants," Church said.

"No, no. Just ask her for directions to Hudson County Park or Avenue C." I was getting a little nervous.

With me tagging along behind him, he cleared his throat and said, "Excuse me. Do you know how to get to Avenue C from here?"

The old lady turned around and muttered sharply, "No, I'm not from here. I cannot help you."

I thought I knew her then, her thick Polish accent, the sharp smell of liquor and onions, the tight knot of her face. As she shuffled off, I turned to Church. "That's my grandmother," I said, not as sure as I sounded, but wanting to be sure. "My dead grandmother."

Every evening Dino Pantuliano surfaced for the cocktail hour, always like that first night: Bloody Marys with celery sticks, Cheez Whiz-ed crackers, the swishy jogging pants hiked up, his balls hanging obviously to one side, the bare chest—how it got tan still a mystery. He poured drinks all the way around—Church and I were now allowed one weak drink each—and chatted. A few weeks into our sojourn at his house, however, he'd started to press. His commentary got pointed: He'd ask over and over when my birthday was, then when my mother was last in Bayonne, when she last saw Anthony. My mother answered honestly but didn't offer anything further. He'd say, "The girl's got an Italian nose, don't you think, Ruby? She could be from the old country, picked right off an olive tree." Church knew not to say a word.

The Friday I thought I saw my dead grandmother alive

and well in the arcade was especially tense, the sun too hot, the neighbor's rap music too loud, Jacko whining to get at his irritated skin. I was distracted, confused by the sight of my grandmother in the arcade. Church was antsy, his knees bouncing. He was convinced that Dino was a mobster on some small scale, which only made him love Dino more. While Dino was trying to pin down my lineage, Church was trying to get Dino to talk about his possibly dirty business dealings.

Church had told me a story of his dad's friend's friend who was about to testify against one of the bosses but died before he got the chance, "of a heart attack," Church had said, "while swimming away from his exploding boat! That's the way Dino will go one day. Mark my words."

"But Dino doesn't even own a boat," I protested.

Church was firm. "Mark my words."

Dino was grouchy, bellyaching about Steinbrenner, "He changes managers as often as he does his boxer shorts! He should have stuck to building ships!" He was also pissed off about the players. "Righetti, Mattingly, Winfield—all prima donnas."

Ruby was really putting the screws to my mother and me. The big euchre party was only a week away, and that afternoon at our lesson I'd played a heart when I'd meant a diamond and she'd lost it, yelling, "You're weak! You play like my brother, the fag in Redondo Beach; like Mrs. Marcucci, that ninety-five-year-old woman without the teeth. Is this what I've taught you?" I hadn't told my mother that I was being stalked by a little old lady with a menacingly large black pocketbook. There'd been no good time.

We sat there in the blue glow of the bug zapper, frying bugs full tilt. My mother said, "It's hot."

Dino said, "It's muggy, not hot. Hot's okay. It's muggy that no one can take. If I had a gun, I'd shoot the sun."

"Don't you have a gun?" Church said. He turned to me. "I mean, I'm sure he's got a gun."

I shook my head, having already had an overdose of Church's paranoia that day.

Ruby said, "You're a bad shot, Dino. You'd put somebody's eye out."

My mother said, "I don't know. Hot or muggy, it's brutal."

"Hot or muggy? Hot or muggy?" Dino rolled his eyes. "Look, it's either one or the other. You can't have both."

Jacko whined plaintively, circling our feet for someone to rub his itchy back.

"Dino, just hypothetically," Church said, "just between you and me, have you ever killed a man?"

"That's not hypothetical," I said. "Do you know what *hypothetical* means?"

"Often, the weatherman says, *'Tomorrow will be hot and muggy,'* " my mother said. "I think he says it all the time, *'hot and muggy tomorrow.'* He probably said it just yesterday."

"The weatherman on channel three wears a bad piece," Ruby said. "Rat fur, I tell you."

Jacko started yipping, sharp, ear-piercing cries.

Church leaned in to Dino. Church whispered, "Nothing out of hate—you know, just business, right between the eyes?"

Dino stood up, burst out, "There are no bastards in this family. A Pantuliano is a Pantuliano. Don't try to confuse an old man about the weather, about guns and his personal business. The only man I'd shoot is a dirty little sniveling thief." He stared at Church. The dog was quiet. Ruby scooped him up in her arms. "Blood. Blood is what matters, am I right?"

We all nodded silently. "And she is my blood." He pointed at me. His voice became a hoarse whisper, like he might cry. "She's my blood."

He was looking at my mother, and she was looking at him, unflinchingly, like she was finally relieved to be forced to say it. "Yes."

"Well, well," said Ruby, clapping her hands like a little girl, Jacko bobbling in her lap.

I looked at Dino and he reached down, pulling me up, hands on my shoulders. He kissed both my cheeks and said, "Yes, I knew it the first minute I saw her. Anthony Pantuliano can expect a call, the cocky son of a bitch. He'll have to claim what's his." And the old man pulled me into his body, my head pressed to his bony chest. I could smell his cologne, musty and sweet, and beneath it his sweat. His heart was beating so fast I thought he might die right there. I imagined him keeling over, his arm locked around my head, imagined Ruby and my mother and Church standing over us. *Well, she'll have to stay there forever; a Pantuliano is forever bound to a Pantuliano.* And I imagined in that quick flash my grandmother, Mrs. Verbitski, knocking the newly dead Dino Pantuliano over the head with her giant handbag. I wondered what she would think, her granddaughter a Pantuliano after all.

12

When my mother talked about the convent, she was totally different, her eyes bright and alert, her mouth open too wide like she was singing. She looked freshly scrubbed, beaming.

"I wanted to be a nun," she said. "I loved everything about them, their black skirts and sweet faces cupped by the wimple, the way everything had its place under their aprons, in the folds of their skirts, files and tiny scissors and the rosary slung from one unseen hitch to another. If you said, 'Sister, I need the *World Almanac*,' presto, it would appear. They were each a bit off, a minor deformity, a wandering eye, a gimp leg, a humped back. Damaged goods. And I was one of them, sitting along the chapel pew, our dry lips scurrying over prayers like hungry mice. I was damaged goods, too. Knocked up and kicked out. And they loved me, even though they didn't know I was pregnant; they knew I was one of them."

She'd heard so many terrible stories from the girls at Mt. Carmel Church who went to the Catholic school about the typically evil nuns, austere, jealous old women with stinging rulers. She'd been nervous. But my mother didn't find any of that to be true. She loved the nuns. They taught her French, and every day at noon, a young muscular local girl who was thinking of becoming a nun would teach swimming lessons while the nuns went to chapel for special nun-only prayer sessions. My mother couldn't swim. She'd try every day to get her French teacher, Sister Katherine Perpetua, an older nun who'd suffered polio as a child and now leaned on wrist-clasp canes, to let her stay and speak French. *"Oui, oui, la piscine,"* my mother would say. *"Mais je ne nage pas, Soeur.* I sink."

Sister Katherine Perpetua would reply, "Does the water make you uncomfortable?"

And my mother would say, "Yes. I can't swim."

"Maybe the water makes you uncomfortable for a reason. Maybe God is testing you. Maybe one day the water will save you. It will be your calling from God." Sister Katherine Perpetua was always claiming that a calling from God was just around the next bend, that everything hinged on it and that it was just about to happen to you if you were paying enough attention. And my mother began to pay attention. As Sister Katherine Perpetua hobbled off to chapel, my mother would watch her and pretend that Sister Katherine Perpetua was her own mother and that she was going to the chapel to pray only for her.

She tried not to think of temptation, not only Anthony's blood-cocked penis but his sweet voice, his shining eye. Nearly everything led her thoughts to him. At the pool she felt self-conscious in her swimsuit, wondering if her stomach was sticking out, if anyone was whispering behind her back. The suit made her feel naked, and feeling naked made her think of Anthony. Sometimes a car would mistakenly pull down the dirt driveway and all of the girls would turn and squint to see if it was someone coming for them. And my mother expected to see Dino's Pinto, Anthony behind the wheel, his thick black hair on his large head, that he'd finally found her. But the car usually turned around in the parking lot and headed out again. It was never someone for her.

The swim instructor gave up on her quickly. She said in a little lisp that my mother thought might be enough to make her damaged goods if she believed in it enough, "I've never known anyone who couldn't float, who could turn so blue lipped and shivery." And so she told my mother to lie down on a picnic bench and practice her stroke in the cinder-block shade of the squat pool house. The swim teacher promised her that one day she could just apply all the dry swimming to water. But on the bench she thought of Anthony even more. Her ribs pressed against the wood, feet kicking over the hard edge, she thought of his hard body, knees and hips, his bones, and she practiced breathing deep breaths held tight in her lungs.

She'd glimpse the blue square, shimmering with girls who rippled below the water, their hair shiny as scales. They bobbed to the surface with their firm breasts, climbed ladders, tugged at suits that inched up their narrow rumps. She breathed, *Baby, baby, baby*, hoping it would come out whole, with a beating heart and all of its fingers and toes, that it would not choke inside of her like her mother said. She wanted it.

• • •

One Sunday after my mother had been at the convent about two weeks, Sister Katherine Perpetua invited her for a talk in the convent in a chamber, which was really just a small room. My mother liked the way they were always changing the names of things; the bathroom was a lavatory, a corner a reading nook. Leaning on one cane, she pulled down a pair of blinds to keep out the sun and placed herself neatly on the edge of a wooden chair with a box on her lap. Every once in a while the wind sucked the blinds into the windows tightly, and the room went dark and orangy and airless. She offered my mother a little tray of cookies. My mother took a cookie with a small cherry in the center. It was just the kind of thing she loved about the nuns, how little and meek the cookies were and the cherries in the center—she'd begun to see Jesus in so many small ways—like His sacred heart.

"Your father," she began, her mismatched teeth seeming to rise from her face as she spoke, "has sent a box of letters from one Anthony Pantuliano. Your father says he doesn't know if it is a sin that he sends these letters. He doesn't know if it would be a sin not to. He says he doesn't understand sin because he is a simple man who owns a fish shop. He wants me to decide whether or not to give you the letters, and I turn to you." She looked at my mother, deeply into her eyes. "Do you want me to give you these letters?"

My mother was poised on the edge of her chair, her back straight, her brow stitched. She didn't say anything at first. She wasn't sure why she was being asked and what exactly was at stake, although she felt it was something very precious.

Sister Katherine Perpetua said, "You know, Dorothy, that when a nun takes her vows, she dresses like a bride, because she is marrying Jesus. Not many girls know that."

"I didn't know that," my mother said. She imagined the entire metaphor, including Sister Katherine Perpetua's wedding night, with Jesus lifting the white skirt to reveal her pale, twisted legs. The bedroom was like her parents' with a crucifix on the wall, but this one was trembling as the headboard knocked the wall, Jesus himself in the act and above on the cross taking it all in, head lolled to get a better angle.

"You know, you could still receive a calling."

My mother thought of Anthony, the backseat of the Pinto, their bodies pressed together, the child swimming inside of her. She thought of my grandmother calling her a whore. Her chin went weak, her eyes flooded. "I don't think I can."

The nun's face turned pink, the tiny veins around her nose stood out as fine as blue pen ink. She said, "You know, I didn't think much of myself at your age. I thought I was ugly, crippled, stupid. The children threw stones at me on the way to and from school; sometimes I was covered with welts. My mother was dead. My father stayed drunk, too drunk to unbuckle the braces on my back and my legs. Sometimes I would be trapped in the braces for weeks and I smelled sour and got sick. But I wanted someone to save me and I prayed, and someone did."

They sat quietly for a minute. My mother's knees felt weak and her hands sweaty. She pictured Sister Katherine Perpetua as a girl her age in a small bedroom, the dark stink of her skin, a curdled powder, her drunk father angry and flustered with the buckles, finally pushing her away.

"Should I give you the box of letters, Dorothy?"

And my mother said, "No, Sister." She stood up. "No, thank you."

• • •

The tiny child swimming inside of my mother at the Oblate Sisters' School for Girls was not me. My mother lost the baby, a miscarriage. She doesn't know how far along she was, maybe eight weeks. It's hard for me to envision my mother in the bathroom stall at the convent school, the detail of blood slipping from her in warm gushes when she kneels to throw up in the toilet and puddling, dark red, between her knees on the white tile floor. I want to step into her life, to hold her hand, wipe sweat from her brow with a cold washcloth, and yet I know that I'm helpless. My mother wiped up the blood with bunches of toilet paper while her stomach cramped in labor, and she was covered with sweat, her hair soaked. It was night, and a little cool air seeped in from a high, small, open window. She felt lightheaded and weak. And she couldn't stop feeling that she was the baby, the one being washed away by all of the blood. She didn't know where she stopped and the baby started, whose blood was whose; and, pulsing through it all, she could hear her mother's heart beating in her ears, her tiny, ugly heart, throbbing with everything it hadn't gotten but felt bitterly that it deserved.

She could hear Sister Katherine Perpetua on night patrol, her wrist-clasp canes clinking and tapping down the hallway. The old nun walked into the bathroom and paused at the stall door. My mother turned her head, and under the stall door she could see the nun's thick-heeled shoes—one heel thicker to even up the length of her legs—her canes' rubber stoppers, and her black hem.

"Dorothy, are you in need?"

"I think so."

"Is it your time of the month, dear?"

"Yes, sister."

"Would you like me to stay with you and pray?"

By then my mother's face was wet with tears. She didn't answer. She rested her head on the toilet seat and stared into the bloody bowl.

She heard the nun pull a chair, scraping against the floor, to the other side of the door. She sat down and laid the canes next to her on the floor. My mother imagined her pulling the rosary from the unseen hitches in her black skirt and then her hands cupped to her mouth, her lips running through the simple recitation of prayers—this time for my mother's body, her bones, her teeth, her bright lungs and slick valves, each fine hair, perfect gleaming egg, and, without knowing it, for the dead child, the beautiful clot of blood.

My mother told me this part of the story the night after Dino had announced that he would find Anthony Pantuliano, my real father, the night after I'd seen her dead mother in the arcade. My mother was lying on the bed next to mine, and I could see her profile lit by the streetlights lining the street. Tears had rolled out of her eyes into her dark hair.

"And your mother never knew?"

"No," she said. "No, no, no."

"I saw a woman just like her today, like her picture on the piano, an old woman with a thick accent," I said.

"You talked to this woman?"

"Church asked her directions. He thinks she's following us."

There was a long pause. "She isn't dead, Lissy. Your grandmother never died, exactly."

"What do you mean. 'exactly'? Is she dead or not?"

"She isn't dead." My mother looked away from me

toward the window. She didn't say any more. There was a distant siren, nothing else.

"Do you think it was her? Would she know we're here in town?"

"She knows," my mother said. "From one mouth or another."

I asked her if she thought my grandmother would be the type to follow me. I asked her what she thought the old woman wanted.

"She thinks love is a weakness, a dirty sin," my mother said. "She would never come to see you, to admit to wanting to see her granddaughter. If she gave in to her weakness, she would do it this way, in secret, the way she drinks vodka in coffee cups."

It was silent between us. Neither of us spoke for several minutes. I was wondering how my mother could lie so easily, how she must have almost believed that her mother was dead, maybe because at some point it began to feel like she was dead. I thought about her in the convent bathroom, bleeding away the baby, how much she needed the baby and how that need went unanswered, in blood and sweat and pain. Then finally I asked her, "Why?" I sat up, straining forward now, propped up on my elbows. "It was so awful. How could you let it happen again? Why did you let yourself get pregnant again? With me?"

"Look," she said softly, "sometimes the only way to fix a mistake is to make it twice."

After the miscarriage, my mother bled for about a week, a heavy period. At night, she dreamed about the

swimming pool, filled with everyone she knew, naked—
her mother, her father, Anthony. Sister Katherine Perpetua
treading water, her weak legs dangling beneath her. My
mother was waiting for Jesus, not just to save her but to
save all of them. Sometimes the water would swirl red as
if he were wading in, the nail holes in his feet seeping
blood. But he didn't show. Instead, my grandmother polished silver, my grandfather chopped the heads off of fish,
arranging their bodies in the chipped ice of the display case
completely submerged with him. Anthony circled on the
surface, like an angel watching over his slaughterhouse
sheep that paddled with their thin hooves. They seemed to
say, *It's just like normal. C'mon in.* And she wanted to tell
them it was not normal. The baby was there, too, floating
away without a cord, farther and farther. She was in the
pool trying to swim and on the edge of the pool, dry as a
bone, watching.

During the day, she tried to pray to Jesus, but she could
hear the highway, the trucks rumbling by, day and night.
She knew she could hitch a ride to Bayonne and find
Anthony. She wondered if she would go, moment to
moment, she wondered if she would get up and walk out.
But each moment passed and she was still there.

Eventually, she found herself at the pool again, bloated
and pale in her blue suit, sitting on the wooden bench in
the shade of the pool house. She watched the girls slip into
the water, their hair fanning out over their heads, how they
nearly disappeared, became a blur, and then broke up
through the water's surface. At noon the nuns poured from
the chapel, their black bell skirts gliding across the court-
yard, their crosses catching sun the way windshields do
when a car is driving toward you, white holes burning on

their chests. Even Sister Katherine Perpetua from that distance seemed to be gliding, her canes like two gold staffs. My mother wanted to know what it felt like to be saved.

She walked to the pool's edge to see if Jesus would make her swim, if Jesus would be the one to save her. She jumped in like all of the rest. The water rose around her, slowly filling her mouth. She wasn't afraid of anything. She put her faith in God, everything going white, brilliant light shooting off the water's surface. But Jesus didn't save her. The spry swimming instructor dragged her up from the pool's floor onto the cement. My mother threw up pool water, heaved until her breaths were clear. She looked up at the cluster of nuns leaning over her, their silver crosses now swinging like pendulums from their chests, their pink cheeks tear stained. She stared up into their skewed faces, their wandering eyes, their bucked and gapped teeth, their thick spectacles, and knotted noses. They were so beautiful, she said it out loud. "You're beautiful. You are all so beautiful." And the nuns reared and giggled, blushing. She knew that she couldn't leave them.

13

Juniper called a few days after Church carried Kitty Hawk, his bride, over the threshold of my apartment. This time in my life is blurry. I remember feeling outside of myself and yet rooted in my body, its nausea, and bloated tenderness. I was exhausted and clammy, my mind whirling in different illogical directions. I spent a lot of time bent over trash cans. I wasn't prepared to have a chat with Juniper Fiske. But there I was, the receiver to my ear, Juniper Fiske's chirpy voice chatting away.

Evidently Church had taken Kitty home to meet his mom, a day trip, and it wasn't a pleasant scene. Juniper had been excited to meet Kitty. Juniper was, after all, interested in Asian cultures and desperate to discuss her *chi* with someone who might find her enlightened. But Kitty wasn't the *chi* type. I'm pretty sure she wore the thigh-high lace-up spike-heeled boots.

On the phone, Juniper sounded at first as if she were

scolding me, as if it were my fault, and then she became miraculously enthusiastic. She had a plan.

"Not that I blame you, Lissy. Really, I don't. And, of course, I don't have anything against the Asians," she said. "I think they are a wondrous people. I take tai chi, you know, twice a week and the instructor is Chinese and we get along famously. I am very open-minded, Lissy. But . . ." She hesitated. "I don't think she's right for my Church. I've been thinking of hosting an intervention. I've always wanted to."

"Well, it's a little late for an intervention. They're already married."

"Better late than never. I would like you to be in charge of getting Church home without his knowing a thing about this."

Well, there was little I could say, considering that according to Juniper this was at least partially my fault. I had little faith in her plan, but I was almost as unenthusiastic about Church and Kitty's relationship as Juniper was. I needed Church. I wanted to have that moment with him, whatever that moment would be, something sweet and gentle, in which I'd know everything would turn out right in the end, the way my mother felt after meeting Bob Jablonski at the punch bowl. I certainly wasn't convinced of Church and Kitty's love. I was pretty sure Kitty was in it for the money or the green card—most likely both. I agreed that although the intervention would happen ex post facto, maybe it would make Church snap out of it, come to his senses, and get out before he got in any deeper. I said I would make something up to get him to her house on the day; lying had become a specialty of mine. But I was suspicious of Juniper's tone, the way at the end of the conversation she got giddy and said, "Okay, so it's

set. I'm throwing an intervention." I was fairly certain that
she had a very different view of an intervention than I did,
but interventions were fairly new to me—actually, this
would be my first so I didn't really know what to expect.
And because it was her son, I decided to just go along.

Evidently Piper often didn't return Juniper's calls, for
what Piper referred to as "political reasons," which meant
nothing to Juniper, or to me for that matter. So I was to
phone Piper, and Juniper suggested that I try to be "polit-
ically sound."

I called Piper that afternoon. "Yes? Piper Fiske here."

I said, "It's Lissy Jablonski."

"Uh-huh," she said. "What is it?"

I assumed that she remembered me. I knew her well
enough to take this as her friendly tone. I was straight-
forward but felt that old nervousness, remembering when
I'd called from Ruby's kitchen at fifteen. "Church is in
trouble. He's married a stripper he met a week ago. He's
lost his mind."

"Church Fiske, I will remind you, is a wealthy white
heterosexual man born with every advantage and privilege,
in a world designed for wealthy white heterosexual men
born with every advantage and privilege. He had someone
cut his meat for him till he was twelve years old."

"Your mother wants to have an intervention."

"For Church Fiske? That is so typical. Do you know that
there are women in China killing themselves by drinking
pesticides? Fuck Church Fiske." And she hung up.

When I called to tell Juniper that I had failed to entice
Piper into coming to the intervention, she said, "Piper is
very busy. She's probably overcommitted herself this
month. Did she hang up on you?"

"Yes," I said.

Juniper sighed a little sigh of relief that seemed to mean *Oh good—it's not just me.* "I've already engaged a caterer. You'll get your invitation in the mail."

When I received my invitation to Church's intervention in the mail on Juniper Fiske's monogrammed stationary, I called my mother. You have to keep in mind it was 1999. By then, my parents had, for all intents and purposes, never been apart aside from one "conference," as my mother put it, during the summer that never happened. I will mention here that my grandmother had been dead, by that point, for three years. She went peacefully, the doctors claimed. I remember my mother saying, "A little presumptuous, don't you think? How can anyone know what goes on inside someone as they die? Since when is sleep necessarily peaceful? Why does everyone think that that's so comforting?"

My grandmother had been at home in bed, found four days later by a neighbor with a key. My mother felt guilty, yes, because anytime someone dies, we feel guilty. But she wouldn't allow herself to take on too much of the burden. She still held tight to their bitter silence, not giving in to a big display of emotion. I followed suit. I felt guilty, too. I was old enough to have forged a relationship with my grandmother on our own terms, which I failed to do. But like my mother, I didn't shoulder all of that responsibility. It was a multigenerational effort at silent unrest. I understood why my mother didn't want her to go peacefully; she wanted her mother to have struggled at the end to make peace with her meek husband; with her daughter, both the infant she loved so easily and the woman that infant grew into; with me; and with herself.

I was curious if, as she got closer to her death, she'd become softer, more like that girl again swinging out over the grain and flax, if her body itself had become more childlike, less the way I think she might have seen herself, as raped and dirty, but finally as again pure. If the doctors were right and she went peacefully, I imagine that was part of the peace she had to make. My grandmother had been raped and it affected my mother; it affected me. My grandmother thought her body was dirty. My mother thought she herself was a whore. My own craziness is lodged in my uterus. I'm aware of it, but I don't know how to fix it. All I know is that I agree with her, that love is a weakness. I can't fix that either.

My mother knew all about the Kitty-Church fiasco; she knew that I'd recently sworn off men and knew the nondetailed version of the breakup with Peter Kinney, a boyfriend she'd never met. And although I hadn't told her that he was a married man, I knew that she knew because she told stories, out of the blue, about abysmal relationships that were born out of "this kind of deceit." Other types of deceit—her own, for example—were completely acceptable. Infidelity was not high on her list of vices. Of course, she had no idea I was pregnant. I asked her if she'd come to Church's intervention with me. I didn't want to go alone.

"It sounds like one of those sensitivity training things where everyone cries and hugs each other. Mrs. Defraglia's son went to one, came home, told her he loved her and hasn't had a job since. She caught him embracing the mailman. I'll never understand people's obsession with expressing themselves. What's wrong with pruning a tree? Your father finds that a nice form of expression and he doesn't have to sit on a couch and talk about how everything makes him feel, for God's sake. And what about Jazzercise? Did I tell you I've started up again? Juniper said my voice sounded fat. Does my voice sound fat to you?"

Obviously, my mother was still pissed at Juniper for the comments she'd made during their last phone conversation. I decided to ask my mother a question more in her field—deceit. "Church won't take the garbage out unless Kitty promises to watch him wave from the curb. How am I going to get him all the way to Cape Cod alone?"

My mother said, "Tell him that Juniper has lost her mind again. That she's shuffling around in her bathrobe all over town. Tell him his mother's a complete loony. He'll believe that."

I used my mother's excuse to get Church to Cape Cod. He'd wanted to take Kitty, but she was taking a bubble bath, alone, sulking about a bracelet Church hadn't bought for her. He had the money, but it wasn't his style to act rich and throw money around, something Kitty did not understand. Also, she had to work that night.

I told Church, who was drinking a beer, absentmindedly flipping through my CDs, "You don't really want Kitty to see your mom all freaked out and huddled up in the corner of her room in an old bathrobe. It won't be pretty."

"I thought you said she was out wandering the streets."

"At first, yes, but she's pretty tightly cocooned right now."

By this time, it had begun to really sink in that I was pregnant. And although I had Church alone, I didn't bring it up. I felt guilty about having lied to Church about his mother, like I was driving an old person to a nursing home

the intervention there in Juniper's black-and-white-tiled
entrance, he laughed.

"My intervention?" And then he asked with mock seriousness, "I'm a heroin addict and you didn't tell me?"

"It's Kitty. People think it's a mistake."

"Oh, I like this," Church said, smiling. "This couldn't
be better." He crammed some mushroom caps into his
mouth. "So, Juni got the Laury Brothers to cater. She must
think it's serious. She knows I'm already married, right?"

"It is serious, Church. Better late than never," I said, trying to sound convincing, but now I wasn't so sure. I felt a
little ridiculous as if trapped in one of my nightmares, a
high school flashback to the time I played a Polynesian in
a production of *South Pacific,* singing "Happy Talk," that
sinking feeling of being trapped on stage with bad actors
and I'm always blanking on my lines. I wished Giggy and
Elsbeth had been invited. I thought they'd have helped me
out. I saw no sign of them or Matt, not that I was mourn-
ing Matt's absence; his definition of a relationship was not
the most sound.

Juniper breezed in from the kitchen at that moment. She
was carrying a glass of white wine, smiling tightly. "Oh,
Church, I'm so relieved to see you." She put the wineglass
on a lowboy, took both his hands, and looked at him with
true concern. "How was the trip?" she asked as if the real
concern here were traffic.

Church said, "Not bad, really. Smooth sailing, I'd say."
And he popped more mushroom caps.

Juniper took my elbow and whispered, "Do I look okay?
I don't seem the least bit off-putting, do I?"

"No," I said. "You look divine, as always."

"Oh, thank you," she said, shy and hopeful.

"Who's the leader?" I asked, glancing around the room. "Did you go with a psychologist or priest?"

"Was I supposed to hire someone?"

"Yes!"

"I've never cared for psychologists, Lissy. They like to blame mothers. You'll agree with me on this point one day. And as for a priest, I mean, no one can relax with that collar lurking about." With that, she floated off.

The intervention was dysfunctionally lovely, everyone much too civilized and polite—with minor exceptions—to mention "the unpleasantness," as Juniper liked to call it. Church walked through the crowd, smiling and nodding, speaking through his teeth like a politician: "No Piper?"

"Nope," I said. "She thinks you're an asshole white male, et cetera, undeserving of an intervention."

"Oh, and she's right. Who could deserve all this?" he said, waving across the room to a clot of whispery women. "Did she say someone cut my meat for me till I was twelve?"

I nodded sadly. It was falling apart, really melting. I felt like a sucker, and I was—taken in. I wanted to blurt out, "Kitty Hawk will turn around and bite you. She wants your money, a green card, something. And everyone agrees with me. Right?" But I knew I'd be met by blank stares, people maniacally searching out crab-stuffed mushroom caps. Really, I thought that Church was head-over-heels for Kitty and I knew it was just a setup for a fall. Yes, I still wanted Church to adore me, to comfort me—that part of me was looking for a savior at the punch bowl as my mother had at Juniper's wedding—but also I genuinely cared about him. I didn't want to have to shovel him up off the floor.

Church's father, Guy, was there with Daisy and their

kids, Littlebit (a nickname for Laurabeth) and the twins Chippy and Chuck. Littlebit was ironically a fat eleven-year-old, sulky and rude, hovering by the marble-slab cheese cutter, eating what seemed like block after thickly sliced block. The twins were taking turns punching each other as hard as they could in the arm, identically freckly redheads in matching tan wide-wale corduroys and argyle sweater vests. Daisy looked flawless, each tiny wrinkle spackled smooth, and Guy looked old, paunchy, exhausted. He was staring into a scotch that he was swirling in a tumbler when Church walked up, breaking his distant focus. He smiled, shook Church's hand, and clapped him on the shoulder.

Daisy gave Church a stingy hug, then said, "There's Littlebit," pointing at the girl's broad, hunched back, "and you remember the boys." She put one hand on each of their shoulders and tilted her head, smiling as if this were the moment we were supposed to snap the photograph, at least mentally.

One of the boys said to Church, giggling, "I hear your wife gets naked on stage."

Daisy gave a fake little shocked expression and then apologized, her voice full of pity. "Oh, Church, I'm so sorry."

"Oh, yes," Church said, sarcastically. "A naked wife. It's such a tragedy. Send flowers. She'll paste them to her tits for the next show."

"Well, I see you have your usual way with words," she said, pushing the twins toward their sister at the cheese tray.

"Church," Guy said in a chipper tone, obviously not having overheard the last comment. "Your Grammy wants to talk to you."

Grammy was a tiny, birdlike woman with a sharp, beaky

nose and tightly pursed lips outlined shakily with pink lipstick. Once upon a time, my mother had spent a lot of time at her house. Grammy had been a very proper uptight debutante mother, a Shriver after all. But age had washed that austerity away. She was sitting in her wheelchair, wiping her nose with a tissue, when we walked up; then she stuffed the tissue up her sweater sleeve, where it joined an enormous bulge of tissues, both of her frail forearms bulging like Popeye's.

"SO THIS IS THE LITTLE CHICKIE." Grammy was fairly deaf and shouted everything at the top of her birdlike lungs and was old enough not to be too precious about what she said. It was a crowd-pleasing combination. The room fell absolutely quiet aside from the *click, click* of Littlebit at the cheese cutter and the fierce wrestling of Chippy and Chuck who were under a buffet table. Grammy was eyeing me squarely, evidently confusing me with Kitty; it was, after all, more like a wedding reception than an intervention. "YOUR GRANDFATHER HAD MARRIED A STRIPPER, A FRENCH GIRL FROM THE WAR. BEFORE HE MET ME, THAT IS. WHEN HE WAS DRUNK, HE'D TELL ME THAT HE UNSNAPPED HER BRA WITH HIS TEETH." She paused. "I TELL YOU THIS BECAUSE HE WAS THINKING WITH HIS JOLLYWAGGER." She wiggled a finger, pointing unsteadily at Church's crotch.

"WHAT HAPPENED TO HER?" Church asked.

"DON'T KNOW. I ENDED UP WITH THE OLD CODGER TILL HE FINALLY DRANK HIMSELF TO DEATH." Grammy seemed unfazed by what she was saying, just being factual.

"I'm not his wife," I said interrupting.

"WHAT?" Grammy said.

"I'M NOT THE STRIPPER."

"LOOK, I DON'T CARE IF YOU SHAKE YOUR BOSOM ON A STAGE WITH THE AMERICAN ANTHEM ROARING AWAY. I'M TELLING CHURCHIE HERE THAT HIS GRANDFATHER WAS A SON OF A BITCH. AND MEN THINK WITH THEIR JOLLYWAGGERS." She lowered her voice to a loud whisper. "Your father, for example, Churchie. And that tramp he's taken up with."

We heard a rustle beside us, Daisy huffing out of the room.

"But women, Church, are thinking of other things." Again she lowered her voice. She pulled Church down close to her wizened face. "She's not stupid, Church. You might be, but she's not. For God's sake, Church, look at her." And Church turned and looked at me, smiling.

I stared back at him, wide eyed.

"She isn't even an Oriental."

"MY GOD," Church shouted. "YOU'RE RIGHT!"

Grammy rolled her eyes and dismissed us, shooing us away with her wrinkly, spotted hands.

Church talked to a few other people. A group of country-club ladies cornered him at the little bar. They caught him up on how all of their children were doing, a list of Ivies and corporate positions, the occasional Peace Corps. And then they'd ask about him. "So, Church, how are you paving your way in the Big Apple?"

"For a while there, I wanted to write a book with a colon in the title," Church said. "You know the type: *Intimate Terrorism*, colon, *The Deterioration of Erotic Life*. But now I have seen the light. I think I'd like to be one of those guys on the construction crew who turns the stop-slow sign, but a dancing one—or a traffic cop, the gloves, the whistle, the complete control. Or a UPS job. They pay over $10 an hour. And Kitty makes a lot of money, you can imagine. Guys just shove the money down her G-string. Couldn't be easier."

But Juniper had been keeping a keen eye on the situation and whisked him away before he could say more. "Remember Margaret Porter? From the stables? She just stopped by to pick up her mother." And she wrangled Church out to the patio, where she planned to have him fall in love with an acceptable girl.

I talked with the country-club ladies. They seemed at first to want to know about Kitty, but actually they wanted to talk about Asian culture. One had been on a guided six-day tour of Japan that she enjoyed mostly because, as far as I could tell, the natives made her feel tall. The others enjoyed sushi from the gourmet deli. They all agreed that Asians seemed to excel at math and violin, which was followed by a short intellectual discussion of the right and left divisions of the brain.

Church's conversation with Margaret Porter was also brief. He told me later that she'd been a weird kid and that when he saw her again he was surprised. He'd said, "Wow, you look totally normal. I'd have thought you'd be the type of meek loner who lives alone and puts her cats' names on her answering machine."

She'd answered, "And what's wrong with that?"

Church had responded, "And your cats get a lot of phone calls?"

She'd told him that her cats were family and that she'd never thought he was at all normal.

Church was ready to call it a day. We were stopped only by one more guest, a neighbor, Mr. Wiggins, who'd served in the Korean War and, quite drunk, wanted to reminisce about a little shop in Seoul where a woman would rub his feet. Wiggins rested his hand on his wide belly and chatted on dreamily.

But Church broke up the story with a comment on the glories of war, something extremely patriotic. And Wiggins snapped to with some strong affirmations about the country and God. We shook hands all around.

Church waved to his mother from across the room, where she was laughing with the country clubbers. She waved back absently, at first, and then she realized he was leaving. She looked around the room, in a momentary panic. I felt sorry for her. It was as if she was looking for the exact thing that wasn't quite right, the flaw held accountable for her failings. Her eyes reached Church again. Suddenly, she looked overwhelmed, tired, fragile. She blew him a kiss, her hand lingering in the air for a moment as if she were touching his cheek. Church looked tired, too, exhausted. I thought, for a second, he was going to cry. He tilted his head, as if giving in to her touch. He closed his eyes. And then abruptly, he opened them, pinched his nose, and stepped outside. I gathered our two light overnight bags that hadn't made it past the oversize coat closet.

It was dusk and cold, the stars just starting to surface in the darkening sky. Church shut the door behind him, stepped into the clipped yard, unzipped his fly, and peed on a bush with a loud sigh.

And I had to ask myself at that odd moment, *Do I love Church Fiske?* He's self-centered, sarcastic, insincere, irreverent. He's improper and asocial, meaning he doesn't abide by social laws. If you look fat in the dress, he'll say you look fat in the dress. On the other hand, he's honest, surprising. He has an internally logical integrity. If I admitted that maybe I loved him, then I had to look at the circumstances: Did I love him one summer because my father disappeared on me, because I confused him with Anthony Pantuliano? Did I love him when he showed up in New York because Peter Kinney dumped me? Because he fell in love with Kitty Hawk and I hated Kitty Hawk? Did I love him because—like Peter—it wasn't possible to have him? Did I want him to love me? Or did I simply want to be him, that sure of everything, that composed and confident?

I could have chosen that moment to tell him. I could have said, "Church, I'm pregnant. What should I do?" And waited for his reaction, breathlessly. But it seemed ridiculous, suddenly, that I would want so much from anyone, much less Church Fiske. It dawned on me that life, in general, isn't always elevated to a series of perfect moments, elemental still points, but sometimes it's a series of smaller moments that we let pass. I decided not to tell him and I rested my hand on my stomach. I could feel the multiplying cells, the folding and unfolding, a curled being, flexing inside of me, taking shape.

And then Church, as if hearing my whirring mind and agreeing with my decision not to tell him, jiggled his penis and zipped up and said, "I love Kitty Hawk, Lissy. What can I say?"

14

My grandfather, Wladyslaw Verbitski, attended his daughter's high school graduation, sitting in the row of wooden folding chairs, nodding from his seat. But after a half hour at the cookies-and-punch reception in the school's gym, he began to get nervous, glancing up at the caged clock. He looked much smaller than my mother remembered him, his fingers more oddly angled and scarred from years of handling sharp knives and fish guts, bones, and meat. His suit jacket hung down from his shoulders, which seemed now to be as narrow as a woman's. He left shortly thereafter, saying he couldn't leave the store for so long alone, but really she knew it was her mother he couldn't leave. That was the only time he visited, and my mother never went home. If my grandmother answered the phone when she called, my grandmother would say nothing. There would be a silence until my grandfather's voice came on the line, or worse, if he wasn't home, just a click.

Sometimes she'd ask about my grandmother. "How's Mother feeling these days?" And my grandfather would say, " 'Bout the same. 'Bout the same," meaning "She hasn't forgiven you. She still thinks you're a dirty *kurwa*."

My mother had spent holidays with an elderly widowed aunt who'd married a military man who passed away in Dover, Delaware, at the air force base, where she lived on alone for the rest of her days. My mother never said too much about her, only that she was bossy, like a military colonel herself. The summer after my mother's graduation, it had been arranged that she stay on at the convent to help out in the library. And then at the end of the summer, her father appeared again, looking even more frail, to drive her to Simmons in Boston to study nursing, where in between her second and third years she would end up marrying Bob Jablonski. She met Juniper Fiske, whose primary objective was to become a doctor's wife. My mother claimed to have been keenly interested in the body, how it all worked, blood, tissues, muscles. But despite themselves, Juniper married a dentistry student and my mother married a med student. They got married halfway through the four-year program, and although both finished their degrees eventually, neither ever practiced nursing.

By the time my mother was in nursing school, the old military aunt had begun to leave the oven burners on and had been put in a nursing home. And so my mother spent the holidays at Juniper's family's home. My mother learned to play tennis and ride horses. She was given presents by Juniper's equally high-strung mother, whom I'd later meet as the straight-shooting Grammy at Church's intervention. My mother got cashmere sweaters, once a little pearl necklace. That first summer between her freshman and

sophomore years, she worked with Juniper in the children's unit of a hospital as a candy striper in a pink-and-
white-striped uniform, and Juniper met Guy at a party in
Boston. He didn't come from as much money as Juniper
did, but his family was definitely well off. The facts
that he was studying only to become a dentist and from
only moderately well off stock were overlooked (they
played up the fact that he was a Harvard man), mainly,
my mother suspected, because Juniper wasn't easy to get
along with or beautiful, and her parents were slightly
desperate. They simply avoided any conversation that had
to do with teeth and matters of high society. Juniper complained about her parents' snobbism and was proud of
Guy and optimistic about the future importance of dentistry in American life.

It was hard for my mother because Juniper was absolutely obsessed with Guy. She spoke of nothing else and spent
as much time with him as he would allow. He liked his
buddies (one of whom was a med student named Bob
Jablonski) and his parties. In the end, Juniper won. She
grew pouty and sullen and threatened to break it off altogether if he didn't propose. She told him it was to ease her
mother's mind and that it would be a long engagement,
years maybe even, before they'd actually tie the knot. But
once he gave in, the wheels were in motion and a date was
set. There was no going back.

Juniper read books on wedding etiquette. She'd make
precise notes in a little notebook. From *Emily Post's Etiquette*
she copied, word for word, things like "If the bride custom-
arily wears makeup, naturally she will for her wedding but
skillfully applied in moderation. Nothing could be more
inappropriate than a bride and her attendants coming down

the aisle of the church made up as though they were in a chorus line in a musical comedy."

Juniper was not nearly as pretty and likable as my mother. But the wedding to Guy had given her another edge over my mother (in addition to money and class and upbringing), and she used it.

"Will you wear white on your wedding day?" my mother remembers Juniper asking her. "What with your tawdry affair with Anthony, you might want to go with a pretty cocktail dress in a pastel shade."

"You aren't a virgin." My mother made the claim on the basis of little information. Unlike her, Juniper kept quiet about anything the least bit sexually explicit.

"No, but I'm marrying the man who . . . well, I don't have to say it. You know what I mean and you know that it's a different case altogether. You wouldn't ever marry Anthony Pantuliano!"

My mother didn't like Juniper's invoking his name. She disliked Juniper fiercely at times and then she wished she could be more like her, in innumerable ways—the sturdy family, the sweet holidays, all the things her money could buy, including Guy. Not that my mother even particularly liked Guy; he was loud and oafish, a bit too happy. But she wanted someone like him who could ensure a certain lifestyle that seemed not just materialistically better but gentler and more loving, the golden life.

When my grandfather's heart seized in his chest, as he was hunkered over some dead fish, my mother blamed my grandmother for years of wearing-and-tearing abuse. It was a month before Juniper's wedding day. He hadn't made it up for a visit that summer. He'd said he was feeling weak, like he was coming down with something, but my mother had assumed that it was an excuse that my grandmother had forced him to create. My mother had been frustrated, but she was used to it by now. She'd learned to want less and less from him and nothing from her mother.

It was a relaxed summer, the two girls living together in a cute little apartment that Juniper had spiffied up with the help of her mother's decorator. Dotty was helping Juniper with wedding plans, despite Juniper's snooty comments. My mother liked sorting the details: shoes, white satin or moiré? Gloves or no gloves? Guy's clothes: wing collar with a cutaway and waistcoat? Hat or no hat? They fretted together over the bridesmaids' dresses, whether to go with paired unmatching colors: two in green, two in chartreuse, two in lemon yellow, and the maid of honor, Dotty, in pale yellow. Or should they be arranged in varying hues of the same color, from American beauty rose to my mother in the palest flesh pink? They worked still as candy stripers—my mother putting in many more hours than Juniper—and studied occasionally, a little ceremony of reading textbooks and eating popcorn while in hair curlers. When my grandfather died, the head nurse had allowed my mother as much time as she needed to help her mother, especially because Dotty was an only child.

It was the summer of 1969, the day before Woodstock, the day before my conception. She hadn't stepped foot in Bayonne for a total of three years. All that time she'd tried not to think about Anthony. She'd tried to replace him first at the convent school with Jesus, the beautiful long body hanging everywhere she looked, eternally dying for her, a lowly, penitent sinner, his love for her as strong as his love for Mary Magdalene, the whore he fell in love with—my mother had sneaked a copy of Kazantzakis's *Last Temptation of Christ*. And then at the nursing school, she replaced Anthony and Jesus with the idea of a doctor, a husband, someone triumphantly rich and strong whose father had taught him golf, whose mother played tennis and the piano.

But her mind, in its weak moments, usually when she was sleepy or occasionally drunk, would lapse back to Anthony Pantuliano, his strong arms, firm jaw, his beautiful penis, and his fierce, dark eye. Every time she saw a photograph of the war, the tired faces of U.S. soldiers, the burning cities, the Vietnamese—their thin, brown bodies, screaming, dying, she looked for his name in the credit. She wondered if he was there amid gunfire, running through city streets with his camera slung over his shoulder. She wondered if he was burning his draft card in one of those lit-up trash cans along with the American flag.

She'd also tried not to think of my grandmother, her cold blue hands and liquor-hot breath. But she appeared also, the sturdy Polish woman, her broad lap covered by a fish-stained apron, the potato-and-onion-and-fried-fish smell of her wool sweaters, her thick-heeled shoes rooted there in my mother's mind.

My mother had taken a bus and then a taxi the day of the funeral itself, not any sooner because she was set on avoiding my grandmother's house. Koch's Funeral Home was packed. Her father had been a weak fishmonger through good times and bad, always letting people run up a tab, always lightening the scale with his pinky for the poorest families, and everyone knew it. They loved him. They crowded his casket and cried.

My mother arrived only a few minutes early. She saw my grandmother next to the casket, shaking people's hands,

nodding, tight-lipped, seemingly sober and without emotion. She looked much older than my mother remembered
her, not so much worn as toughened. My mother walked up
to her father's casket, ignoring the line. The couple placing
a flower inside stepped back, gave her room.

It was her father, but not. He was tiny now, small
enough, it seemed, to lift up and sit in her lap. His cheeks
were painted, eyes closed. He looked like a little girl who'd
gotten into her mother's makeup. It made my mother
think of Juniper's wedding notes. She could hear Juniper's
voice: *There's nothing more inappropriate than a dead man in his
casket made up as though he were in a chorus line in a musical
comedy.* She was embarrassed for him and for herself. She
loved him and she hated him, too, for being weak, for
being small, for confusing love with selflessness. When my
mother stood over her father's body in the stuffy parlor of
Koch's Funeral Home, she was tired and confused. Juniper
was getting married. Her father was dead. She wasn't sure
who she was or what she wanted. She was unraveling. She
cried, her chest heaving, sobbing for a moment, but then
she felt my grandmother's disapproving eyes on her. She
wiped her cheeks with a handkerchief, stood up, and took
her place next to my grandmother without speaking to her,
without looking at her. The procession continued; each
person giving his condolences to my grandmother and then
to her.

The two women didn't say a word to each other until the
car ride to the burial in Holy Name Cemetery in Jersey
City. My mother's Uncle Joseph was driving, an old, jovial
man, even at a funeral. He hugged my mother, saying,
"Your father was a good man." He glanced at his sister and
then whispered, "Maybe a saint!" My mother barely recog-

nized him from photographs. My grandmother had estranged herself from the family, an estrangement she'd always blamed on her husband's low social status, but now my mother wasn't so sure. My grandmother was a champion at estrangement.

Uncle Joseph and his wife sat in the front; my mother and my grandmother sat in the backseat, the middle empty between them. During the fifteen-minute ride, my mother stared out the window onto the streets of Bayonne. A lot had changed, it seemed, this shop for that, and the people looked different, too, more divided into camps. There'd been some hippies three years earlier, but not this many. She'd seen hippies up north, too, especially when shopping or going to parties in Boston, but they were nonexistent in the nursing school, where hair and dress were strictly regulated, and they were equally rare in Juniper's tight wealthy circle. It was strange to see them everywhere in this town she thought she'd known so well. They were slouching down the streets, sunning on front stoops, so much skin and hair, large poofed Afros and long, swaying shiny blond hair. She wondered if Anthony was a hippy, if he was smoking dope—she'd been warned vigorously against its evils in nursing school and had never tried it— if he was as angry as so many people her age seemed to be, angry at the war, their society, their parents.

My mother was angry, too, don't get me wrong. She hated the war. She hated the treatment of blacks. She was sickened by the assassinations of Martin Luther King Jr. and Bobby Kennedy. The news coverage of the war turned her stomach, made her body ache. It made her think of blood and death and her own dead baby, lost that hot night in the convent dormitory bathroom. She never went to protests, though. They weren't suitable to her life with Juniper Fiske who, like Julie Nixon with her bouffant poof-flip hairdo, didn't want to be lumped with the hippies of her generation, calling the youthful war protestors "a very vocal minority." It wouldn't have been appropriate or grateful for my mother to side with the likes of Dr. Benjamin Spock at Juniper's parents' Sunday dinners, for example, as they agreed with Spiro Agnew's comment on the "spirit of national masochism encouraged by an effete core of impudent snobs who characterize themselves as intellectuals." Covertly, however, my mother had begun to listen to Eugene McCarthy, who really seemed like he wanted the war to end. He sounded sensible and sincere. In the 1968 election, she'd decided to write in his name, but there hadn't been a blank space as she'd expected, and so she refused to vote.

The car was quiet, somber. Finally, my grandmother spoke up. "You do good at your school?"

"Yes," my mother said, not taking her eyes off the passing street scene.

"I no longer can support your *education*." She said the word *education* as if it were something dirty or untrue, as if my mother's education had been a grand hoax, a lie she'd fooled my grandfather with for years. At this, Uncle Joseph turned on the radio, quickly flipping from an inappropriately happy polka to classical, to give them privacy.

My mother hadn't really thought that without her father, she'd have to quit school. She already had a partial scholarship, but there was no way she could replace the money her father sent each month to cover the remainder of the tuition. She had two years left. But she turned around quickly. "I don't need anything from you." She missed her father. Not that he would have defended her. He was never capable of that. But she wanted him to have overheard the conversation, the way he'd overheard her mother's insults all her life, like an uncomfortable stranger seated on the same park bench. She missed the solace that he would give her later, behind her mother's back, some shy smile, a small stroke of her hair. But he was gone now.

My grandmother nodded and turned to the window. "When you were a baby, you cried out once, so afraid. I waited until you were asleep, poured melted wax into a pan of water over your head. I repeated three Hail Marys. This was all to find out what had frightened you, to see the image that would appear from wax. It was my face. It was my face in the wax. You were afraid of me." She glanced at her daughter. "But I can see that is no longer true."

My mother didn't say anything, but she was thinking, *You're right. I'm not afraid of you.* She was surprised, too, by the image of her young mother, melting wax into water to see what had frightened her child, surprised that at one point in her life, her mother had been interested enough to go through a ritual like that. But she remembered my grandmother's speech the night after she had found out about my mother and Anthony, how my grandmother had said that as a baby she'd been so perfect. She felt that old dirtiness creeping into her, the dirtiness my grandmother seemed to store inside of herself.

"This will be the end of it," my grandmother said. "There's nothing more between us."

My mother nodded. "Fine," she said, and she meant it. That was fine with her.

My mother didn't remember much about the burial except that the eulogies would have embarrassed her father.

He'd have hated the fuss. He'd have wanted to insist on leaving, but he'd have been too embarrassed to call any more attention to himself. She imagined him shaking his head vigorously, saying, "No, no, no," wagging his hands, his cheeks flushed, that he'd glance at his wife, who would be angry at the attention—as if it were undoing or at least denting her life's work. And my grandmother did seem annoyed, her feet shifting, the little O of her mouth puffing out not grief-filled but exhausted sighs.

It was a hot day, breezeless, suffocating. My mother was wearing Sbicca spectator shoes, black-and-white wingtips with sling backs, and a sleeveless black Dacron-wool knit dress with two white stripes around the waist, carrying a black wooden-bead shoulder-strap pocketbook. It wasn't perfectly appropriate—they were Juniper's hand-me-downs but not what she would wear to a funeral. My mother could barely hear the soft-spoken priest over the noisy traffic on West Side Avenue. When they lowered the casket into the ground, my mother threw in her flower, but she was mostly surprised that what she felt was not a new ache but the same old ache she'd known for years. She told me she'd lost him long before his death.

She wasn't planning on riding again with my grandmother in the backseat of her uncle's Ford Galaxy. She looked around during the final prayers, maybe wondering where the closest bus stop might be, maybe because she sensed someone watching her, and that's when she saw him far off, leaning against a tree by the entrance. Anthony. It was as if she'd been expecting him—he'd obviously been expecting her—and she simply peeled away from the crowd and walked toward him. He was a hippy, the wavy hair on his oversize head brushing his loud color-swirled tie-dyed T-shirt collar, his bell-bottom blue jeans faded and patched. He was barefoot. She remembered the street shimmering with heat, for a moment wondering if he was a mirage, but he wasn't. She walked up to him without saying anything, put her hands on his face, pressed her body up against him, and they rolled to the other side of the tree. She was about two inches taller in her high heels. She stared into his one dark eye and remembered what it was to be in love with someone real, someone not nailed to a cross, someone more than a wealthy figment of her imagination.

The first thing Anthony said to my mother was, "Come on, I want to show you *everything*." And he started to run out of the cemetery, hopping over gravestones like a leprechaunish track star, and she zigzagged after him. At the gates, he grabbed her hand, and they started walking quickly, breathless, up West Side Avenue. My mother stopped to take off her high heels; three blocks later, she peeled off her stockings, the soles ruined with nubs and runs. She tossed them into a garbage can. She hooked the swingbacks of her shoes with two fingers. It was dawning on her that she was on her own, that she'd been cut loose, permanently. Juniper wouldn't miss her, as she was so distracted with wedding plans. And her boss had set her free. Of course, my mother wasn't going to move in with my grandmother, the supposedly grief-stricken widow, to nurse her back to emotional health. And her father, whom she wouldn't have hurt for anything, was dead. For the first time in her life, no one really knew where she was or what she was doing.

Anthony was different, freer, and yet serious, too. He was thicker, broader, and he no longer carried the heavy smell of death from the slaughterhouse. My mother had forgotten how deep Anthony's voice was, or maybe it had become more resonant—three years of speaking that she'd missed—and she was surprised, too, by what he was saying. And he was speaking so quickly that she could barely keep up.

"You never got the letters, did you? I wrote hundreds of them. At first your father took some of them, like he might get them to you, but I don't know, maybe he buried them somewhere. I begged him to let me know where you were, but he wouldn't." He stopped on the street. "I'm sorry about your dad. Dino got word to me. He thinks I'm an American ingrate. He won't talk to me anymore, but he made sure I knew. He still feels bad about the last time he saw you. He didn't think it was an emergency. He left me a note that said you'd been crying, but you'd be okay. It was the next day before I got the whole story out of him. After Bitsy died, he got more sensitive. He realized there's always something you still want to say to someone."

"Bitsy died?"

"Yeah, she got hit by a milk truck. Look, I'm sorry about your dad. I know how you felt about him."

My mother shook her head, lifting up her hand. She didn't want to talk about it and start crying.

"I still think about my mother," he said. "I know how it can be."

"Do you still think about the flying circus?" she asked, trying to sound light.

"I've become a circus freak," he said, standing back from her, his arms outstretched. "One day the Fetucci Flying Circus plane will come for me," he said. "To take me away from all of this societal constraint, nice middle-class barbarism, to a land of happy freaks." He paused a moment,

but it was a held-breath pause that my mother didn't inter-
rupt. "I let them out, you know, the sheep and pigs and old
run-down horses. Not that first night but a week later
when I figured you weren't getting my letters. They
wouldn't go. I opened the pens and shouted and flapped
my arms. I screamed at them, but they wouldn't leave their
stalls. They sat there scared to death, wide eyed, paralyzed.
Isn't that perfect," he said. "Just like us, too, us human
beings, going around scared to death of freedom." And
then he shouted it. "Freedom!" He jumped up on a mailbox and raised his hands in the air.

My mother was shocked. She started to giggle nervously. He slid down off the mailbox and landed in front of her.
They were eye to eye now that she was barefoot, too.

"You're perfect," he said. "More absolutely you than I
remember. Dotty Verbitski. I've said it in my mind a million times. I thought you might have, you know, rebelled
a little. Changed. But you're still you. I like that. I can be
the one to give you the message. It's wild, Dotty, out there
in the world. I want you to come with me, into the world!"

My mother told me that he could make her stop breathing. He could say something that was completely arresting
and she would have to remember to let the air out of her
lungs.

They took the bus back to Bayonne to his one-room
apartment that he shared with Elvin and Cathy, a couple,
although neither one was into "ownership." When my
mother walked in, Cathy was sitting cross-legged on a
mattress on the floor, staring at the palms of her hands, her
stringy light brown hair hanging down in planks, hiding
her face. Elvin, tall, black, and rail thin, was packing up.
He took one look at Dotty Verbitski and said, "Far out! She

looks like she's about to do a commercial for toothpaste."

My mother definitely stood out in her black knit dress, holding onto her wingtip sling-backs, her hair in a chignon with ringlets in front of her ears. The room was cluttered with bongs, blankets, and pots coated with burned rice, and she said there were books, stacks of them everywhere. My mother remembers titles like the *I Ching, The Way of Zen,* Norman Mailer's *Armies of the Night,* James Joyce's *Ulysses, The Tibetan Book of the Dead,* Abbie Hoffman's *Revolution for the Hell of It.* Anthony was carrying around a copy of *The Making of a Counter Culture* by Theodore Roszak. He was telling Dotty about Woodstock, that it would be better than the gigs in Atlanta and Atlantic City, better than the Yip out in Central Park's Sheep Meadow.

Elvin continued stuffing clothes into a large backpack. He pulled off his T-shirt and slipped on the white Indian silk shirt. "Do I look like Leary?" he asked. "A black Leary."

Anthony snorted, stuffing things into a backpack. "Leary's an idiot."

"Who's Leary?" my mother asked.

"Leary's for the people," Elvin said. "Drug-based equality for all."

"Who becomes a Buddhist at West Point?" Anthony said. "Who's a psychologist whose wife kills herself?"

"Who's Leary?" my mother asked again.

"No one really listens to Leary," Anthony said. "Not even Elvin. He thinks every white man has a credibility gap like Johnson. Tell her you don't listen to Leary," Anthony said to Elvin.

"Leary's got a credibility gap, if you ask me, like Johnson and Nixon and all those white guys."

"And me," Anthony said.

"You're white, aren't you?"

Cathy suddenly jerked her head up. She flipped back her hair and her plain freckly face appeared. She piped up, "Leary is the high priest of LSD. You wouldn't have heard of him. They've never mentioned him on *Laugh-In*."

Elvin told Cathy to get Dotty some clothes. It was obvious that Cathy didn't want to, but it was equally obvious that she did what Elvin said. She added under her breath, "Yeah, so when we get there, people won't think I brought my mom."

My mother tucked the nasty comments away. It's the way she operates. She planned to sting Cathy with a zinger when she least expected it. She watched Anthony jump around the room, getting everything ready. He was deep in concentration, sorting bongs and books.

Cathy handed my mother a tie-dyed shirt and a pair of low-cut bell-bottoms. My mother went to the bathroom to change. It had just one bar of soap, one hairbrush, and a half-empty bottle of aspirin. The shirt was too high cut, the pants too low, leaving her middle exposed. She felt very uncomfortable, soft and pale, like one of her father's fish with its white belly. Her suitcase was in the back of her uncle's Ford Galaxy, probably parked in his driveway by now somewhere in Bayonne. She had only her pocketbook, inside it some money, a bus ticket back to Massachusetts, and a pale-pink lipstick. She folded her funeral clothes and left them neatly stacked on the back of the toilet lid, along with her shoes. She freshened up her lipstick. Still clutching her navy blue pocketbook, she walked out of the bathroom, a little hunched to hide her belly.

Elvin drove Cathy's shiny-new Day-Glo VW van. They took Route 17 to Route 87, which led them past Cathy's hometown, Paramus, New Jersey, not yet famous for its malls. She gave the whole town the finger, waving it angrily out the window, throwing her whole body into the effort, her stringy hair flipping around her head. She singled out her high school and her parents: "Fuck you, Bergen Catholic! Fuck you, Mom! Fuck you, Dad!"

When she settled back down into her seat, she hugged Elvin's thin, muscular arm.

My mom said, cheerfully, "Nice van. It must have been expensive. Did you buy it yourself?"

Cathy turned around and silently glared at my mother, who shrugged innocently.

They passed around a couple of joints. My mother was nervous about getting stoned, but she was curious. She shook her head the first few times the lit joint passed, but then once she saw that it didn't cause seizures, she took a few hits. Nothing happened at first. Eventually she got fuzzy-headed, giggly, and sleepy. She laid her head down in Anthony's lap, and he stroked her hair. It finally hit her that she was here, with him, like this, after so many years. She felt peaceful for the first time in as far back as she could remember.

Anthony rattled off questions. He wanted her to tell him where she'd been, what she'd seen, what she'd done. He said, "What do you think of this country? All of our hostility? It's all so ugly. And everybody dead. Bobby Kennedy and King."

Elvin spoke up. "And Vietnam's got 542,000 of our brothers."

"This is one fucked-up world," Anthony said.

"But," my mother said, "we landed on the moon, too. It isn't all tragedy."

"I don't know," Anthony said. "It seems like a hoax to

me. I mean, if you look close at the pictures, you can see the air bubbles. It was probably all Hollywood underwater bullshit. I don't trust anyone, especially not anything government-run officially American."

"I would believe that," Elvin said.

"Me, too," said Cathy.

My mother thought about telling Anthony about the miscarriage, the blood, the polio-stricken nun; about how she almost drowned because she wanted to be loved. She could have told him about Juniper Fiske and her fiancé, Guy; how she was helping Juniper plan the wedding, now only four weeks away; how she'd glimpsed the golden life, but that she didn't feel like she fit in there any more than she did here. She said, "I'm almost a nurse."

Cathy glanced at my mother and rolled her eyes, which my mother read as a feminist critique, something like *Typical women's work.*

My mother quickly switched the subject. "Do you still take pictures? I thought you'd be shooting the war."

"A Buddhist threw my camera out of a bus. He told me that I shouldn't document and witness but should experience life. I work part time at a magazine shop. I want to buy a new camera, I think. I don't know. Maybe he's right—you know, experience life."

"And are you going to school?"

"This is my education. This and genus *Psilocybe* straight from the Mexican highlands."

" 'Shrooms," Cathy explained before my mother had time to ask. "Magic mushrooms?" she said, her voice rising, meaning *Ever heard of them?*

"But did you get drafted?"

"I'd never serve."

"Did you burn your draft card?"

"No, I'm 4-F, because of my eye," he said, a little embarrassed. "But I would have burned my draft card. Dino wanted me to serve any way possible. He wanted to pull some strings and get me a desk job or something. He wants me to do my duty, serve my country, and all of that patriotic bullshit. I told him I'd rather save the world than take part in blowing it up. He didn't get it. Some people just don't get it. Nothing's so simple like it used to be. I'm not so innocent. Are you?"

"No," she said. "Not at all."

But they *were* still innocent, something within them pure and sweet, or I wouldn't be here. I imagine them on their way to Wallkill, New York, back to a time when I wasn't myself but two parts, that I was swimming inside Anthony with my small, flicking tail and that I was the ticking egg waiting patiently inside my mother, and the two of them in the Day-Glo van, a sleek ship hurtling them toward an unavoidable future.

They made it up to Wallkill, pulling over only once to pee by the roadside. It was around seven o'clock. The concert had already started. Eventually, the cars in front of them stopped, the road jammed up tight. The curtained windows had kept the van dark even when it had been midafternoon. They stepped out, blinking. My mother felt disoriented. By the time they walked to a spot where they could pop their tent, my mother was covered with little red mosquito bites and it had started to rain. She hated it there, the crowds, the mud-smeared bodies, everyone so out of control. She was soaking wet, trying to pull her shirt away from her chest, her bra completely outlined in revealing detail, seams and all. No one else seemed to mind the rain. Cathy's white shirt was plastered to her little braless tits. Elvin's Afro glistened, his white Indian silk shirt sleek against his skin. Anthony took off his shirt and let the rain beat down on him.

Cathy shoved her guitar case into the tent—my mother had already been subjected to a number of renditions of "There But for Fortune" and "It's All Over Now, Baby Blue" in Cathy's high, shaky voice, which sounded nothing like Joan Baez even on a very bad day—and she was relieved. Elvin wanted to see what kind of mushrooms they could get, and so eventually he and Cathy headed off into the crowd.

The tent had enough room for only two—plus a guitar case. Dotty and Anthony climbed in. This was their chance for privacy. And this is the moment that is the hardest for me, the moment I see my mother at her weakest, feeling desperate and alone—she was truly lonesome, her father newly dead, her mother now no longer really her mother. And yet there they are in my mind, two kids, working at buttons and zippers while they kiss, and soon enough he is inside of her, their bodies rocking together slow and then fast and I am shot out and swimming for love and I am the love waiting. That's all it took.

I imagine them after, the tent so hot they can barely breathe in it, only a small breeze kicking open the front flap. I imagine them grinning like kids holding sparklers in the dark. And as many times as I have wished I could have stopped my mother, as hard as this romance was for my mother, this doomed love affair, I would not change it now if I could. How could I change it without sacrificing myself? There is something so right about the scene, sweet and sad, their young bodies flushed with blood, so perfect.

Finally they jiggled into their clothes and climbed out of the tent. They couldn't hear the music, it was so far away, but they could hear roaring in the distance, the crowd all around them. Everyone was now pressing in, touching each other. My mother felt out of control as if the crowd around her was becoming the body of an animal, a snake maybe, and she was only one small muscle, one tiny scale. She was hungry. She had to go to the bathroom.

Anthony told her to just squat, that no one would care. He said, "You'll never find a Porta Potti without a ten-hour line."

"I wouldn't pee in one if I did," she said.

He gave her a banana from his bag. It was bruised and overripe. He turned to her. "I've got to step inside it, deeper. Let's live it. Come on, Dotty. Come with me." And it seemed to her like a proposal, not quite of marriage but a commitment to him and to an experience, an entire life with him that stretched out in front of her, wildly twisting like a snake. His one eye shining, his black patch wet, he stared into her eyes. He held her hands up next to his chest. He was serious, honest; this was what he wanted. "C'mon," he urged. "I've been waiting forever to be a part of something this cosmic. Come with me."

She said, "No, I can't." It was simple. She couldn't go, and he had to. He threw back his head and stared up at the sky; the rain washing over his face. His hands slipped from hers.

"I won't be gone too long," he said. "I'll come for you." He turned away from her without looking back. She watched his bare muscled shoulders as he made his way through the crowd, deeper and deeper, until it swallowed him whole, and he was gone.

My mother crawled inside the tent and listened to the crowd shifting around her, pressing in. She waited for an hour or two. Cathy and Elvin never returned and neither did Anthony. Finally someone fell onto the tent, bending the support beam, and so my mother got out, leaving it there crumpled. She headed away from the music, until finally she found a spot that wasn't so crowded. She pulled down her jeans and squatted in the mud to pee. She ate the banana and trudged on, head down, winding through the mud-caked bodies. She sat down now and then to rest and even doze a bit.

Eventually dawn broke. By midmorning, she got to the road. She saw a garbage truck rumbling by with a load of trash. It passed her, rolling along slowly, and holding onto the back was a kid with curly hair. He was also covered in welts. She called out to him and ran after the truck. He held out his hand and hoisted her up. He was younger, going into his senior year of high school, as it turned out. He talked a lot, about basketball and his coach and his dad. He said he'd temporarily misplaced his good friend, but just after he'd said it, he mentioned the garbage, its sweet awful smell, something poetic that made the loss seem more permanent. She was thinking about her clothes folded on top of her shoes on the back of Anthony's toilet and it made her cry. She and the kid were quiet, watching the endless road that was crammed with cars and people, face after face, and Dotty took them all in, each one, until she thought she would explode.

15

The euchre party was set for a Thursday, but that morning Marianne Focetti called to tell Ruby that her Italian tiler, Aldo, hadn't finished the bathroom. "He's an artist, Ruby. You can't rush art."

Because the euchre party was held under the auspices of a casual get-together and not all-out war, Ruby couldn't refuse to have it at her place, so she consented to hosting. She was frantic, charging around with her mop and bucket, clipping at our heels with the vacuum, all the time saying, "This is what she wants. To get me all upset. She's playing hardball. Can't you see it?"

My mother helped Ruby scrub, and I was in charge of a kitchen counter of egg timers for Ruby's *spezzato* and *muffuletta*: one timer for simmering rice, one for bread in the oven, and one for a pan of mushrooms, peppers, and onions that I was to stir diligently, slowly, without stopping, except to get Ruby if a timer dinged.

Church and Dino were ordered around, hauling her heavy velvet furniture from one spot to the next to make space for card tables. When Dino wasn't lifting, he was pacing back and forth from his study where there was an important ball game on his TV, which seemed to make him extremely nervous. He hated to miss a second of his Yankees on the field. In retrospect, I suspect that Dino was a little compulsive about his routines, always five o'clock, always the same drink, always the same pants, but this time, although he was investing a lot of energy into keeping up with the game, play by play, I think he was also anxious about finding Anthony. He said he'd "put the word out," which seemed like code for some underground system of family connections. Of course Church smelled mafia. In any case, Dino was nervous about getting the news, worried about what he might learn. Even Jacko was more tense than usual, his nails clicking and skidding as he jogged after Ruby, his stunted face bobbling in the plastic funnel.

I was feeling a lot of pressure as well, to perform, not only at euchre but at appropriate euchre conversation and mores. Was I good enough to mingle with the euchre elite, the euchre intelligentsia? Despite the fact that I looked the part—hair teased, nails done, dressed in the acceptable uniform of matching-separates flashy leisure wear—I wasn't absolutely confident.

My mother, however, seemed not the least bit rattled. It was a Thursday, and the mail carrier had brought a letter forwarded from Keene by Mrs. Shepherd, the maid, from Tati and Bobo. It was a chastising letter from Tati, really; Bobo only signed her named in faint pencil at the end. "Why didn't you tell us that my brilliant Robert was chosen for the conference? We had no idea he was so highly regarded."

My mother laughed, a loud cackle so perfectly euchre appropriate. She was dressed impeccably, her hair so stiffly sprayed it would go up in a blue flame if lit. "So," she said. "He's coming back."

"How do you know?" I asked.

"Conferences end. He could have made his excuse more permanent, an illness that required treatment in Arizona, something chronic, if he planned on staying. But this, well, he'll be coming home, that's all; it's clear."

"Then what?" I asked, not rudely, just curious, naïve. "What are you going to say?"

My mother stopped laughing. "He won't know what hit him," she said.

This news didn't relax me at all. I envisioned both fathers coming to claim me: Anthony Pantuliano being escorted in by a pair of Dino's henchmen—a vision supplied by Church's mobster-populated imagination—a wild, rugged, bushy-haired, big-headed man, his one eye darting around nervously because he is bookended by the two blockheads in big-shouldered suits and dark sunglasses, and then Bob Jablonski limping up the front steps in his Bermuda shorts, his real leg a guilty Arizona tan but his fake leg still true to us, loyally pinkish white, still shiny and hairless with its little black sock and shoe and laces, maybe getting down on his knees, maybe not. And my mother, the third point of the triangle, smoking casually, almost cocky in her euchre party outfit, and me standing in the middle, not knowing what to do, my chest a buzzing hive.

The euchre party started at two. The regulars were a mangy group. Ruby complained about Mrs. Totello because she would always argue that it was better to get your meat at Malone's, not Scaglione's, when everyone knew she was just sticking up for her husband, an Irishman whose cousin owned Malone's. Mrs. Allesandrini always wanted to brag about her disastrously untalented children, one a garage attendant, one a house painter, both in and out of rehab, always between jobs, with illegitimate children. Ruby could mimic her perfectly: "Oh, Donny's hoping any day to get a call to park cars over at the lot in Jersey City. He's a good boy." Mrs. Totello and Mrs. Alessandrini were no real challenge, not to mention the aged, toothless Mrs. Marcucci, who couldn't tell her hearts from her diamonds.

Marianne Focetti was the true danger. She was really after Ruby—and capable of throwing anything at us. We were her targets, Ruby claimed. Nothing was sacred. Where Ruby got her lamp shades, for example, was an opportunity for intense scrutiny. "If you don't know the right answer," she warned, "just say you can't remember. You're from out of town. Eat a cannoli."

Marianne Focetti arrived with her own entourage of small chubby women in stretchy clothes. She was ferret-like, chewing a small wad of gum fiercely, her eyes clipping around the house. Dino kissed her cheek, said his hellos, and retreated, pulling Church with him, into his study. Jacko sniffed the polished toes poking out of their open-toed sandal pumps.

Marianne said, "Oh, this color!" pointing at the walls. "Avocado! It brings back memories. It matches the kitchen appliances I had in the '70s. Remember?" She lowered her voice and said to Ruby, "Don't you hate inheriting the previous owner's mistakes?"

Ruby said crisply, "We've lived in this house for twelve years. You can assume all the decisions are mine."

It was a bad start. Marianne came across amusing, and

Ruby, defensive. My mother and I shifted nervously; Ruby's kitchen was filled with avocado-colored appliances from the '70s. We glanced at each other conspiratorially, agreeing via mental telepathy to keep Marianne out of the green kitchen. The euchre began slowly. I was overplaying, reacting too quickly, not being patient. My mother kicked me under the table. Ruby was dishing out the cards, shuffling maniacally, like a card shark, smoking like a fiend. It was tense. The smoky air was humid and thick despite the air conditioner rattling in the window. Marianne was winning, up by two games. And then there was a knock at the door.

It was a boy about my age at the time, fifteen, maybe a scrawny sixteen. Ruby let him in, Jacko yipping. He swiped the baseball cap off his head and nodded at the ladies. "Sorry to innerupt," he said. "But I got news for Mr. Pantuliano, if you don't min' and it's not much trouble and all."

"Dino!" Ruby screeched. "Some kid for you."

Dino charged out from the back room with Church at his heels. "You Sal's kid? You got word?"

He nodded. "Sal wrote it down for youse."

"And where is he?"

"Sal?"

"C'mon, kid," Church said, irritated, doing his best Corleone impersonation.

"Anthony Pantuliano!" Dino said.

"'Ant'ny Pantuliano,'" he read from a small slip of white paper unfolded from his back pocket, "'sells cars in Queens. Buicks, good prices, some deals. He's been there two and a half years.'" He looked up to see if everybody was watching him, and everyone was. "'He's had two different wives before this, no kids with either of them. His girlfriend's name's Josephine, but call't Jo. They've got a two-year-old girl.'" He looked up. "Real cute kid." And then he returned with seriousness to the paper. "'Only a little record, a disorderly in '70 and '72, a possession in '69, that didn't stick. He was called in for questioning, somethin' political, in '72. Nothing after that but parking tickets, and not many.'"

"You got an address?"

"Two," the kid said. "Home and business. He's a manager at the car dealership. Buicks, like I said. Before that"—and he returned his attention to the slip of paper—"'He worked installing windows, as a postman. He parked cars at a hotel, but then he wrecked one.'"

"A car salesman!" Dino said. "And this is American morality? I thought he was going to save us from the horrors of capitalism. He buckled! You see it? He gave in!" Dino pointed his finger in the air, vindicated. "And he is so morally respectable!" He shook his head.

I was surprised by this news, too. I'd heard Anthony Pantuliano was a visionary, an angry god intent on changing the world. I'd heard he'd read *The Making of a Counter Culture*, but now I thought maybe he'd just carried it around. I agreed with Dino that he'd sold out. I wasn't angry but sorely disappointed. If he'd sold Volkswagens, even—but Buicks? I felt sorry for him a little and for myself, too: he already had a daughter, an adorable toddler, an entire life.

"What's this?" Marianne snapped, the cigarette sticking to the inside of her lip like it was attached to flypaper. "Look, I'm up two games. Are we going to play here or not?"

But one of the chubby women from her entourage asked, "Who's Anthony Pantuliano?" She asked my mom, because that's who everyone else was watching—Dino and Ruby and Church and I were all fixed on her now.

My mother was sitting there, her back straight, her eyes filled with tears that didn't spill onto her cheeks but were just poised on the brim of her lids. And she told them an unsorted, jumbled version of her life, almost poetic in its ellipses. As she spoke, she blinked back tears, wiping them with the back of her hand. She told them about falling in love on a downtown bus, about a fire, my grandmother polishing silver until she collapsed. She told them about a boy with a camera—the penned animals he smelled of and his mythical penis, about having sex in Uncle Dino's Pinto. She told them about a crippled nun with a drunk father, and a dead baby, and a swimming pool, about beautiful, beautiful nuns. She told them about a plain-faced rich girl and frilly wedding plans with chorus girls. She told them that her father died and the man she loved showed up, and they made love in a hot tent, and how he walked away from her into a crowd. She told them about her husband and a punch bowl. She told them about having a daughter, and the old women turned to me, their faces streaked with mascara, each blowing her nose into a cocktail napkin. It seemed to make no sense, and yet every woman understood her.

Marianne Focetti was crying, too, her whole face screwed into a tight knot. She said, "I loved a man like that once." And every woman nodded, sobbing.

The euchre party broke up quickly after my mother's long, impassioned speech. Not one of the women could have reaffixed her makeup properly, and it would have been impolite to go on without any, all pale pucker, lashless, their bald faces staring at each other like bloated fish, more uncomfortable, it seemed, than if they'd been sitting there completely naked. And so they all went home, but not without first hugging my mother, then hugging me, lightly petting our hair. They hugged Ruby, too—both camps. Even Marianne kissed Ruby lightly on the cheek. "She's an angel from heaven," Marianne said about my mother in that way one mother compliments another on her child. Ruby shrugged modestly.

After the room emptied out, the five of us stood there awkwardly.

Dino said, "Should I get the car?"

"No!" my mother almost shouted. "Look at me!"

Ruby translated. "It's been . . . what, fifteen years? She's got to get spiffied up."

"But today?" Dino asked.

My mother nodded. "But I want to drive. Just me and Lissy. It's family business."

Dino nodded. Ruby, too. Little Jacko looked around at all of our concerned expressions. Only Church protested by rubbing his hands through his hair and sighing with agitation. He was ignored.

I had no idea what to imagine and I didn't really understand my mother's intentions. She wanted to look good, of course, but I knew she didn't really expect to rekindle a flame, even with my putative father gone. Bob was coming back. She was sure of this, and she seemed sure that she would be there when he did. But, looking back, I assume that my mother didn't know what to expect either.

While my mother was in the shower, I fished Anthony's picture out from under my mattress and put it in my pocketbook. My mother wore a white sleeveless dress, the least flashy of Ruby's new wardrobe for her, and I wore a miniskirt and a paisley shirt, something she'd picked up for me at The Limited in one of her outings with Ruby, paisley being the rage. Ruby was a little disappointed that we didn't wear the euchre-party uniform, but she was still beaming about the party's success. My mother could do no wrong.

Once again, my mother and I were on the road, this time in Ruby's Cadillac Coup de Ville. It was a cool evening for midsummer, and we buzzed the electric windows down only an inch or two, the wind just kicking around lightly, not messing up our hair. Queens was only twenty minutes away over the Verrazano-Narrows Bridge. I didn't say anything until we were off the highway and it looked like we were almost there.

"What do you think he's like?" I asked.

"I don't know."

"What are you going to say?"

"I don't know."

"Do you think you still love him?"

My mother didn't answer for a long time. "He's a father," she said finally. "I'm not a twenty-four-year-old bank teller from Walpole. I know better."

"Are you going to tell him about me?"

She stopped the car at a red light. "What would I say? How can that make things better?"

And she saw my chin start to crumple like I might cry. I'd come all this way. I was so close. I had his picture pressed together in my hands. She put her hand on my head. But I didn't cry. I refused. A car behind us honked. The light had changed. My mother took her foot off the brake.

We found the car dealership where Anthony Pantuliano worked in 1985 and where he still works today. It sits on a corner, the last in a long row of dealerships, all waving enormous American flags. It was six o'clock when my mother pulled into the parking lot of Tucker Buick. A representative was there to help her out of the car, but she just buzzed down the window.

"Is Mr. Pantuliano here?"

"No," he said. "He leaves at five every day."

"Oh," she said.

"Can I help you with something? We've got great trade-in deals right now." He was an older man, but with one of those chubby, sweet faces that never ages and could sell you anything.

"No," my mother said. "No, thanks." But he insisted on giving her his card, slipping it through the window to her before she'd buzzed it all the way up.

I was disappointed. My mother gave out a little gust of a sigh.

"We have his home address," I said quickly. I thought she might be fading, losing her gumption, giving in to better judgment, something.

"I don't know, Lissy."

"We've come this far," I said. I didn't mean just that night, but far from Keene, New Hampshire, and our nice house on Pako Avenue. "It's a long way to come."

"Okay," she said, the energy in her voice rising. "Okay."

We started the hunt for his house somewhere in Queens. I had a map spread on my lap, one of Dino's, an ancient collapsible paper accordion of a map, anything in the folds absolutely lost forever as fray and eventually the air of dime-size holes.

"I hope he doesn't live in a crack," I said, joking, but my mother didn't laugh. She didn't hear me.

We found the house tucked into a modest row of houses, much like Dino's house in Bayonne, with a small, well-kept yard, a kid's slide parked in the middle of the grassy square, an old shaggy dog asleep under it. We parked across the street. My mother scooted down in her seat and sighed.

"What do I want?" she said.

I knew what I wanted. I wanted desperately to see him, to put together piece by piece what my life could have been. Not that I really thought it possible, but I had already begun to imagine this as my house, that as my dog, what it would be like to have a little sister, the alternate reality. We sat for a long time, our eyes fixed on the metal screen door.

"Your father—Bob Jablonski—loved me," she said. "When you were born, too big for premature, everyone knew it. The nurses, the other doctors, his colleagues. I remember one joking in front of us, 'Was there a shotgun at your wedding?' Your father smiled. He looked at me. He said, 'Can you believe she made this little miracle?' Like I'd made you all by myself. He was a man of science, and he turned his head. He looked the other way. You see," she said, "he took me in. It was an act of love."

Sitting there across the street from Anthony Pantuliano's house, my mother told me the rest of the story of the summer of my conception, 1969. She was a bridesmaid in Juniper's wedding. Juniper finally decided on the gradation of pink hues, my mother's as the maid of honor, the pale flesh pink, which made her feel completely naked, as if the white boutonniere were pinned directly to the skin of her chest. Juniper's mother paid for the dress.

My mother's period was late. She thought she was pregnant, maybe, she told herself, but she would always echo, "Probably." She was scared but was trying to have fun. If she had been a good dancer, she would have danced to prove she was enjoying herself. But my mother has no rhythm.

Bob Jablonski wasn't dancing either. He'd lost his leg early in the war—in fact, he'd joined up, taking leave from Harvard's med school to enlist. He'd traded in his life with women, their pantyhose slung over the tub, the whole house smelling of lilac powder, the conversation always turning to decoration and gossip, for men and war. In any case, he'd met Guy when he'd returned to med school, always limping along now with his one fake leg, the memories he never talked about, the war still trudging on. If war was mentioned at all even later when I was growing up, my father would leave whatever room he was in; he'd push his chair away from a friend's dinner table mid-fondue. He never talked about it. I knew he'd carried stretchers in from the field, that he'd helped administer some first aid, assisting nurses and doctors, but that's all he ever said.

He was a shy young man, not the type to go crazy cutting a rug even if he'd still been all in one piece. He fell in love with my mother. And she fell in love with him. It might be the hardest part of her story to believe—his love is easy to believe—but her love wasn't as simple. After losing Anthony a second time, could she fall in love again so readily? It's easier to believe she was a little desperate, already thinking she was pregnant, and along came a med student, shy, quiet, who so easily fell in love with her that she could coax him into an amazingly short courtship, a speedy wedding two weeks later. But I maintain that she did fall in love with Bob Jablonski, that he was exactly what she was looking for, especially on the heels of Anthony Pantuliano. Both of the loves of her life were lame, only three eyes and three legs between them. In the end, my mother wouldn't choose the one she'd have to follow, but the one she could lead, her mother's daughter after all. Bob Jablonski was steady, loving, predictable, and deeply sensitive. Most of all, he loved her unconditionally and he didn't need anything else. It all fit together and my mother got her second chance. This time, the baby swelled inside her and she pushed it, screaming, into the world. A daughter.

Anthony Pantuliano's door opened, just an arm at first, a thin arm, someone talking over a shoulder to whoever was still in the room. And then a woman stepped into the yard, wearing a man's T-shirt that hung down to the middle of her thighs. Her long, dark hair was pulled back loosely, uncombed, into a ponytail, although she was almost too old for a ponytail. She clapped her hands, calling to the dog, "Dulcie, Dulcie." The dog lifted its head slowly and staggered a bit to stand up, but then its legs folded beneath it. The woman came out and picked the dog up from under its belly and struggled back to the door. A man's arm opened the door for her. She bent over to drop the dog onto the floor, her white underwear glowing for a second. She disappeared inside.

And then the man stepped out. I could tell by the way my mother drew in her breath that it was Anthony. He was short, broad. He had no patch and his eyes, from a distance at least, looked normal, perfectly matched. He had a little gray in his hair and was wearing a T-shirt, too, a V-neck, and khakis. He tucked a folded newspaper under one arm. Both hands in his pockets, he looked up at the moon for a moment and then turned back to the house, staring at the gutters, it seemed, the slant of the roof. I wondered if he ever thought of my mother, how much he loved her, of those paralyzed sheep. If he still checked the sky for Fetucci's Flying Circus plane, finally coming for him after all of these years.

Now, when I think of Anthony Pantuliano as a grown man, when I try to envision what he might be doing at this or that very moment, I see him in his yard, looking at the moon and then at his gutters, trapped somewhere between the two.

He bent down and picked up a garden hose that had been hidden in the grass. He wound it, elbow to palm, elbow to palm, dropped the circle of it beside the house, and then went back inside. The screen door clapped, and he shut the heavy door behind him.

The night didn't end there. My mother took a different route home, driving this time straight through Bayonne's downtown. We ended up in front of the video store that had once upon a time been Verbitski's Fish Shop. My mother pulled Ruby's car over and parked it by the gutter. It seemed inevitable that we would find ourselves here. I knew better by now than to ask my mother if she was going to go up to the door. It was not her nature, and yet my mother was always surprising me.

"This is where I end up," she said, "the nights I'm out alone in this car."

"Oh," I said.

"You know who lives here?"

"Yes."

She looked at her watch. "She'll be calling for the cat soon out the alley door. She'll scoop it up and take it upstairs. She'll sit there, drinking from a coffee cup— vodka, no doubt—and she'll fall asleep in front of the television."

My mother and I sat there, waiting, and then she picked up her pocketbook. "C'mon," she said.

I was shocked. I jumped out of the car and followed her down the alley, which was lit by a street lamp. She paused about twenty feet from an alley door to light her cigarette.

"Why does she hate you?" I asked her.

"She can't love anyone," she said. "It makes her sick. It's a weakness. She hates weakness. She hates herself." She paused a minute, looked up at the side of the building, its dimly lit windows. She took a drag on her cigarette, held it, then exhaled. "We took you to see her once as an infant. Your father and I rented a car. We called from a pay phone downtown. I said, 'I'm married. I thought you should meet my husband and the new baby. You're a grandmother.' I thought that would fix everything. You were in the car with your father. I said, 'I married a doctor. We're here in Bayonne visiting.' It was early afternoon, but I could tell she was drunk, disoriented. She said I was too good for her with my schooling and my doctor husband. 'Why bring him here?' she asked me. 'To show him your terrible mother, an imbecile, an old Pollack.' "

My mother stopped to listen for my grandmother, but there wasn't a sound. "She wanted to know one thing," my mother said, "if you were a boy or a girl. And when I told her that I'd had a daughter, I thought I heard her cry, a small sharp sob. She said, 'Throw her in a river,' and she hung up the phone."

We waited in silence for another few seconds, and then the door opened and an old woman stepped out, scolding, "Kitty, kitty, kitty," with its sharp *k*'s and *t*'s. She turned quickly when she saw our shadows and stepped back inside, closing the screen door. She squinted at us through the mesh. "Who are you? What do you want with an old lady?"

My mother was calm. She said, "It's me. Dotty." She paused. "And your granddaughter, Lissy. But you two have already met." It was the coldest I'd ever heard my mother. She tossed her cigarette to the ground, twisting it into the grit with her shoe. "Are you going to invite us in?" But her tone seemed to indicate that she knew the answer would be no.

My grandmother said, "I'm getting my cat. It's a good cat." At this, she opened the screen door and stepped into the light. She was a small, heavy-breasted woman, with rolls under her chin. She wore a gray dress, her white hair pinned up on her head. She put her broad hands on her knees and called, "Kitty, kitty, kitty," this time more gently, more sweetly, and a cat appeared at the end of the alley and padded to her. She bent down, with one hand still on her knee, and scooped the cat up with the other.

I looked at my mother. Her eyes were filled with tears. "Well," she said, "that's that. I guess you have nothing to say to me. To Lissy."

She was stroking the cat, a yellow tabby, and she looked at me then. "Yes," she said. "To the girl." She pointed at me. "It's better this way, for you," she said, "that you do not know me. On this," she said to my mother, "you and I would probably agree."

My mother said nothing. Her eyes level, she stared at my grandmother. I thought that she must want to answer both yes and no, angrily. I saw a stitch in her eyebrows, her eyes flooded, her mouth opened just slightly. My grandmother opened the door and walked inside. When the door shut, my mother clutched her pocketbook to her chest and fell back against the brick wall of the alley. She stood that way for a minute or two, her eyes squeezed shut. She shook her head, chiding herself, I assumed, for feeling so much. Her pocketbook slid down her stomach. She straightened and tucked it under her arm.

"Now you know," she said.

I said, "I guess I do." But, of course, I couldn't really. I figured that my mother had been right, that love made my grandmother sick, the weakness of it, the giving in, and guessed, too, that the alcohol helped numb her to it. I knew that I wanted to reach out to my mother just then at that moment, but I couldn't. I followed her, unsteadily, back to the car. Once inside, I glanced up to the window. I could see my grandmother's profile, lit blue from the television. I could see the tabby, too, in her arms, nuzzled up to the folds of her neck.

16

My father, Bob Jablonski, started having chest pains on
the tenth hole at the Keene Country Club. I got the
news on my answering machine when Church and I got
back from the intervention. We'd driven home that night,
a four-hour trip. Halfway through, I said, "Look. I feel terrible about this whole thing. I'm sorry I lied to you."

"What lie? You told me my mother was crazy. Is that a
lie? The woman has lost her mind." Church had regained
his unflappable exterior.

I decided to attempt to say what was wrong with
Juniper Fiske and Dotty Jablonski by taking a look at
advertising from a historical perspective. It's one of my
favorite pastimes: how advertising lays it all out for you,
our dirtiest secrets, our favorite lies, our most desperate
fears, more honestly than anywhere else, the ugliness of my
job. I've looked through magazine after magazine, especially the ones from that 1969 summer my mother's father

died and I was conceived in a tent at Woodstock. My mother was reading Juniper's *Ladies' Home Journal*s. My mother was trying to envision the rest of her life, looking at articles on brushing her eyebrows and recipes for pot roast and, between those pages, the advertising promising what could be hers.

"Our mothers were afraid of the untidiness of the subconscious and bang! there's an ad for Perma-Prest sleepwear from Sears, two girls waking up wrinkle free and happy. They were afraid of their bodies, and there's the feminine hygiene spray." I glanced at Church to see if he was following. He seemed vaguely interested. "They were afraid of the bomb, the end of the world as they knew it—and this is my favorite—there in the back is an advertisement for sunglasses, special lenses that would darken instantly to protect observers' eyes from the blinding light flash of an atom or hydrogen bomb. They developed Substance N, in honor of Admiral Nimitz, who received the surrender of the Japanese on the deck of the battleship *USS Missouri* in Tokyo Bay, and put it in their sunglasses to keep Juniper's and Dotty's eyes safe. They called themselves the Military Optical Company, located in Kansas City. It was such a beautifully worded advertisement that our mothers could get the impression if they had a pair of these sunglasses and the bomb dropped, they would be "observers," sipping martinis on a veranda, watching the distant fireworks of an atomic holocaust."

"I don't think Juniper was ever really afraid of the A-bomb. Maybe you don't realize how much money she comes from."

"It's so perfect," I said. "It's a perfect example."

"Of what?"

"Of what we're talking about! Look, I'm not just selling a product, marketing research, targeting my truest consumer in my little office all day long. I'm psychoanalyzing a culture, putting the nation on the couch. I'm not only monkeying with the American mind—"

"—and that's a delicate thing—"

"I'm creating the American mind. I had a friend tell me that she actually wanted to start smoking because the people on the nicotine patches looked so damn happy."

"You know what's wrong with you, Lissy? It's that you don't believe in anything. Do you believe in God?"

"I believe I'm ignorant."

"And Jesus?"

"It's a great story. I know it inside and out."

"It doesn't matter what you believe in; you just have to have the ability to have faith. You think because you can't believe in what your mother believed in—and you can't, I agree; it's not possible—then you don't believe in anything. You lack inventiveness."

"What should I have faith in?"

"If you believe in total crap, then crap will save you." He paused. "Look at me, for example. I believe in the American middle class—you told me that, right? My own private religion—and one day, if I believe in it strongly enough, it will save me."

"The American dream didn't save my mother," I said.

"But didn't it?" With that, Church took off his sports coat, balled it up into a makeshift pillow against the window, and dozed off. I agreed with him at least that I couldn't believe in what my mother had believed in. But Church didn't understand what was at stake, that this wasn't just rhetoric; I was pregnant. I had made sure that I was on the other side of the advertising game. I was selling the golden life through minivans and new siding, lemon-scented dish detergent and nonstaining lipsticks. Buying bit by bit, in tiny ways, but not buying the entire dream at least. Not the way my mother had. Not completely selling out like Anthony Pantuliano, hawking Buicks—their slogan being A New Symbol for Quality in America. But Church was right. I had no faith in anything, not even my own body. I'd always been afraid of my crumbling ovaries, my flimsy fallopian tubes, my dank, possibly tumorous uterus—it was a safe way to live, in fear. But now swollen with life, I had to make decisions, and I wasn't sure what those decisions were. I felt like I had nothing to go on but my mother's example—an effect of my habit of living her life. But I was going to be a mother. What would I teach my child about life? Could I keep making the same mistakes?

I learned later that when my father's chest pains started, he had been wearing a yellow golf shirt and bright yellow golf pants with migrating geese stitched into them. He'd been playing alone, because his normal Tuesday-Thursday partner had to have some bridgework done. But he'd bumped into Bill Ragsdale, a podiatrist who'd done my mother's bunions, and Arch Polkey, a professor from Keene State College, an odd bachelor, a quiet chubby fellow. They'd been laughing because Arch was wearing pants identical to my father's, bright yellow with the migrating geese stitched into them. And then my father's face blanched. He grabbed the front of his golf shirt and sat down on the green.

There were three messages on the machine that night, two from my mother (one from the hospital and one from home) and the last call from Kitty. She hadn't been at my place when we arrived, not answering at her new number, and Church had been a little worried. It wasn't her night to strip and it was getting late.

"Your father's in the hospital." My mother had left the message. "He had chest pains. We're at the hospital still. I'll call you back. Now there's no need to rush home. We're fine." I translated this as: *Rush home.*

The next message was better news. He was doing very well, but my mother sounded no better. He'd been feeling fine, shooing doctors away from him, asking to go home, and the doctor had released him. They were at home now, trying to rest. My mother sounded exhausted, her voice shaky. I was shaky, too. My hands were sweaty, my head light, and I was already tired and hungry, from the morning sickness, that dizzy washed-out feeling from travel and, now, fear. I ate some bread, balling up the soft center, but it was hard to swallow down. I drank three glasses of juice.

The third message was from Kitty. It was short and sweet. "I am with a movie guy, Churchie, who make movies. I love this guy now. Talk to you later. Bye-bye."

Church fell back on the sofa like he'd been punched. "What does that mean?"

"That's Kitty Hawk," I said.

I walked to my bedroom and started to repack. Church followed me, incensed as if it were my fault Kitty was going to ditch him for "a movie guy."

"What's that supposed to mean?"

"Look, I've told you how I felt about this from the start. There are no surprises here."

Church plopped down on my bed. "You know he doesn't make movies. You know that, don't you? He's lying to her."

I picked up the phone and called my office secretary, the

type who's always home but never answers because she's busy eating popcorn and watching *Star Trek* with her five cats, the type of shut-in who mistook a Hacky Sack sitting on someone's desk for a pincushion although she's twenty-five and should know better. I told her I'd be out of the office the next day, that I'd call soon. I didn't call my parents. I didn't want to wake them. When I walked back into the living room, Church followed again and sat down on the couch.

"You don't understand Kitty," he said. "She's a lost soul. Her mother was a whore, Lissy. Growing up, she saw her mom fucking guys all the time."

"I don't know if you can believe everything she says," I said, even though what he said sounded right—it sounded like the truth of that toughened sadness I'd seen in her, the feeling I'd gotten that she was a survivor.

"Lissy, who would lie about her mom being a whore, about 'sucky fucky' and shit like that?"

I didn't want to have to think about Kitty Hawk, about her terrible childhood, about her soul, but I could feel my heart give a little in my chest. I offered to take Church home with me, to get away from the whole scene. "It won't be an upper, but you won't be alone," I said.

"I won't be alone, because she's coming back. I'll call up Matt. I'll drag Giggy away from Elsbeth's harness. We'll do vodka water ices and bitch about women. She'll come back, Lissy."

"Okay," I said, trying to sound positive. "You're probably right."

Church's dad called the Pantulianos again one night late in the summer that never happened. He had a

brief talk with my mother first. Church and I were eating
Oreo cookie ice cream. My mother walked as far away from
us as the cord would allow, saying things like "How
awful," and "How long has this been going on?" and "Oh,
I had no idea." Guy and my mother made some sort of
arrangement. My mother jotted down dates and times on
one of Ruby's memo pads from Assumption Church that
read NEED DIRECTIONS? ASK GOD. And then she cupped her
hand over the phone and handed it to Church. Their conversation was short, and after Church hung up, he went
straight to his room without saying anything to anybody.
It was then that my mother explained, "Juniper's gone over
the edge. Dinah's going to take over for a while. His dad
wants him home."

Juniper Fiske had had a complete nervous breakdown.
She was admitted into McLean Hospital in Belmont,
Massachusetts. It was plush and privately run. She would
end up staying there for two weeks. This was a few days
after my mother and I had seen Anthony Pantuliano in his
front yard in Queens, the night my mother formally intro-
duced me to my grandmother.

We'd gotten back that night to Dino and Ruby's feeling
tired, our mood somewhat reverent. Dino and Ruby and
Church were up watching David Letterman. Ruby jumped
up. "You need some coffee. I'll get coffee. We'll talk." Dino
and Church looked at us questioningly.

My mother declined. "I think we'll just go on off to
bed."

"Women only," Ruby said. "Just us gals."

My mother shook her head, smiled. We went to bed and
made an unspoken pact, true to the Verbitski tradition of
silence.

I even held out on telling Church, who'd begged me for the whole story the next morning. He whined, "It's not fair. It's like ripping the last page out of a novel. It's like going to *The Empire Strikes Back* and not finding out that Darth Vader is Luke Skywalker's father and he dies."

I just shook my head.

Dino and Ruby were also trying to read our expressions, to find out some small detail.

The night Guy called my mother to tell her about Juniper, the Pantulianos took my mother out to a fancy Italian restaurant, what I suspected to be an attempt to get the story out of her before she left for good.

Church and I had the house to ourselves. We sat at the pool's edge, lit from the pool's tiled sides, our bare feet dangling in the water. Jacko was asleep in the blue glow of the bug zapper. Church was nervous. He wasn't talking about it, but I knew he didn't want to be sent to another boarding school, much less a military academy, if his father could pull it off. He didn't want to see his mother, whom Piper had told us "looked like a little shriveled weed wasting away in a housecoat, totally pathetic," and he didn't want to see Piper either, who'd be attempting to capitalize on the family's delicate balance of power, making a race for head of the household while their mother was at her weakest. He knew Dinah wouldn't let her, but he also imagined it would be an ugly struggle.

Church said, "C'mon, Lissy, tell me the story. What happened? Is he your dad or what? Could you tell? Is she still in love with him?"

I couldn't refuse him. "She didn't say anything to him. We stayed in the car. We watched him in his front yard."

"I knew it," he said. "You didn't even get to talk to him! See, we have no control. All I want is control over my own life."

"She still loves him." As soon as I said it, I knew I was going to cry. I didn't want Church to see me. I hopped off the edge of the pool and went under, holding my nose. My T-shirt, a red Indian print, lost some of its dye, a little pink cloud swirling as the shirt billowed up around my bra.

When I came up, Church looked bleary eyed, as if he might cry, too. He pulled his polo shirt away from his stomach and wiped his face. It was then that I loved him most, not sadly or gently, but almost breathlessly, the way that my mother was desperate about Anthony, the kind of love that comes from so many needs unanswered. And I think it's this moment that anchored inside of me, that anchored Church deep inside of me, forever maybe, as some kind of answer.

I swam up to him, tugged on his shorts. I said, "C'mon in." He slid into the pool and we were face to face. Our first kiss was more like we'd bumped into each other, but then we started kissing as if we did it every day. We were up to our necks. I was balanced on my tiptoes. He dipped underwater to take off his shirt. I struggled mine off over my head. I was nervous, afraid suddenly that I might slip underwater and try to breathe, that I'd come up sputtering and coughing. I was worried about being naked for the first time in front of a boy. I glanced over Church's shoulder at Jacko and was disturbed to find him watching us with his popping eyes. Our clothes drifted and settled piece by piece to the pool's floor. We were bony, a striking white where our tan lines faded. My limbs felt rubbery, and I was shaking despite the water's being end-of-summer warm. I wondered where we would stop—I knew he didn't have any protection—and then he was suddenly inside me, my legs wrapped around him, my body light, and I thought how amazing it was to have my hands on his skin, his skin on my skin, skin sliding against skin. There was no blood, like I'd heard there would be, and no real pain. It was just our bodies locked together, more out of fear than passion. But I wasn't able to really feel everything. My mind was reeling. I was mostly afraid of pregnancy, of course, but even at this age it was a mixed bag of emotions. I'd just heard the stories of my mother's romantic youth while lamenting my own dull life. I wanted to be desperately in love, but I *couldn't* be, either. I knew too much. I put my hands on his shoulders and pushed him back. The bug zapper crackled, the drain glugged.

"We can't do this?" It was a question.

"We can't?"

"I don't see how we can."

"Sure we can. People do it all the time."

"I can't," I said.

"Yeah," he said. And he looked into my eyes for the first time, really, deeply. "But you know we should. You know that it's what we *should* do." I knew that he was right and I knew exactly what he meant: that we shouldn't be so afraid, that it's no way to live, that we should *do* something. I've thought about this moment many times since, and I've wondered what might have happened, not pregnancy, really, but what would have happened to the two of us if we'd have been able to fight against that helplessness, that desperation. I've wondered if we would have become different people, stronger, less guarded—not that having sex would have made us fall in love with each other, but having sex might have made us the kind of people who could have fallen in love with each other, who would have let ourselves fall in love with each other.

Church backed out and he slid from me. I knew that we had made the right decision and a terrible mistake. We stood there for a minute, too embarrassed to move, and then slowly we let go of each other. He dove underwater to collect our clothes, piece by piece, handing me mine, both of us politely intent on our own nakedness, not watching each other. Half in the pool, half kind of out, we put on enough clothes to cover essentials—Church in sopping boxers and me in my wet underwear and bra—and went to our own bedrooms to change into something dry.

When Dino and Ruby and my mother came home, we were lying down in front of the television, our heads resting on cushions pulled from the sofa, Jacko on a pillow between us. I had hidden my wet clothes in a plastic bag, stuffed in my suitcase. I assume Church shoved his wet clothes in with his dry. I wondered, too, whether the stolen goods were there, the fridge magnet of Jesus, the beer-can baseball hat, the patriotically crocheted toilet paper cover. The bowling ball had reappeared miraculously in the closet from which it had originally disappeared. I guessed Church hadn't thought through how exactly he was going to smuggle that one out of the house.

We headed out the next morning after an enormous breakfast of over-easy eggs and triangles of buttery toast. Ruby paced and smoked and made sure we ate until we were stuffed. Dino was quiet. As we got to the door with our bags, Dino pulled out a Yankees cap for Church. He hugged Church and then me. Ruby kissed our cheeks, leaving red lip prints. Soon, we were in the car. Ruby and Dino waved from their front stoop, like the grandparents I never really had, Ruby in her pumps and popping black-eyelined eyes and painted-on eyebrows, Dino in his swishy jogging pants, and Jacko scratching tenaciously at his head guard. I knew that I would miss them.

We arrived after a few rest-stop breaks at the Fiskes' house on Cape Cod midafternoon. Dinah came out to greet us. She hugged Church, and he responded weakly, the backpack an excuse not to use both of his arms. Piper lingered in the door frame, her arms crossed. I waved from inside the car. She nodded. Church came around to my side of the car. He said, "So, I guess we'll keep in touch and all that bullshit, right?"

"Right," I said.

He seemed okay with that, and he backed away from the car. My mom put the car in reverse, and then Church added with a cocky grin, "See you later, *Tiger*."

And I started to laugh, and so did he. My mother turned to me as we were pulling out. "What was that supposed to mean?"

"Nothing," I said. "Just Church being weird."

When we got home, the house smelled like layers of Mrs. Shepherd's Pine-Sol and Pledge. It was clean, and empty, so empty it seemed to echo. We stood quietly for an awkward moment in the entranceway, like trespassers. But then my mother said, "I'll put on a pot of coffee. Go turn on the radio or something."

As soon as we were home, my mother reverted to her old self, her Izod shirts, Bermuda shorts, and her pulled-back hair. She cut back on cigarettes and gum, bought a new Weight Watchers scale, her old one beaten up from travel,

and began weighing her food again. She gardened. She told
neighbors about my father's prestigious conference in
Arizona.

Meanwhile, I called up Louisa Eppitt. Her slovenly
father, of course, hadn't given her the message that I'd
called, just as I had suspected. But she didn't really carry a
grudge. She had changed considerably during the summer.
In my absence she'd taken up with the prettiest-girl clique
in school, led by its founder and president, the breathtaking Julie Milty. Louisa had quit clarinet and went from
awkward to stunning, finally shaving her legs, painting her
toenails. She wore lip gloss, hair spray, padded bras, et
cetera. I began to try to fit in with her new group of
friends, thinking that obviously they took on charity cases,
Louisa Eppitt having set a glowing precedent, and what
with the return on their investment in Louisa, maybe
they'd accept me, too, in that same way Juniper must have
first taken my mother on as her own personal responsibility, her social charge. I told Julie Milty and Louisa that I'd
lost my virginity with a rich kid named Church Fiske
while visiting family friends in Bayonne, which took on a
dirty, inner-city feel. I'd lost it in a swimming pool, no less,
with my mom only moments from walking through the
front door. I played up the mafia suspicions. All of this was
a big hit. Julie Milty screamed over each new twist.

Although I enjoyed talking about my sordid summer, I
was aware that it had changed me, that my mother's girl
talk had given me a weird perspective. Deep down, I had
the inkling that I was a strange person who knew too much
about something in an area where I should have remained
ignorant. I envied Louisa ever so slightly for having a dead
mother, although I loved my mother—don't get me

wrong. But Louisa was a clean slate, and I wondered if I would be normal, like Louisa, if my mother had never decided to go after my father that summer night to catch him in the act with the redheaded bank teller, if she'd decided instead to confront him one night in bed and go to marriage counseling at our cinder-block church, if she'd decided that it was not her maternal duty to tell me every sexual detail of her youth. I tried to fit in. I bought bangles, like Madonna, and I blow-dried my bangs so they stuck up and I rode around in the backseat of Julie Milty's Rabbit convertible singing along to the Smiths.

So when my father appeared, magically, one morning at the breakfast table a week before school was to start again, our lives were already back to their regular patterns. When his head popped up from behind the newspaper, I didn't even flinch.

He said, "How've you been?"

I said, "Fine." I looked around for signs of Vivian, but there were none. His face was suntanned, yes. His nose still a little pink. I looked at my mother, calmly pouring me a glass of orange juice.

She said, "Well, your father's Ivy League education finally paid off." She smiled and he smiled.

"Yes, yes," he said, sipping his coffee.

I had no idea what they were talking about—to this day, it's a mystery—whether his Harvard education had helped him find his way home, had given him the sense necessary to dump Vivian, or whether it had helped him get invited to the bogus conference, and at the same time, I didn't really care. I was friends with Julie Milty. I was going to be taking driver's ed. I had my own life and was tired of sorting through the muck of theirs. Once he'd come back, it was as if his absence had been planned. I wouldn't have been surprised if he'd given me a little souvenir from his trip, as he had once before when a real conference had taken him to Florida for three days and he came back with a can of Florida sunshine.

My mother had packed up that summer of her truth-telling spree, stuffed it into an unlabeled box along with her metallic leisure wear and her teasing combs, and shoved it into a crawl space in the attic. And I followed suit. I slipped the picture of Anthony Pantuliano at sixteen into the thinnest Nancy Drew mystery, put the books in a box along with my clarinet, and shoved them into the back corner of my bedroom closet.

She said to me two or three days before my father showed up, "It never happened, did it?"

I said, "I guess not."

"You can choose to be happy," she said. "You can pick it up, like a dress from a hanger, and slip it on. Don't waste your time, Lissy," she said. "If there's a spot of milk, don't stare at it all day long. Wipe it up and go on." That was our pact; that is what we did for years.

17

The last time I saw my father, he was dressed as a gardener, standing over a row of shrubs with a rusty pair of clippers. It had looked like rain all afternoon and he'd paced nervously by the bay window while my mom and I chatted on the sofa. I had arrived early the morning after the intervention and stayed at my parents' house just two nights. I ended up sleeping most of the time. Even after long naps, I woke up exhausted and nauseated. My father insisted that he was absolutely fine, that he'd be out on the links in no time at all, better than ever in his yellow golf shirt and matching golf pants with geese stitched into them; he was kidding, seeming chipper. And so I was getting ready to leave.

My mother had just given me a present, rug mats. "So your throws won't slide on the kitchen floor," she said. I didn't have throw rugs in my kitchen and so I took it to mean that I should have throw rugs in my kitchen the way she has throw rugs in her kitchen. In that silent language between mother and daughter, she was saying, *Be more like me,* although if I'd called her on it—the whole idea of a daughter becoming her mother—she would have said, *No, don't become me.*

My father was a little bit deaf—despite his denial of deafness—and so I spoke up. "Go on out and get at that hedge before the rain comes on. I know you want to. We can say our good-byes now."

"Oh, please," my mother said with a sigh, and then raised her voice. "Let it wait till tomorrow. It won't clip itself between now and then." She was a little angry at him for having chest pains. It wasn't rational or fair, but it was a threat, and she didn't respond well to threats.

My father had barely spoken. He rubbed his hands together and watched them fold over each other. For the first time, he looked quite old to me. He cleared his throat and said, "But the rains here can last a good long bit. Once a rain starts, it can settle in and then you're up to your hips in snow: It's winter in New England."

My mother relented. "Do what makes you happy!" she said. But it wasn't the type of thing she'd normally have given in on, and I knew she was afraid he might die on her and that she didn't want to feel guilty for not allowing him his little pleasures. It was a current beneath the conversation, as usual, an entire language they'd invented for communicating without communicating. She was actually, in her own weird way, telling him that she loved him.

Before I zipped out of the driveway, my mother waved from behind the glass door, and my father, from the hedgerow. He shielded his eyes with his hand and looked up at the dark sky. He then curled over the hedge and went back to work, snipping the stray branches, which then collected at his boots. I wish now that I had gotten out of the car and told my father, there in the front yard under the cloudy sky, that I was pregnant, that everything was unclear for me but that there was one simple fact: He was going to be a grandfather. But I didn't. I pulled the car out of the driveway and lightly beeped the horn.

Two weeks later, my father came inside from yard work on a similarly gray afternoon and had a piece of peach pie. He took off his work boots, placing them neatly beside the sofa, lay down, and died.

I drive a Buick bought from Tucker Buick in Queens. I bought it after I'd worked a couple of years and saved some money. No one knows that Anthony Pantuliano sold it to me. Anthony doesn't even know that he sold a car to his daughter. I drove it right off the lot. The coincidence wasn't overlooked completely. My mother raised her eyebrows, saying, "I didn't think you were the Buick type," and Church commented on it, too—"A Buick, huh?" But I said I loved the car, and it was left at that.

Sometimes I stop in the dealership to take a look around. If Anthony is there, I talk about possible trade-ins. He writes down figures, neat numbers stacked up in tidy rows, and pushes them to me across his desktop. He's been working there for almost sixteen years. His daughter is seventeen years old, a beauty, Maxine. He keeps a family photo on his desk, a picture of Maxine and Josephine, now his wife, and himself in front of a fake fireplace. I imagine myself, sometimes, stuck into the picture, pasted in, but it's a tight snapshot with little background. I don't really seem to fit anywhere.

The last time I was there, I told him that I was pregnant and that I would be needing a safe, reliable, family car. I told him that it was a girl, although I haven't had any tests. I told him, "I can just tell." He congratulated me. "I love kids," he said, and I could tell it was true. He showed me around the lot, and I let him take me by the elbow, guiding me gingerly in and out of wide-bodied cars, as if I were suddenly breakable.

I've had to make peace with my mother's deceit. Omission, I've decided, is a sin only if, in the process of deceiving, you forget the truth. Lying is a sin only if, in the process, the lie becomes the only truth. Anthony is one version of the truth of my life. There are many truths to each story. Take the Bible—Judas's death, for example. Catholics prefer the version in which he commits suicide by hanging himself. But there is the other version in Acts of the Apostles where he buys a field with the blood money and one day falls into that field and explodes. I believe both are true. I know that people have a difficult time with this. People love truth, but no one can really offer the truth; and if someone does insist something is true, don't believe it. Trust me on this; I hand over truths for a living.

I have tried to imagine my life without the summer that never happened. If my mother hadn't decided to confess, if she hadn't switched the cars, if my father hadn't fallen for Vivian Spivy, if Vivian Spivy had had a normal upbringing, if my mother had had a normal upbringing, if Anthony had never been compelled to take her picture, if my grandmother had never started that fire, if a landowner in Poland had never raped her and turned her bitter on life . . . maybe

I wouldn't have my fears, my problems. I wouldn't have taken up with a married man. I wouldn't be pregnant. Regardless of my close attention to detail, my years of poring over the moments of my mother's life, I have never been able to step inside. There was no intervention, divine or otherwise. And now I'm not so sure I would have intervened if I could have. What would I have changed? Would I rather not know my mother's life? Isn't the series of sad events what led to my creation? I am my mother, stamped with her DNA. If her decision to tell the truth was like a gangster opening violin cases to show his kid his guns, then wasn't it also an initiation? A gangster's kid doesn't go off to become a dentist. A gangster's kid is a gangster. That kid has got to know that unchangeable truth about himself. My mother wasn't just showing me guns; she was showing me what I'd need to arm myself.

Before my father, Bob Jablonski, returned and my mother informed me that that summer hadn't happened, she was cautioning me; she told me to choose my truth and move on. That's what I have been trying to do. I have decided in the end to see Dotty and Bob as two kids who fell in love at a wedding, that during their marriage there was give and take, but their love is what saved them. And Anthony? I couldn't return him to the mythological figure that he was before I saw him at the end of that summer in Bayonne. I knew too much about him, and yet I want him to remain pure, the way my mother first tried to describe him. It isn't completely possible, and yet I try to hold the thought in my mind: He is my pure father.

My child will have to make peace with me one day, too—that's a fact of growing up. One day I may have to lay my decisions down in front of her, but I will say that the decision to have her, to raise her alone, was my own, and that it was the most important decision of my life. I'll tell her that no one is just one person. I'll explain who I am, let her decide who she is, and, when she's old enough, I'll let her decide whether that definition includes Peter Kinney or not. Until then, I'll drive her around in Buick after Buick sold to me by Anthony Pantuliano—sturdy, reliable, inelegant Buicks, big safe family cars built with the American dream in mind, but I'll be alone behind the wheel.

Every time I visit Anthony in his office, I carry the picture of him that I stole from Dino's shoe box of family photos, the one of him at sixteen with his firm jaw and his black eye patch. One day I might say, "If we were on a downtown bus in Bayonne, I would pull out a picture of you as a young man—this picture—" and I'll hand him the picture, "and I would say, 'I am Lissy Jablonski, your daughter.'"

I imagine now what it might be like, that he'll start to cry. He'll wrap his arms around me. He'll say he's been waiting for me all these years, that he knew all along that I was his. He'd been expecting me. He knew I'd come.

Vivian Spivy didn't come back from Arizona with my father. My mother had heard through the underground network that she stayed out there, taking college classes in journalism, waitressing to support herself. Once when I was in my senior year of high school, I saw her mother, Ruth Spivy, loading twenty-pound bags of dog food on the flat bed of a truck in front of the O.K. Fairbanks, our grocery store. I was there with Louisa Eppitt, picking up mint gum, zinc pink lipstick, and a pint of cream for my mother's

penne pasta dish, an old recipe from Ruby. Louisa was asking me about the checkout boy, someone she had a crush on
despite the fact that he was a checkout boy.

"Do you think he bags like that for everyone? I mean, we
only had three things. We didn't, like, need a double bag!"

Ruth Spivy's husband, Dudley, was slumped behind the
wheel, and a kid, whom I took to be the once unweanable
Tig, was hanging out the window. I stopped and stared for
a moment, and she looked up at me, arching her back. But
she didn't seem to recognize me. At least she didn't say
anything.

"What?" Louisa asked. "What is it?"

"Nothing," I said. And we scurried across the street and
drove off quickly in my mother's Mazda, the station wagon
having disappeared shortly after we'd returned from
Bayonne.

Vivian Spivy did, however, show up at my father's funeral. I was there with Church, who was glum, having gotten
his second message from Kitty, something like, "I divorce
you, Churchie, okay? We get divorce now." But she never
left a number, so technically, he was still married and not
inclined as of yet to do much about it.

He was, in many ways, the same sad little boy of the
night we lost our virginity together in the Pantulianos'
swimming pool just before he was shipped back to Cape
Cod, to his increasingly disenchanted sister, his mother
recovering from a nervous breakdown, and Dinah, the only
one who kept the family grounded. He was scared momentarily but also determined, always optimistic about his
search for an out.

He said, "I think I'd like to be a priest when I grow up.
Not Catholic or something, not Buddhist, really—maybe

Hindu. A Hindu priest. Is there a vow of chastity involved in that?" Church is somehow ageless.

Despite Church's prediction that Dino would die of a heart attack swimming away from his exploding boat, Dino was in good health. He and Ruby showed up, too, which brightened everyone's spirits. (Jacko had long since passed, a combination of old age and asthma.) Although Church and I hadn't kept in touch with Dino and Ruby ourselves, my mother had maintained contact over the years with occasional phone calls and Christmas cards. The couple had shown up at my graduations from high school and college, and because no one was really able to talk about who they were exactly without breaking certain unspoken agreements, they were always treated as distant relatives, so distant that it wasn't worth trying to make out the lineage. I had always passed along to Church any news that my mother gave to me. Once Sal's kid had given Dino Anthony's addresses, Dino tucked them away, he told me, probably in the shoe box. He sends Anthony's daughter anonymous presents sometimes, giant stuffed bears, money. "If he wants to talk to me," Dino says, "I'm here. He cashes the money orders, though, I tell you that. A stranger's money." I knew he never talked to him, but I still half expected Anthony to show up, to know by instinct, like in some old-fashioned romantic story line. He'd shown up once before right on cue, but not this time.

Dino and Ruby were a good balance for the grim presence of Tati and Bobo, both still alive—Tati, the older sister, now valiantly, if not aggressively, pushing Bobo around in a wheelchair, Bobo chirping "Excuse me's" for her stern older sister. In her dotage, Tati had become what my mother and I call inspirationally senile, meaning that she's senile when it suits her. She enjoys mistaking my mother for people that she's openly hated for years—her next-door neighbor, her sister-in-law Eloise—once she looked my mother right in the eye and said, "Oh, you—you remind me of my son's ill-bred wife who thinks she's the Queen of Sheba." I was trying to keep Tati as far from my mother as possible.

It wasn't a huge crowd, not like my grandfather's funeral in '69. People in general are more likely to attend their fishmonger's funeral than their gynecologist's. But it was a respectably sized gathering of neighbors, golfers, a smattering of relatives. Louisa Eppitt did show up, surprisingly. She'd retreated back into her drabness, however.

"Do you keep up with the clarinet?" she asked. Evidently she played with an auxiliary band somewhere in Keene.

"No," I said, "I never went back to it."

She seemed embarrassed suddenly, as if she'd just realized it was my father's funeral, not a high school reunion. She apologized for the death of my father, the way everyone seems to, as if we are collectively responsible for death, and then she walked quickly away. My mother had kept me updated on her anyway. I knew that she worked at a florist and still took care of her dad. I was amazed, really. I'd once been jealous of her, because of the fact that her mother was dead and that she didn't have to become her mother and yet there she was, fulfilling her mother's role, unavoidably.

Guy didn't show up, although he'd once been a good friend of my father's. But Juniper was there. She was frazzled, "not centered," she said, but she sat on the other side of my mother, her back straight, her head tall, dabbing her eyes lightly with a tissue, like a professional mourner. She said to me at one point, "I know something about loss."

And although I wasn't buying her perfect performance, I believed that she'd become good at suffering because she'd had to.

Of course, I was keeping my eye out for Vivian. Even though the crowd was a nice size, there weren't enough people for Vivian to blend into. She didn't go through the reception line. She didn't sign the book. She kept her red hair tucked up in a wide-brimmed black hat. She wore sunglasses, even indoors. She was taller than I'd imagined her, more sure of herself, too—but that could have been age and experience, not a misinterpretation of Vivian during the summer of '85 when she was just twenty-four. She was striking in her hat and sunglasses, but then she took off the glasses to wipe her eyes, and when I got a good look at her face, she wasn't as pretty as I'd envisioned her. It wasn't just age, either. She was a plain-looking woman who'd always been plain. It was shocking to see her so different from the woman in my imagination, deeply unsettling. It started a chain reaction of doubt, and I could feel the other stories shift restlessly in my brain, a kind of nervous giggle passing through them, whispers of *Is this right? Is that?*

When she went up to the casket, she put her hand on my father's chest. She kneeled down and whispered something to him or to God—I couldn't tell which. And then she left. I wanted to run after her, catch her by the arm, and tell her that she had changed my life, but I couldn't decide if it was for the better or for the worse. And I also wanted to hug her because I'd always been kind of in love with her and still plagued with that instinct to take care of her, although now it didn't seem she needed to be taken care of. I realized that maybe it hadn't been her that I'd wanted to take care of so intensely but myself at fifteen, a kid whose life had suddenly shifted, a kid without bearings; and despite the fact that I suddenly had two fathers, what seemed an abundance, I really had no fathers. I wanted to tell her that I'd tried to become her, in a way, and that part of me would always be her.

But I also wondered if my father had seen something in Vivian, softer, gentler, that had allowed him to tell her things that he couldn't tell my mother or me. I wonder still if he confided in her about the war, about his leg. It dawned on me while I was sitting there, not running after Vivian Spivy, that I didn't really know my father, that I couldn't really know him without knowing that moment of his life. I've tried to envision him running the wounded soldiers from the rice fields of the Mekong delta in Vietnam to the camouflaged medical tents, his hands clamped on the stretcher, a soldier's boots bobbling at his chest, and then, as if hit by a gusted boom, his body thrown to the worn field where bloated water buffalo rotted, hooves reaching—and his leg, scattered clumps of wet red flowers, sun-polished, dazzling. I imagined him waking up every morning, his fake leg propped up, leaning casually against the wall. It always shocked me as a young girl when I came across it unattached, like part of a lover I might have one day. And for him, what was it like for my father to see this unaging reminder, his fake leg always pink and young? I wanted to know if he had told Vivian his secrets.

But, as I said, I didn't charge after her. My mother wasn't steady. She didn't see Vivian and I don't think she remembers the funeral much at all. She was a statue of herself, almost stone. She let people hug her, shake her hand, but she didn't respond to them. At one point during the priest's eulogy, she grabbed my hand. She said, "Help me, Lissy. I'm drifting up. I cannot breathe." I thought back to that first night my father was gone, how in the kitchen I felt we were underwater, and then of my mother almost drowning in the convent pool. I thought, *She wants to be saved, but from what? Drowning or surviving?* I held her hand in my lap. I wrapped my arm around her arm. I said, "I won't let go."

After everyone had filed out and my mother had been helped into the backseat of Juniper's car, I went up to the casket alone to say my good-byes. I didn't want to see my father dead. I was afraid I'd see him as my mother had last seen her father, the rosy-cheeked formaldehyde-steeped version. I expected a chorus girl, something shrunken and doll-like. But I had to see for myself. I put both hands on the edge of the casket and tipped forward slowly. The body looked like him, but sagged, lifeless. I decided then to remember him not as this stiffened version in its suit and tie, but as a gardener, the way I'd last seen him, steady but uncertain, concerned about the thickness of the hedge and if the rain would hold off long enough for him to get through the row. His uncertainty, his nervousness is one that comes from experience, not the way we usually think of experience and certainty but equally true. I loved my father, and I cried softly alone at his casket because I wished that I had told him that I was his child, because that's the truth I've chosen, that he was going to be a grandfather, which would have made him intensely proud, and, too, because it seemed profoundly unfair that my father's nobility was unremarkable. I would have liked there to have been a more glorious death, a more glorious rite. But, like Joseph's passing, my father's passing was quiet, biblically overlooked. I think if people tried to live their lives like Joseph, not Jesus, capable of difficult common commitments, like fatherhood and marriage, not expecting reward, not expecting their sacrifice to grant them a seat at God's abundant table, the world would be a better place. I still cry when I think of my father. I close my eyes tight and I can still see him, poised with clippers over the hedge, looking up at the sky, the distant rolling clouds.

When my mother can't sleep, she calls me up late at night for girl talk. Tonight, she says, "Lissy, do you think my hair's too weak to hold another permanent?" Her hair is overworked, brittle at best. I sit up in bed, prop the pillows behind my back.

"No, your hair's fine. Go for it."

Church is gone, working his way across the country in a rented Winnebago with Matt, who'd just gotten back together with Sue, the ab roller issue resolved and forgiven if he'd move out of his parents' basement. Matt agreed but threw in the trip with Church, to postpone the inevitable. Before Church went to pick up Matt a few days ago, he double-parked the motor home outside my apartment building, leaving only the narrowest strip for angry drivers to pass through. He gave me a walking tour of the cramped facilities. I was wearing an oversize shirt to hide my slightly pouched belly. I'm four months along. I knew that by the time he came back, I wouldn't have to tell him. It would be obvious. I'd wait until then.

"So what are you going to be when you grow up?" I asked.

"I wouldn't mind declaring something dead. You know, being famous for that."

"God's already dead," I said.

"Yes, and history is ending. I've read it in the *Times*. And science is dead; well, there's a rumor going around about it at MIT—a friend of mine goes to grad school there. It'll come out in the science section sometime soon. Literature's dead, of course, poetry especially. It's a hot ticket."

"Could you declare death dead?"

"That's nice. Death is dead."

"But can you pull it off? I'm still looking for a loophole."

"Like Nietzsche really pulled off killing God. It's just a declaration."

"Youth could be dead. Being young didn't feel like being young."

"How about culture?" he said, and then we laughed. "Culture is dead in America!" We slapped our knees and then we fell silent a minute. Church got serious. "Why don't you come with me?"

"What? I can't come, Church!" I said, my eyes wide, incredulous. But, really, I considered it for a split second, imagined selling my sturdy Buick, putting everything in storage, and riding out across country, heading west, a seemingly endless frontier, in Church's shiny Winnebago. My nesting instinct would kick in. I'd stitch curtains by hand, little tiny ones to match the windows, and booties for the baby. But no, I couldn't. I knew too much. "I can't just trade one insanity for another," I said. "I have to stick to my own insanity. I'm trying to ride it out."

"Oh," he said. "I guess so." And he put his hands on his hips, looked around his little Winnebago, and smiled broadly, saying, triumphantly, "God, I feel so American middle class!"

I imagined somewhere down the road, Church would cover the extra toilet paper roll with Ruby's red, white, and blue toilet paper cover crocheted circa 1976. He'd string up the fridge magnet of Jesus and hang it on the rearview mirror and cruise across country, sipping beer out of Dino's beer-can baseball hat. As he pulled the Winnebago out, he waved wildly and beeped the horn to the tune of "shave and a haircut, two bits." It was, so far, his crowning achievement, his most glorious hour.

When my mother calls tonight, I'm alone, the bed empty. There's no lover to roll over (this never was my love story), no husband to pat my leg to acknowledge the good-daughter role I can't seem to beat. My breasts are tender. I keep one hand on the soft pouch of my stomach. When I tell her, she will help me. I know this. She will be wonderful and say all the right things, because she knows exactly what I want to hear. I want to be sure that when I tell her, though, I am already strong, that I no longer need to hear the things she'll say, although I'll still want to.

My mother tells me how she saw Mrs. Defraglia scurrying around in her backyard wearing a thin white nightgown, calling, "Kitty, kitty, kitty," and that now she can't fall back to sleep. "It reminds me of my mother," she says. "At the alley door, that last time." She believes now that we all confuse one thing for another. My grandfather confused selflessness with love, and my grandmother confused love with weakness, and my mother says, "I've been guilty of both." She adds, "Don't let me define love for you." But I believe they are all right, that love is selfless, it is a weakness, a giving in, a constant falling, something I am just beginning to understand.

Eventually, my mother asks tonight as she always does, "Why don't you come and visit with me for a while?"

"I have to go to work tomorrow. I live six hours away," I remind her.

Sometimes, like tonight, she cries and whispers, "We never said a word. Year after year, we held our breath." It's hard on her now, all of that silence. She worries if that silence was really saying what she thought it was saying. I remind her sometimes of the advice she gave me before my father showed up after the summer that never happened, not to stare at spilled milk, and now it seems all we do together is pour it on the floor and ponder. Nothing is ever wiped clean. She has regrets.

And I suppose my father did, too. Tonight I imagine him coming out of Vivian's place on Hamilton Avenue, how he shuts the door gently behind himself because she is still sleeping and takes a few steps toward the car before he notices it—my mother's big blue station wagon. For a split second, it just seems out of place, a dull, ordinary object, a simple explanation; then slowly it washes over him, that my mother has been there, that she knows. He runs his hand along the hood, steps inside, and starts the car with the extra set of her keys on his ring. He adjusts the seat for his long legs and sits there in the idling car for a long time, before he goes back inside to wake Vivian, to begin what he thinks is a new life. Tonight my mother says, "Our mistakes lead us to grace."

But she doesn't regret what she says was the most important thing—and this is the part of the story I try to remember, the one moment I try to hold inside of me like a tea light floating in water; maybe with effort, it can become my own brand of faith—how late during the summer that never happened, when my mother and I were home again in Keene, she heard a car in the driveway. I can see her now as she walks downstairs to the front door and turns on the porch light. She opens the door to find her husband. I imagine them blinking like two unlikely saints caught in a brilliant halo. It is a confession, repentance, forgiveness. They are both desperate, both afraid. It's the way we should live our lives.

She says, "What are you doing out there? Come in. It's late." And he steps inside.

Tonight my mother is quiet. I can hear the thin static of the line between us. Out on the street, people are laughing; in the distance, a car alarm. My mother says, "I'm surprised to find myself alone. I still expect him to come to bed."

I say, "It's funny how a life suddenly becomes your own." And then I imagine us again as swimmers, now at night, alone, our wet heads moonlit. This time we're calm. Our toes push off the silty floor, and we let our bodies rise. This time, we aren't stretching away from the water. We let the water hold us up, a buoyancy the child inside of me already knows, by instinct. We drift on our backs, stare up at the sky, the fattening moon. We wonder how we couldn't have known it before, how to give in, to float.

ABOUT THIS GUIDE

The following questions and author interview are intended
to help you find interesting and rewarding approaches
to your reading of Julianna Baggott's *Girl Talk*.
We hope this guide enriches your enjoyment
and appreciation of the book.

For a complete listing of our Readers Club
Guides, or to read the guides online, visit

http://www.SimonSays.com/reading/guides

girl
talk

Julianna Baggott

A Readers Club Guide

Q: One of the most refreshing things about *Girl Talk* is its unique combination of so many different themes and genres. It is at once an exploration of memory, a coming-of-age story, a comedy of contemporary manners, a love story, and, of course, an engaging portrait of the mother-daughter relationship. What inspired you to tell this particular story? And how do you describe your novel to people?

A: I don't think I ever once thought to myself: *I'm going to sit down and write a memory-exploring, coming-of-age, comedy of manners/love story about mothers and daughters.* I have an instinct to collect things—not Hummels or snow globes, but memories, small moments in my life. My mother once woke me up to ask me if her bathing suit was flattering. I tagged it and put it on a shelf in my brain. It slipped its way into an essay. The essay became a short story about a woman waking her daughter for a girl talk that leads them one night to try to catch her husband in an affair. I mused: what if it wasn't just one night, but if he disappeared for an entire summer? The plot exploded. I had a novel. While writing it, I rummaged all the tagged shelves in my brain and took down all the things that seemed to fit, and all the while, I never forgot my mother in her bathing suit. I never forgot that these were real people in a very real world.

Q: Lissy is charming and funny and twisted and poetic. But what really makes her work as a compelling protagonist is that she's also so very ordinary: her perspective is so easy to identify with; her ambivalent reactions to her mother's behavior during "the summer that never happened" are so real; and her preoccupation with the past is poignant and, I think, universal. Did her voice, and her choices, come easily to you?

A: At times, Lissy was very easy for me. I enjoyed writing her hysterical scene with Peter and the "Love that Lemon" campaign, her harangues about Freudian theory, and the dialogues with Church were pure pleasure. And a number of aspects of Lissy come from my own life (for example, although I'm married with three kids, I've spent a small fortune on unwarranted as well as warranted pregnancy tests). But Lissy was often a witness to what was going on. Like I am as a writer, she stood back and watched, and I wanted to make sure that she wasn't on the sidelines, but really present, and so I had to go back through, making sure she was speaking her mind, reacting and being reacted to.

Q: Along with novel and short-story writing, you're an acclaimed poet, a fact that is abundantly evident in the vivid imagery that fills *Girl Talk*. Does either type of writing come more easily to you? In what ways does your poetry feed your fiction, and vice-versa?

A: I'm a cross-trainer. When I get bored of sprinting, I do a marathon. When I get too wearied by the marathon, I go back to sprinting. I find it liberating to have an idea, an image, an eavesdropped conversation and to be able to decide what genre it's most suited for. There are images that repeat no matter what I'm writing, including essays and screenplays. My poems are more personal, more autobiographical. One friend has called my book of poems "a backstage pass to my fiction." I don't think my poems would be happy to be dismissed as such, but I understood exactly what she meant when she said it.

Q: There are many moments in *Girl Talk* when you manage to convey so much emotion with very few words. For example, the scene when Dino realizes that Lissy is Anthony's daughter. He doesn't really analyze—he just reacts by immediately hugging her. Tell us about your choices in writing scenes like this? Is this an instance of your poetic instincts coming to the fore?

A: This scene is pure theater. My father has a stack of index cards which list every production from po-dunk community theaters to Broadway that he and my mother have ever seen. To many, many of them I was dragged along. My sister, who's nine years older, was a struggling actress living in New York by the time I was ten. My parents took me to the city to see all of her shows, including the ones where you had to cross the stage to get to the only bathroom. I love theater, and writing this scene was purely an act of bringing five irritable people, each with a strong motive, to one spot and letting them duke it out. As for Dino, he isn't an analyzer, by nature. He got the answer he'd been angling for. He hugged Lissy. He's an emotional man.

Q: The characters in *Girl Talk*—especially Dotty and Juniper Fiske—often shift seamlessly from comedy to tragedy, from blithe asides to poignant revelations. But all the while, their choices and behaviors are utterly believable. Are these women based on any real-life models?

A: When my mother read *Girl Talk* as a short story, she gave it to her friends, saying, "The mother is me." This, of course, confused people since we don't live in New Hampshire; my father wasn't a gynecologist; he didn't have an affair with a red-headed bankteller; my mother is from Raleigh, North Carolina, not Bayonne, New Jersey, et cetera. But there are undeniable similarities: my mother's accent comes back when she chews gum, she adores girl talk, she believes that nuns, in many ways, saved her life. And so I've taken bits and pieces, little details, and created something completely, extravagantly untrue. As for Juniper, she's whimsy. I'm not sure where she came from, but she did so with such strident confidence that she became immediately real for me, and therefore easy to write.

Q: From Kitty Hawk to Church and Piper Fiske to Jacko the dog, your characters have such unusual, quirky names. Where do they come from? Do you plan and mold a character's personality and then pick his or her name based on the personality, or does the name drive the character?

A: Most of the time, I don't know where the names come from. I adore names. And, when one of them comes to me, the character becomes real from that moment on. Names are incredibly important. I couldn't write a character without a name, and think, *Oh, I'll fill that in later.* While writing *Girl Talk*, my husband and I rented out rooms to foreign students, mostly Asian. They often would take on an American name, like Sally. I always loved this. So I came up with Kitty, and then it was a natural association: Kitty Hawk. My husband works at a prestigious boarding school; it's an endless source. I look through phone books and often rely on last names of people from high school (I went to grammar school with a Nancy Pantuliano, for example. The bully in my son's preschool class, at that time, was Dino). There have been times that, for one reason or another, I'll have to change a character's name and it's terribly uprooting, virtually impossible.

Q: If you were to write a coda of sorts to this novel, what would be going on with Lissy and Dotty? How will Dotty react to Lissy's pregnancy and motherhood?

A: Oh, Dotty will be thrilled about the baby. It will fill the void over the loss of her husband. It will redirect her life. Lissy will have to deal with her mother's intense focus of love, but she will need her, too, as a single mother. They will form a new family unit. I've actually envisioned the last scene in screenplay terms, and I think of the three of them about seven years in the future, having returned to that lake where Lissy had vacationed as a kid: the three of them, Lissy, Dotty and the little girl, holding hands, floating on their backs.

Q: You've rendered the settings in *Girl Talk* so vividly as to almost make them characters in themselves. What sorts of research did you do, geographically or otherwise, to write this story?

A: My husband grew up in Keene and so, through his stories, it already has inhabited my imagination. I had a live-in fact checker. As for Bayonne, I went shopping for it. I knew that I had to describe a place in a time that I wasn't yet alive, so my own perceptions wouldn't be as important as my source's impressions. So, I interviewed my parents and their friends, looking for the person who had the deepest, most storied memory of the setting of their youth. Isabelle Murray won. I asked her about the Catholic church, and she said, "Which one, the Polish or the Italian?" And in that detail, she was giving me not only factual setting, but conflict, plot. Kathleen Middleton's book on the city was also very helpful. I fell in love with Bayonne. Who wouldn't? My second novel is also partially set there.

Q: Can you tell us a little about the specifics of writing *Girl Talk*? Did you come up with a complete outline early on? Were you surprised by the course the story ultimately took?

A: I always have a map. I always know what decisions the characters have to face, but I don't always know which route they'll take. *The Miss America Family*'s ending was written a number of different ways. I was most surprised while writing *Girl Talk*, not by how it ended, but by all of the unexpected twists and turns in the middle. The intervention, for example, came out of a phone conversation with a friend whose big family had planned an intervention for their brother, but everyone was too polite to bring up the subject, so it went undiscussed. I used it immediately. It was a wonderful surprise.

Q: Which novelists and poets do you most enjoy reading? And which of these would you name as the primary influences on your own work?

A: I adore Gabriel García Márquez, Italo Calvino, and Fred Chappell. They were huge influences early on. I'm a fan of John Irving, Lorrie Moore, and Stuart Dybek. I love the poets Andrew Hudgins, Linda Pastan, and Rodney Jones. Right now I'm reading Michael Cunningham's *The Hours* and a book of poems by Olena Kalytiak Davis, *And Her Soul Out of Nothing*. Both are fabulous.

Q: Is it accurate to describe *Girl Talk* as a feminist book?

A: I never write with politics in mind. I only think of my characters. I fall in love with them. *Girl Talk* is about two different generations of American women in the sixties and today, therefore it will deal with feminist issues. It's inevitable. I consider myself a feminist, but I wouldn't label my fiction as such. Feminism is complicated and I think this novel talks about the generational complications and evolutions of feminism, but that wasn't my goal. It was a product of the characters that I was committed to writing about.

Q: You've spoken elsewhere about your hopes to one day write a book about your grandmother. When can we look forward to some Julianna Baggott nonfiction?

A: My grandmother was raised in a whorehouse, and she's a natural storyteller. It's the kind of writerly gift that you have to accept. Although I've no idea what shape it will take, I will certainly write about my grandmother's life. There's no question.

Q: Can you tell us about your next novel, *The Miss America Family*?

A: *The Miss America Family* is about a former Miss New Jersey (1969-70) and her sixteen-year-old son, Ezra. In the summer of 1987, it seems like she has the perfect American family: a son, a daughter, a second husband more reliable than the first. This time around she's got an ex-quarterback with a solid dental practice. Ezra, however, is not convinced. He feels disconnected and has set out to define himself by inventing his own list of Rules to Live By, falling in love with Janie Pinkering, the rich podiatrist's daughter. But when his grandmother, disoriented from a stroke, reveals dark family secrets, his mother reclaims her tragic past through a series of odd, dangerous choices. Ezra is a wonderfully sweet, smart character, and his mother is mysterious and unpredictable. Together they try to find a way to turn it all around.

Reading Group Questions and Topics for Discussion

1. *Girl Talk* features a rich cast of lively "minor" characters—
   Juniper Fiske, Ruby Pantuliano, Kitty Hawk, Peter Kinney,
   Jacko the dog. How does each character contribute to the overall
   flavor of the novel? Compare Julianna Baggott's narrative and
   characterization techniques to the techniques of such writers
   as John Irving, Jane Smiley, and Anne Tyler.

2. What is the particular role of humor in this novel? Discuss
   the ways the author fuses comedy and pathos in many of *Girl
   Talk*'s scenes. How would you describe the tone that results
   from this delicate combination?

3. Discuss Baggott's novel alongside recent films, plays, and
   other novels which similarly illuminate: the dynamics and
   intermittent fracturings of family relationships; the transition
   from girlhood to womanhood; the alternately comforting and
   haunting specter of the past on our present lives.

4. The persistence of memory—the ways in which remembering
   one's past continues to color and influence one's present—is
   certainly among the chief concerns in Baggott's story. What
   does the author achieve by switching back and forth between
   the present and the past?

5. One of the dominant motifs in *Girl Talk* considers the subtle
   distinctions between honesty and truth. Lissy tells us that her
   mother instructed her to "choose the truth." But later, Lissy
   realizes "that nobody seemed to know the truth." And elsewhere,
   the act of lying is held up as a sort of art form, one to be honed
   and developed. What is Baggott up to here? Is truth inherently
   subjective? Dotty's ultimate lesson for Lissy is to, again, "choose
   [her own] truth and move on." Which of Baggott's characters
   seem to have the firmest grasp on truth and reality?

6. How do sexuality and sex figure in the lives of Dotty, Lissy, Juniper, Ruby, and Kitty Hawk? What compels Dotty to share such intimate and often graphic details about her sex life to her young daughter? Discuss Baggott's portrait of Dotty as a whole. How does Dotty's relationship with her own mother, Evelyn, for example, come to color Dotty's subsequent relationship with Lissy? And how does Dotty's alternating candor and ambiguity with regard to talking about sex seem to affect Lissy's attitude toward and relationship with her own sexuality, both as a girl and as a woman?

7. "The summer that never happened" was, in fact, possibly the most influential summer of Lissy's life. So why the "never happened" label? Discuss the disparate elements of irony, repression, and melancholy which inform Dotty and Lissy's largely unspoken feelings about that pivotal summer.

8. Julianna Baggott is a celebrated poet, and to read *Girl Talk* is to understand exactly why. Discuss Baggott's vivid use of recurring imagery (especially that of water), her lyrical evocations of Lissy's memories, and her skillful use of rhythm and well-placed silences to convey different emotions.

9. Talk about the mothers and the fathers in this novel; the ones who disappear, physically or emotionally, the ones who stay and the ones who never come into the picture in the first place. Is there a pattern here? Who is the ideal parent? Is Juniper the sort of person who should not have become a parent? Why? What sort of mother is Dotty? What sort of father is Bob?

10. Lissy imagines Bob's homecoming after the summer that never happened. Likewise, she pictures her own consummation in a tent at Woodstock. Discuss these scenes alongside others in which Lissy endeavors to imagine events that she can never know firsthand. In Lissy's renderings, what clues can we glean about Lissy's feelings for her mother—whether of resentment, understanding, or affection?

11. Is *Girl Talk* a love story? If so, whose love story? Lissy claims that it's certainly not hers. Why not?

12. In the particular emotional realm of this novel, what does it cost to love—and what does it finally mean to love? Considering what happens to her characters and their relationships in *Girl Talk*, what does Julianna Baggott seem to be suggesting about love and the ways it has evolved over the course of the novel's two generations?

13. Lissy chooses in the end not to follow Church across the country. Dotty chooses not to follow Anthony into the crowds of Woodstock. What parallels and distinctions exist between these pivotal decisions?

14. Imagine an alternate version of *Girl Talk* in which Bob does not come home at the end of the summer that never happened. Or one in which Dotty actually knocks on Anthony's door—and he welcomes her in? What if Lissy told Peter she was pregnant with his child? Would any of these choices ring true, considering the characters we've come to know? Why or why not?

15. "You can choose to be happy. You can pick it up, like a dress from a hanger, and slip it on." Dotty's conviction here contrasts sharply with the way Church comes to see the world. "We have no control," he says at one point. "All I want is control over my own life." Here, Baggott underscores the principle tension plaguing her novel's heroine—the struggle between notions of an immutable fate and an ever-malleable free will. Who in this novel would you say ultimately wins the most control over her or his own life? Explain.

16. Lissy tells us that she is "more like my mother than even my mother." At what points in your own life—including the present—have you been able to identify wholeheartedly with this statement, for better or worse? Discuss the ways Lissy has come to feel caught between choosing not to follow Dotty's path in life and being unable to break the pattern. How much, in fact, does Lissy resemble Dotty? And in what ways is Dotty like her own mother, Evelyn?

17. "There's only a tiny sliver of this story that I can tell with any precision," states Lissy. Is Lissy a "reliable" narrator? Why? Discuss the richly comic irony in the fact that Lissy—a narrator so tirelessly preoccupied with the relative truth and honesty and accuracy of her story—is ambivalently pursuing a career as, of all things, an advertising copywriter.

18. Dino says growing old allows you to pile up more and more regrets. What do you suppose Dotty regrets? Evelyn? Explain.

19. Discuss the intermittent mythological and biblical references in *Girl Talk*. Lissy likens her father's affair to a "miraculous" event, and she compares her own mother to Mary and Bob to Joseph. Later, a therapist tells Lissy she suffers from two Electra Complexes as a result of her having two fathers; and the one-eyed Anthony comes to resemble Cyclops in Lissy's mind. How do these allusions contribute to *Girl Talk*'s central themes?

20. "Sometimes the only way to fix a mistake is to make it twice." Dotty's assertion to Lissy is echoed later in the novel with an even more hopeful—and vaguely spiritual—tone when she says that "our mistakes lead us to grace." Does the truth of these statements bear out when we look at the major choices and mistakes made in this novel? What "grace" is discovered by Baggott's characters in the end?